Christmas at Silver Dale

LUCY DANIELS

H

HODDER

First published in Great Britain in 2019 by Hodder & Stoughton
An Hachette UK company

I

Copyright © Working Partners Limited 2019

A CIP catalogue record for this title is available from the British Library

Paperback ISBN 9781473682450
eBook ISBN 9781473682467

Typeset in Plantin Light 11.75/15 pt by
Palimpsest Book Production Limited, Falkirk, Stirlingshire

Printed and bound in Great Britain by Clays Ltd, Elcograf S.p.A.

Hodder & Stoughton policy is to use papers that are natural, renewable
and recyclable products and made from wood grown in sustainable forests.
The logging and manufacturing processes are expected to conform to the
environmental regulations of the country of origin.

Hodder & Stoughton Ltd
Carmelite House
50 Victoria Embankment
London EC4Y 0DZ

www.hodder.co.uk

Special thanks to
Sarah McGurk, BVM&S, MRCVS

To Ross W Syme Bsc (Hons), BVM&S, MRCVS and
to Sarah Syme for feeding him for all these years

Chapter One

Mandy Hope awoke with a start. It was almost light, though there was a grey tinge to the late October dawn. A gust of wind sent a spatter of raindrops against the window. She blinked at the clock. It was a few minutes before seven o'clock.

Her much-loved collie dog, Sky, was curled up on the floor beside her bed. Apart from Sky, Mandy was alone. For the past two years she had shared almost everything with her boyfriend Jimmy Marsh. They had renovated the little house at Wildacre together, but now Jimmy was in the far north of Canada with his childhood friend Aira Kirkbryde, tracking polar bears.

Mandy felt a pang of sadness as she glanced at the empty pillow beside her. It wasn't just his absence which was troubling her. Two and a half months ago, she had proposed to Jimmy over a romantic meal, down on one knee, hoping for marriage and children and a guaranteed future in his arms. But he had turned her down, saying that he wasn't ready for that kind of commitment, not when he was already helping to raise his twins Abi and Max from his first marriage. Now

Mandy had no idea what the future held, or what would happen when Jimmy returned from Canada.

Footsteps thundered on the narrow staircase and the bedroom door swung open. Sky woke up and barked once, then began to wag her tail. Abi and Max stood on the threshold, panting. Eleven years old, they had grown over the summer and Abi was sporting a new short hairstyle. They looked more alike than ever with the green eyes and thick brown hair they had inherited from their father. Three more dogs, Simba, Zoe and Emma, a German shepherd and two huskies, rushed into the room and ran around exploring with their noses. Sky greeted them briefly, then leaped onto the bed, almost winding Mandy.

'Can you come?' Max gasped.

'The door of the chicken house is broken and all the hens have got out.' Abi's eyes were stretched wide. 'We tried to round them up, but Emma chased Butter under a bush and then Peckerill and Damson tried to fly away. I think Damson's stuck on the barn roof, but it's raining hard and Tippy was squawking like anything!'

'We were trying to get them inside without waking you,' Max promised anxiously.

Mandy nudged Sky off her knee and threw off the covers, sending a reassuring smile towards him. 'On my way!' she said. She pulled on some trousers and a thick sweater, then cantered down the stairs.

Abi and Max were waiting for her. They shut the dogs in the kitchen and hurried outside. The chicken coop was in a sheltered corner of the garden, but a branch had blown from a large beech tree that overhung the lawn and landed on the wire frame. The wooden framework had cracked and the door to the henhouse was hanging at an angle. Mandy decided to relocate the chickens to the old henhouse inside the barn until she fixed the door and the frame.

To Mandy's relief, despite the damage, three of the chickens were still huddled inside the nesting boxes along the side of the henhouse. She lifted Tippy, the plumpest of the Rhode Islands, into Max's arms and Red, Tippy's daughter, into Abi's. Then she picked up April, the long-legged silver Leghorn that Jimmy had bought her for Easter. Heads down, they waded across the wet lawn and into the shelter of the barn.

Damson and Peckerill were huddling in the long grass under the garden hedge. Mandy scooped them into the arms of the twins and set off to hunt for Butter. Of all the chickens, Butter, a stately golden Buff Orpington, was Mandy's favourite. Helen Steer, Mandy's friend and the nurse at Animal Ark, the veterinary practice that belonged to Mandy's parents, had jokingly named the chicken after a curry dish from Roo Dhanjal's take-away. Despite the fact that Mandy was vegetarian and there was no chance of Butter ever being eaten, the name had stuck.

Mandy eventually found her huddling underneath an azalea. She gripped Butter firmly with both hands, then shuffled out backwards. Although the hen was distinctly ruffled, there was no sign that Emma the young husky had made contact during the chase. Mandy handed the light feathery bird over to Max and he carried her off to the barn.

Mandy battled through the gusting wind to inspect the battered hen run. She would need to buy some new chicken wire to repair the outside cage but the door to the coop needed to be fixed at once or there was a risk it'd come right off its hinges.

'I'll get the toolbox,' Abi said. 'Pity Dad's not here, but we can do it, can't we?'

'Of course we can,' Mandy said. Her memory flitted back to one of the first times she'd spoken to Jimmy. He'd been up a ladder, working on the barn. It hadn't been called Wildacre then; it had still been Lamb's Wood Cottage. The elderly owner, Robbie Grimshaw, had just been taken into hospital and Jimmy had stepped in to help save the animals left behind. Mandy had been touched by his concern and mesmerised by his craftmanship as he repaired the barn.

Abi reappeared with both Max and the toolbox. Mandy took out a screwdriver, then dug through the plastic tubs until she found a screw that looked about the right size. She reattached the door to the broken hinge and wedged it shut. It would need to be rehung properly but she'd do that when she had some more wire for the frame.

In the kitchen, Mandy hastily put cereal boxes and milk on the table. She was on a tight schedule today and the escaping chickens hadn't helped. 'Wash your hands and have some breakfast,' she told Abi and Max. She dashed upstairs to shower, leaving the twins to help themselves. As she came out of the shower, she heard a car draw up, and then Helen Steer's voice greeting the twins. She was going to look after the dogs today.

'Hi.' Helen beamed at Mandy as she rushed back down the stairs. Helen's long brown hair was tied back in a ponytail and she was wearing dark blue jeans and an Animal Ark sweatshirt.

Abi and Max were playing with Isla, the little Bedlington cross that Helen had adopted in the summer. Isla had been abandoned and brought, newly blind and very nervous, to Hope Meadows, the rescue centre Mandy had set up behind Animal Ark. The little curly-haired dog had been a challenge at first, but today she seemed full of joy as she rolled onto her back when Max pretended to shoot her.

'Don't blame me.' Helen held up her hands. 'Seb taught her that, along with sitting up to beg and giving high fives.'

Seb was Helen's fiancé. He had objected to Helen adopting Isla at the beginning, but adored the little dog now. Lucy, Helen's shiny black flat-coated retriever, zoomed into the kitchen with Sky. Simba, Zoe and Emma were in hot pursuit. Suddenly the room felt very small and full.

'I'll take them out when you've gone,' Helen promised. 'Though I might have to organise a rota. Even for me, six at once would be a challenge. I'll have to do nose counts throughout the day to make sure nobody's missing.'

The doorbell rang and the knot of dogs careered out of the kitchen and into the hallway, barking loudly. Mandy had to fight her way through the sea of hairy bodies to open the door. Belle Jones, Jimmy's ex-wife, stood on the doorstep. She was smartly dressed in a pink cashmere polo neck with a cream gilet and immaculate brown cords tucked into long boots.

Mandy had found Belle rather intimidating at first. Mandy tended towards jeans and jodhpur boots for every occasion and the only beauty routine she did was to wash her face and apply a lick of mascara. But as she and Belle had got to know each other, Mandy found that Belle was unexpectedly down to earth, and she felt they were on their way to being good friends. Belle hadn't objected at all when the twins had asked to continue their visits to Wildacre, even though Jimmy was away.

Despite her flawless appearance, she didn't flinch as all six dogs launched at her. Instead, she grinned as she bent down to pat them, then followed Mandy into the kitchen where, as if by magic, the dogs fell silent and conversation became possible.

'Are you ready?' Belle asked the twins. They nodded. 'Go get your bags, then,' Belle told them, and they squeezed past the dogs to the stairs. 'Good to see you both,' Belle said to Mandy and Helen. 'Sorry to rush the kids out, but we're going to Sheffield to visit my parents.'

'How's Dan?' Mandy asked. Belle was married to Sergeant Dan Jones, who worked as a policeman in nearby Walton. Mandy and Helen's fiancé Seb, who was an Animal Welfare Officer, sometimes worked with Sergeant Jones in the course of their jobs.

'He's fine. Working this weekend, though.' Belle rested her hand on Zoe's domed silver head. 'It's good of you to have the twins when you're here on your own,' Belle said to Mandy. 'Bet you can't wait for Jimmy to come back and help with the chaos!'

'They're always welcome,' Mandy replied. She wondered what Belle would think if she knew that Mandy and Jimmy's future was up in the air. The thought of losing Abi and Max was almost as painful as the idea of losing Jimmy himself.

Belle must have caught a look of unhappiness on Mandy's face, because she smiled. 'Don't worry,' she said. 'You'll get used to Jimmy going off on these adventures with Aira – they're like a couple of Boy Scouts! It'll be harder when you have children,' she added. 'But for now, make the most of having the house to yourself!'

Mandy fought to keep herself from wincing. There was nothing she wanted more than to start a family with Jimmy, but he had told her very clearly that he didn't want their relationship to change. He had gone away to Canada so soon after Mandy's proposal that they had never had time to sit down and talk about it all. They had spoken as often as possible on Skype while he'd been away, but sometimes the children had been there, and even when they weren't, it wasn't an easy subject to raise with him so far away. And Jimmy certainly didn't sound as if he was missing Wildacre – or Mandy – terribly. Their brief chats had been full of his adventures with polar bears, rare birdlife and colourful local characters. Mandy hadn't wanted to drag him back to the tedious details of her own everyday routine, or issues of what would happen when he returned.

The door burst open and Abi and Max exploded into the kitchen. They threw their arms around Mandy and squeezed her tight. She bent down and buried her face in their soft, clean-smelling hair. 'See you soon, perils,' she told them.

'Not if we see you first,' Abi teased, and Mandy laughed.

She watched Belle and the children extricate them-selves from the dogs and close the front door behind them. To her dismay, there were tears in her eyes. *You'll see them again soon,* she reminded herself.

'Isn't it time you were leaving?' Helen reminded her and Mandy pulled out her phone to check the time, then flicked through to the Manchester airport arrivals website.

'It is,' she agreed. She unhooked her handbag from the bannister and fished out her car keys.

'I brought you these,' Helen said, holding a creamy white knitted blanket and a small teddy bear. 'In case Taresh is cold and anxious,' she added.

Mandy beamed. 'That's a lovely thought. James will be thrilled.'

James Hunter, Mandy's best friend since childhood, was returning to the UK today with his newly adopted son. James's partner, Raj Singh Bhuppal, had asked James to adopt Taresh, whose mother, Raj's cousin, had died when Taresh was born. Mandy was collecting them from the airport as Taresh arrived in England for the very first time. 'I can't believe James and Raj are bringing their son home!' Mandy said, looking down at the cute brown teddy.

'I know.' Helen looked at Mandy, her head on one side. 'It only seems like yesterday that Raj told us about Taresh, doesn't it?'

Mandy felt herself smiling as she dashed out to the car and climbed in. She glanced into the back seat, where she had installed the brand new child seat that James had brought over before he and Raj set off to Agra in India, where Taresh had spent the first sixteen months of his life. It would be a shock for the little boy, moving from the warmth of India to Yorkshire in autumn. But Mandy couldn't wait to meet him.

'Hang on, Taresh,' she murmured as she steered the car down the narrow track. 'Your new Aunt Mandy is on her way!'

Mandy followed the signs to Terminal Two and pulled

up in a parking bay on the second floor of the multi-storey car park. Her phone beeped with a message from James. 'Landed safely. All well. Waiting for luggage.' He had added a photo of Raj, who was hugging a sleeping Taresh to his shoulder. Taresh had his thumb in his mouth and was clutching a bright yellow blanket.

Mandy followed the signs for Arrivals. Two brown-skinned, dark-eyed children were running up and down, waving windmills made of shiny foil. The automatic doors slid open and with a whoop of delight, the children made a rush for the door. 'Daddy!'

A tall man in slacks and a white shirt dropped his suitcase and held his arms open. The little girl reached him first, then the boy. He scooped them both up into his arms. He kissed them both, then set them down to hug his wife. Mandy watched the family head for the exit, then turned as the sliding door sighed open again.

'Mandy!'

Mandy wasn't sure if she had ever seen James look happier. Though there were lines of exhaustion around his mouth and eyes, he grinned as he stepped through the doorway. He was pushing a trolley loaded with cases, guiding it skilfully with one hand. His other arm was tightly clasped around Taresh, who was gazing around with enormous black eyes. The little boy was wearing blue and red Spiderman pyjamas under a cosy blue dressing gown, and Spiderman slippers on his feet. Raj looked as happy as James as he set down the three carrier bags he was holding and let go of the handle of yet another suitcase. He gave Mandy a hug, then held out his arms to Taresh, who uncurled his fingers from James's collar and shifted into Raj's embrace. Mandy hugged James, feeling his thin frame vibrate with joy.

'Mandy, this is Taresh,' James said proudly. He reached out to hold his son's tiny starfish-shaped hand. 'And Taresh, this is your Aunty Mandy.'

Taresh had a sweet, round face with thick black eyebrows and a very shiny mop of thick hair. Mandy held out the little teddy bear, and the already huge eyes widened. Taresh turned to James, who nodded and smiled. 'You can take it,' he urged.

Taresh curled one hand around the bear and hugged it close.

'Thank you so much,' Raj told her, kissing his son's hair.

'It was actually Helen's gift,' Mandy said. 'She sent a blanket as well. You might need it when we get outside.'

James rolled his eyes. 'Arriving back to lovely Lancashire weather,' he said.

Mandy laughed. 'Because Yorkshire weather's so much better.'

'How was the flight?' Mandy asked as she manoeuvred the car out onto the middle lane of the motorway.

'So-so,' James replied from the back seat. Mandy

could see his face in the rearview mirror. He seemed unable to take his eyes off Taresh. 'I don't think Taresh understood what was happening.'

'The flight was on time, at least,' Raj put in from the seat beside Mandy. 'And luckily we had an extra seat in our row, so we could spread out a bit.'

A spatter of rain hit the windscreen and Mandy switched on the wipers and flicked the sidelights on.

'He's fast asleep,' James announced from the back seat. Mandy smiled. Her dear friend deserved every bit of this happiness. Back in the summer, when Raj had first announced that he had adopted his cousin's baby, James had seemed truly shell-shocked. He and Raj had only been together for a year, and James was still adjusting to life following the death of his first husband, Paul. Mandy hadn't been sure that Raj and James's relationship would survive, yet they seemed closer than ever. Both were obviously besotted with their new son.

A movement beside her caught Mandy's eye. Taresh wasn't the only one who was sleeping. Raj's head had nodded to one side and his eyes were closed.

'You should get some sleep too,' Mandy said to James in the mirror.

'I feel too wired,' James admitted. 'It all feels like a dream, and I'm scared of waking up and finding that Taresh isn't here.'

'Oh, he's here,' Mandy murmured, glancing at the reflection of the little boy.

For the next few minutes, Mandy had to concentrate

on the road as she changed from one motorway to another. It was raining harder now and the wind was getting up again. The next time she glanced in the mirror, James's eyes were shut.

'That seems to be everything.' Mandy put the last of the bags down in the hallway of James and Raj's flat.

'I'll put the kettle on,' James said. He glanced at Raj. 'Shall I hold Taresh?' he offered. 'You can show Mandy his room, if you like.'

Taresh still seemed very sleepy as Raj handed him over to James. Mandy couldn't help but feel impressed as James opened the cupboards and began to pull out mugs one-handed. Adoptive fatherhood seemed to be coming naturally to both of her friends. She wondered what it had been like when Adam and Emily had taken her home. They had adopted Mandy when she was just three months old, still a very tiny baby. Had they taken to it as easily?

'What do you think?' Raj asked as he showed Mandy the spare bedroom that had been converted into a nursery.

'Did you paint those?' she asked, pointing at the wonderful wildlife mural, complete with blue tits, a robin, a pair of boxing hares and a shy-looking doe with a white-spotted fawn huddled against her.

Raj laughed. 'I wish,' he said. 'Douglas MacLeod did them.'

Douglas was a well-known children's author and illustrator who was the boyfriend of Mandy's friend Susan Collins. She and Douglas had got together over Christmas the year before. 'I should have recognised his style,' Mandy said.

They walked back into the kitchen, where James was pouring the coffee. He put out a plate of biscuits and set the mugs on the table, then sat down, shuffling Taresh onto his knee, but as he reached for his mug, Taresh's face crumpled and he let out a howl.

James hugged the small body closer again, cradling Taresh's head against his shoulder. He stood up and started to sway gently from side to side, stroking Taresh's shiny black hair, but the keening sound continued. James put his head on one side and looked calmly into the huge, watery eyes. 'Would you like some milk?' he asked. Still rocking, he poured a small amount into a sippy cup and handed it to Taresh, who took a sip and then dropped the cup, holding out his hand as if he had let go deliberately. James picked it up and set it on the workbench. 'I'll just check his nappy,' he said, his voice matter of fact. He came back a few minutes later and shook his head. 'All fine,' he said. He had given Taresh his new teddy bear and his yellow blanket but the little boy was still grizzling.

'I think he's just confused by everything,' James said, nuzzling his chin on his son's head.

'Not to mention he must feel just as jet-lagged as we do,' Raj added.

Mandy smiled. 'He's still gorgeous,' she said.

James looked at her with his head on one side. A humorous frown knitted his eyebrows together. 'Who are you, and what have you done with Mandy Hope?' he demanded.

Mandy laughed. It was a well-known fact that she had always preferred animals to children. 'I'm right here,' she said. 'But in the absence of Seamus and Lily, I have to have something to croon over.'

Seamus and Lily were James's much-loved dogs, but for now, they were staying with James's parents. 'I might have known,' James teased.

Mandy reached out a hand and very gently touched Taresh on the shoulder. For a moment, she felt a fleeting sense of envy. If only she and Jimmy were setting out on their own adventure with an infant. The feeling lasted only for a moment. No one deserved this moment of joy more than James and she was determined to feel happy for him. 'It was lovely to meet him,' she told her friend, 'but I really do have to get back.'

'How's your mum?' James asked.

'Doing well, thanks,' Mandy said. It wasn't quite true, but she kept her voice bright. Emily Hope had been unwell for the past two and a half years with multiple sclerosis. Even on good days now, Mandy could see that Emily was very quickly exhausted, yet she seemed unable to stop pushing herself. 'Determined as ever,' Mandy added, and James nodded.

He hugged Mandy with his spare arm. 'I think we'll

get this little one to bed,' he said, 'then we'll try to get some rest too. Thanks very much for the lift.'

'My pleasure,' Mandy replied.

'Give my regards to your mum and dad,' James said.

'Will do.' Mandy hugged Raj and then James and Taresh once more, before heading down the stairs to her car.

Mandy was glad that Helen had offered to stay at Wildacre all day. It was four o'clock by the time she arrived at Hope Meadows. It was still pouring with rain and the trees, heavy with crisp brown leaves, were blowing wildly back and forth. She rushed out of the car and pushed open the door to the rescue centre without lifting her head.

'Hello, love,' Emily greeted her from behind the reception desk. Emily's once-red hair was washed with grey and her pale skin often looked taut over her high-cheekboned face, but she smiled her familiar warm smile.

'Hi, Mum.' Mandy pulled the door closed against the tugging wind, then walked across and stood behind her mother. Emily was updating the Hope Meadows website. She turned the computer screen round to show Mandy.

'I got a lovely picture of Peewit and her babies,' she said.

Peewit was a guinea pig that had been dumped

outside Hope Meadows two weeks ago. Three baby guinea pigs had appeared a week later. Mandy was amazed, as always, by the instant independence of baby cavies: so very different from rabbits, or even kittens and puppies, which took several weeks for their eyes and ears to open. Somehow, Emily had managed to get all four of the blunt-nosed fluffies to look at her at the same time. It really was a lovely photo.

'Your dad's just looking at Jasper,' Emily said. 'We haven't done the other dogs yet.'

Mandy felt a pang of guilt. For the past two years Nicole Woodall had worked part-time at Hope Meadows, but now she had left Welford to join the army. Mandy missed the teenage girl's ready smile and boundless energy. Mandy's grandfather, Tom Hope, came in to help now and then, but he was eighty, and with the cold, wet weather, he wasn't able to come as often as he wanted.

'Why don't you go home, Mum?' she urged. 'Dad and I can finish up.'

'Would you mind?'

Mandy shook her head. 'Of course not,' she said. She watched as Emily pushed herself slowly up out of the chair. It wasn't fair on her parents to have to look after the Hope Meadows residents on top of all the work they did at Animal Ark. Even though the other vet, Toby Gordon, was on-call this weekend, this should have been Adam's weekend off. *I really need to find a new assistant*, Mandy decided.

Chapter Two

Adam Hope looked up with a lopsided grin as Mandy opened the door of the examination room. In contrast with Emily, he seemed to have barely aged at all, though his hair was a little greyer and the lines around his eyes had deepened. 'Just checking Jasper's heart,' he said. Mandy raised her eyebrows and Adam shrugged. 'The murmur's still as loud as ever, but I think his lungs are a bit clearer. He didn't cough as much this morning.'

'That's good,' Mandy said. Jasper's long thin tail swept from side to side as he looked from Mandy to Adam. He was an elderly grey whippet with rheumy-looking eyes and a muzzle which had long since faded to white. He had belonged to an even more ancient man who had lived in the village of Kimbleton, but the old man had been taken into hospital and had died a few days later, leaving Jasper without a home. Mandy had started him on tablets to reduce the fluid on his lungs as soon as he had been brought into the rescue centre, but she knew that it might be difficult to rehome him unless they could get his heart condition under control.

'I wondered if it was worth putting him into the isolation unit,' Adam said. 'It's empty just now and I don't think he's getting much sleep in with Mustard and Olive.'

Mandy ran her hand along Jasper's knobbly spine. 'We could,' she agreed. Mustard and Olive were Hope Meadows' other canine residents. Mustard was a young brindle Staffie, who had been seized from a squat in York, and Olive had been found straying on the moor. Both of them were barkers, and despite her best efforts, Mandy hadn't been able to quieten either in the weeks they'd been with her.

'I'll take him for a few minutes outside first,' Adam told her. 'Then I'll put Olive and Mustard in the paddock and come back and give you a hand with the rest.'

Mandy was cleaning out the last of the cats by the time her dad returned. Sixpence was a young tabby tom who had been taken from the squat at the same time as Mustard. He was deeply suspicious of Mandy, hiding away at the back of his bed whenever she entered the room. Mandy was using tuna to try to entice him out, but it was an uphill struggle. For now, he would only come to the front of his kennel if she sat outside the wire door.

'Jasper definitely looked happier to be on his own,' Adam reported. 'I thought we could start him on the enalapril in the morning, now his chest has cleared a bit.'

Mandy backed out of Sixpence's kennel, closed the door and surveyed the cat room. There were three other inmates at the moment: a beautiful tuxedo cat called Luna, whose owners had divorced, and two recently weaned kittens, Goldie and Patchy, whose mother had been rehomed the week before.

'Good idea,' she said to Adam. 'We should take more bloods, too. Recheck his kidney function.' She felt a rush of affection for her father and walked over to put her arms around him. 'Thanks so much for helping out today,' she said. 'You and Mum.'

Adam hugged her back. He had always been good at bear hugs, ever since she'd been small. 'You work so hard,' he said. 'It's great to see how this place has taken off. You know we're very proud of you, don't you?'

Mandy was secretly pleased, but she pretended to roll her eyes. Her dad told her at least once a week how proud he was. 'You work just as hard,' she pointed out.

Adam stepped back and grinned at her. 'Which makes you a chip off the old block.'

'Isn't Mum joining us?' Mandy asked Adam as she sat down at the scrubbed pine table with a cup of tea in her hand. Mandy had grown up here until she'd left to go to university and had moved back in when she first returned to Welford. So much of her past was centred around this cosy kitchen.

'She's fallen asleep on the sofa,' Adam said. 'You're welcome to stay for dinner, if you like?'

'Thanks, Dad,' she said. 'But Helen's at Wildacre looking after the dogs and I need to go and relieve her.'

Silence fell as they sat cradling their mugs. Mandy could hear the wind rising again, though the rain seemed to be holding off for now. The kitchen felt strangely empty without Emily, and it struck Mandy that her dad must feel very lonely when he lost his wife to bouts of illness.

Mandy had read so much about multiple sclerosis that she felt as if she should be prepared for anything, but the course of her mum's illness seemed totally unpredictable. There had been guilt and pain too, the more she learned. While MS was not directly hereditary, there was evidence to suggest that there was a genetic element. Watching her mum's frightening deterioration, Mandy had felt for the first time ever that it might be a good thing that she and Emily were not related. Which had brought the nagging realisation that Mandy knew nothing of her biological parents: nothing about the illnesses that might run in their families, that she might pass onto any children of her own. When she looked up, Adam was watching her.

'Not too long until Jimmy's due back,' he ventured.

'Another couple of weeks,' she told him, keeping her voice light. Her parents knew nothing about the rejected proposal, but she wasn't going to pretend that she was uncomplicatedly looking forward to Jimmy's return.

She finished her tea and stood up rather abruptly. 'Thanks for the help today.'

'Any time,' Adam told her. He pushed his chair back. 'See you tomorrow, love.'

'See you, Dad.' Mandy hugged him hard before heading back into the turbulent October evening.

'Morning!' Emily called to Mandy from behind the reception desk when Mandy arrived at Animal Ark next morning. As was often the case on a Monday morning, there were several animals to be seen whose owners had phoned over the weekend. Toby and Adam were in their consulting rooms already, opening their computers. Helen was in charge of the operations list and was bustling around handing out consent forms.

'Sorry I fell asleep on you last night,' Emily said as Mandy joined her behind the desk.

Mandy shook her head. 'No need to apologise,' she said. 'You helped me a lot yesterday, thanks.'

'My pleasure.' Emily smiled. 'Have you heard from James yet?'

'Not today,' Mandy said. 'I expect they're all exhausted. Hopefully James will bring Taresh over soon and we can all meet him properly.'

'That'd be lovely,' Emily said.

Toby emerged from his consulting room. 'Morning, Mandy.'

'I see you had a busy weekend,' Mandy commented,

flipping through the diary. 'Three calvings and a caesarean on a bull mastiff. Impressive!'

Toby pulled a face. 'It'd have been more impressive if I hadn't had to call your dad out to give me a hand with the mastiff,' he replied.

Adam appeared and clapped Toby on the shoulder. 'No shame in calling for help when you need it,' he said. 'That was the worst tear I've seen in any uterus, ever. Definitely two pairs of hands needed to stop the bleeding, and Helen had enough to do reviving the puppies.'

'All sixteen of them,' Emily put in, looking up at Mandy.

'Sixteen?' Mandy couldn't keep the amazement out of her voice.

'And all of them made it,' Helen announced with a grin. She held up the extra-length artery forceps – the biggest in the practice – and waved them at Adam. 'Will you want these for the spay later?' she asked. 'Fat Labrador?' It was often difficult to reach the ovaries in large, overweight dogs.

'Helen, you're a treasure,' Adam said. 'I'm not sure if I'll need them, but if you can run them through the steriliser, then if I do, they'll be ready.'

The waiting room door opened and a wiry woman in a red sweater was dragged in by a Bernese mountain dog. 'Morning, all!' she called in a cheery voice.

'Come on in, Mrs Harriot.' Adam held the door of the consulting room open.

23

'Here comes my first,' said Toby as the waiting room door opened again and a tall man staggered in with a heavy-looking cat basket.

'Any farm visits or house calls for me?' Mandy asked Emily.

Emily pulled the daybook towards her. 'Just one for now,' she said. 'Molly Future called about Marlowe. He kicked himself this morning. Quite a nasty cut, apparently.'

Molly Future ran Six Oaks, a riding stables that lay on the edge of Welford at the end of a narrow valley called Silver Dale. Helen Steer's horse, Moondance, was stabled there, as was Bill, a retired Shire that Mandy had rescued from Wildacre. Mandy sometimes rode out with Molly, though with the autumn calvings and all the rescues, she hadn't had much time lately.

Marlowe was Molly's new competition horse. Molly had described him wryly to Mandy as 'spirited' but when Mandy had seen him, she could easily understand why Molly seemed so smitten with the beautiful dappled grey.

It was a quick drive out of the village and up to Silver Dale. Mandy pulled up in the familiar cobbled stableyard. The hanging baskets were empty, swinging in the breeze, but the stones were spotless. No mean feat, Mandy thought, after yesterday's storm.

Molly looked over the wooden half-door of the largest of the stables, her face uncharacteristically grim. Her red hair, usually well regimented in its pixie cut, was standing on end as if she'd been rubbing her head. 'He's made a right mess of himself!' she exclaimed as Mandy walked towards her. 'Silly sod.'

Mandy joined her at the stable door. Even from here, she could see it was a nasty injury. Dribbles of blood stained his off-fore from halfway up the cannon right down to the floor.

'I tried to hose it down so I could have a look,' Molly said. 'But he wouldn't let me near it.'

'Looks like we're going to have to sedate him,' Mandy decided.

She fetched a sedative from the car. Marlowe snorted and shook his elegant head as she approached, but Molly took a firm grip on his halter. 'Enough now,' she said. 'You gorgeous idiotic beast.'

Mandy had long ago concluded that Molly preferred challenging horses. The more bad-tempered and aloof they were, the more Molly liked them. Which seemed to match her taste in men, sometimes . . . Mandy pressed her thumb into the jugular furrow to raise the vein and injected the sedative. 'That's it,' she told Molly as she ran a hand down the smoothly rounded muscu-lature of Marlowe's neck.

Once Marlowe was standing quietly, his head hanging low, Mandy washed the cut down with saline and inspected it. 'Full skin thickness,' she reported, 'but as far as I can see, not deep enough for tendon damage.' She pulled the skin edges together. 'We should put a couple of stitches in, though.'

She opened the suture kit on a bale of hay. Despite the sedation, she decided to put in some local anaesthetic. To her relief, the big grey horse stood as still as a rock as she carefully set in five stitches. 'I'll put a bandage on,' she said, 'and give him a tetanus anti-toxin as well. That should do for today.'

Molly frowned. 'Won't he need antibiotics?'

Mandy shook her head. 'It looked clean,' she said. 'The honey dressing should be enough. If any signs of infection appear, then we'll think again.'

Bandage on, they let themselves out of the stable and stood looking over the door at the still dopey gelding.

'The stitches need to stay in for twelve days,' Mandy explained. 'If you can change the bandage every three to four days, I'll come out in a week to check how he's doing. He'll need strict box rest until a couple of days after the stitches are out.'

'No problem,' Molly said. 'Not that he'll be happy,' she added, 'but it's his own fault for trying to keep up with the Biscuit Twins in the next field.'

'The Biscuit Twins?' Mandy wondered if she'd heard right.

Molly grinned. 'Haven't you met them yet?' she asked. 'My two Welshies?'

Mandy shook her head.

'You're in for a treat,' Molly said. She strode across the yard, turned right, crossed the paddock and led Mandy up the track that rose towards Silver Dale. At this end the fellsides, though steep, were lined with silver birch and rowan trees.

A wooden gate stood at the entrance to a sloping grassy field. As Mandy and Molly approached, a pair of gorgeous Welsh Section A geldings cantered towards them and skidded to a halt, snorting.

'Oh, they are beauties!' Mandy exclaimed.

'This is Bourbon.' Molly held out a carrot stick to the dark bay, which had a long black forelock that fell bewitchingly over one eye. 'And this is Party Ring.' Molly offered a carrot to the other gelding. 'He's actually a lovely palomino, though he seems to be permanently mud-coloured at the moment.'

Mandy laughed. She reached out a hand and Party Ring snuffed at it, then threw his head in the air when he realised that she wasn't holding a treat. 'How did Party Ring get his name?'

Molly rolled her eyes. 'I know, it's ridiculous,' she said. 'It was Nicole Woodall's fault. She was eating the biscuit version of a party ring and he snaffled it. The name stuck.'

Mandy grinned. 'It could have been worse. She could have been eating a fig roll!'

'Can you have a look at Bill while you're here?' Molly asked.

Molly had kept Bill at Six Acres for two and a half years now and for most of that he'd been very comfortable, despite his great age. His teeth had been so worn when Mandy had found him that she hadn't been able to tell exactly how old he was, but he had been well past retirement. Mandy had diagnosed his COPD, a chronic lung condition, earlier in the year, when he had started to cough and wheeze. He'd probably had it for years, but now the deterioration was speeding up.

'Has he been able to stay outside?' Mandy said. Bill's condition meant that he was allergic to dust and had difficulty breathing when he was moved into a stable.

Molly nodded. 'So far,' she said. 'He's in the paddock with the field shelter. I've got my fingers crossed that he can stay there for the next few months, but you know what it can be like up here.'

Mandy did know. In the Yorkshire Dales, it was common for some of the higher valleys to have quite a bit of snow, even when other areas escaped it. Six Oaks, set at the end of Silver Dale, was particularly prone to drifting snow. It wouldn't come for a month or so but by December, anything was possible.

'And he's eating the haylage okay?' Mandy checked.

'Oh yes. He loves his haylage.'

They rounded the corner and the elderly bay Shire came into view. He was still as lovely as ever, Mandy thought, with his patient face and kind eyes. As they drew closer she could see that his nostrils were flaring as he breathed and each breath seemed to take a little more effort than it should have done. Heartbreaking though it was, Mandy knew that Bill was not going to get any better.

Bill had pricked his ears when Molly and Mandy

appeared and blew on Mandy's hair as she ran her hand down his mighty shoulder, encased in a thick waterproof rug. 'I'll just have a quick listen.' Mandy pulled her stethoscope out of her pocket and unbuckled the chest straps. As she expected, Bill's lungs were full of crackles and wheezes. Mandy took the earpieces back out and shoved the stethoscope back into her pocket.

'Have you had to use the clenbuterol lately? That should open up his airways.'

Molly sighed. 'I've been giving it to him every couple of days,' she admitted. 'I know you said he could become resistant if he had it all the time, but he really seems to need it.'

Mandy raised her arms and put a hand gently on either side of Bill's neck. Bill put his head against her ear and nibbled at her hair. Despite his illness, he had never once been grumpy. 'You're a good old boy, aren't you,' she told him, stepping back. 'His glands are a bit swollen,' she said, 'but I don't think he needs antibiotics.'

'Fancy a coffee?' Molly offered as they trudged back across the field. 'And a piece of chocolate fudge cake?'

'That would be wonderful,' Mandy replied.

They kicked their boots off and walked into the kitchen. Mandy always felt at home here. The black and white floor tiles were never perfectly clean and there were mugs in the sink as usual, but the walls were bright with photographs of horses, past and present, and there were two comfortable chairs on either side of the Aga. Mandy sank into one of them as Molly bustled around, cutting pieces of a luscious-looking chocolate cake and making coffee.

'Just milk, isn't it?' Molly checked, looking over at Mandy with eyebrows raised. She added a large slug when Mandy nodded.

'So,' Molly said, dropping into the chair opposite, 'how are things going with Jimmy away?'

'Not bad,' Mandy said, trying to keep her voice light. Much as she regarded Molly as a good friend, she didn't want to get into any deep conversations about Jimmy at the moment.

'Not missing him too much, then?' Molly grinned at her. 'You're like me, aren't you? Nice to have a man about now and then, but fine without one as well. That's the good thing about having animals, isn't it? Marlowe's more reliable than any man.'

Mandy pressed her lips together. Part of her wanted to admit that she was missing Jimmy like crazy. Much as she loved Sky, her dog was no substitute. She avoided answering by taking a mouthful of cake.

Molly picked up a piece of chocolate curl with her fingers. 'I just hope Aira's looking after your man,' she commented. 'I know I didn't go out with him long, but he always seemed a wild one. I wouldn't trust him as far as I could throw him. Do you think Canada would be teeming with pioneer women? They'd be right up his street.' She popped the chocolate into her mouth.

Mandy decided it was time to change the subject.

Jimmy had mentioned that a couple of postgrad students were helping with one of the studies. It hadn't occurred to Mandy to wonder if they were providing anything more than academic and practical support. 'Have you got anything planned for the weekend?' she asked, pushing images of leggy, laughing students out of her head.

Molly shook her head. 'Mucking out,' she said, 'same as every other day. How about you?'

Mandy laughed. 'I'll be working too,' she said. 'What a pair we are.'

'Ah, but you have Jimmy winging his way home to you soon,' Molly reminded her. 'While I'll have to start the dreaded online dating again if I don't want to end up a boring old maid!'

Chapter Three

Mandy had just thrown her stethoscope into the boot and slammed it shut when her mobile phone rang. To her surprise, it was Toby calling from Animal Ark. Toby had been a high-flying vet at Glasgow Vet School before coming to Welford. He had originally intended to start his own practice, but he fitted in so well at Animal Ark that Mandy hoped he wouldn't be in any hurry to leave. He'd had a fling with Helen back in the summer, but that had passed quickly. Mandy could imagine him on the other end of the phone, all blue eyes, blond hair and cheekbones.

'Mandy, it's your mum.'

Fear crashed over Mandy like a tidal wave and she couldn't speak.

'I'm afraid she collapsed this morning,' Toby went on. 'Your dad's taken her to the hospital in York.'

'I was just on my way back,' she said, scrambling into the driver's seat. Her voice sounded too high. 'I'm just finished here, I'll be a few minutes . . .'

'Mandy, stop!' Toby interrupted gently. 'Your mum didn't seem too bad by the time they set off, but I know you'll want to get over there. Helen and I have done some phoning round. Rachel's coming in to help and we've managed to reschedule some of the appointments.'

Rachel Gill worked part-time as a receptionist at Animal Ark. Married to one of the local farmers, she was very practical and often willing to help out at short notice.

Mandy blinked. If she wasn't needed at the clinic, then she could head straight to York. She knew Helen and Rachel would take care of the animals in the rescue centre for her. 'Thanks, Toby,' she said. She put the phone on the seat beside her. A flurry of rain hit the windscreen as Mandy turned the key in the ignition, her hand trembling. Five minutes later, she was driving along the Walton road.

Emily and Adam were still in A&E when Mandy arrived. She had wondered whether Emily would have been taken straight to the MS team, but without an appointment, it seemed she had to go in through the normal channels.

Emily was lying on a bed. Her face looked pale and her green eyes were shadowed.

'What happened?' Mandy found it difficult to keep the fear out of her voice. She took Emily's hand. 'Toby said you collapsed.'

Emily managed a half smile, though Mandy could see the effort behind it. 'That's a bit dramatic,' she said. 'My legs gave way, that's all.' She squeezed Mandy's fingers as if she was trying to comfort her. 'They're going to do an MRI, but they think there might be a new lesion on my spine.'

Mandy looked down at the bony, achingly familiar hand that lay in hers. Her mum had what was known as relapsing, remitting multiple sclerosis. Up until now, Emily had mostly suffered from headaches, tiredness and pain. This was the start of more serious symptoms. 'Have they said anything about treatment?' she asked.

Emily rubbed her thumb over the back of Mandy's hand. 'They're going to try some intravenous prednisolone,' she said. 'They seem quite optimistic that the feeling in my left foot will come back.'

'Is it just the left side that's numb? What about the right?'

'Pins and needles,' Emily replied. She managed another smile. 'Not sure which is worse.'

A nurse put her head round the curtain. 'Okay?'

Emily nodded. 'Not bad, thanks.'

'We'll be taking you up to the ward in a minute or two,' the nurse said. Like all the other staff, she was dressed in scrubs. Her name badge identified her as Marion Campbell, Senior Charge Nurse. She disappeared for a moment, then returned with a tall man with dark hair wearing a white polo shirt and black trousers. 'This is Billy,' Marion said. 'He'll take you up.'

Billy nodded at Emily. 'Got everything?' he asked. He squeezed behind the bed head and started to push Emily along the passage towards the lift. Mandy followed, walking beside Adam. She wished her dad would tell her that it was all going to be okay and that her mum was going to be fine.

Another nurse greeted them on the ward and started running through some questions with Emily. The mobile phone rang in Mandy's pocket and she jumped. It was James. 'Just going to take this,' she told her parents. 'It's James,' she added. She didn't want them fretting that something might have gone wrong at Animal Ark. She hurried out of the ward, onto the corridor and stopped at the end beside a window. Outside, she could see the clouds scudding across the grey October sky.

'Hi Mandy, how are things?'

He had his phone on speaker: Mandy could hear Taresh babbling in the background and Raj talking to him quietly. For a moment, Mandy wished she was there with them. 'Not so good, actually,' she said. 'Mum collapsed this morning. We're in the neurology department in York Hospital.'

The background noise abruptly stopped. James must have switched the phone to be more private. 'Oh, I am sorry.' James's voice was sympathetic. 'Is it the MS?'

'They think she might have a new lesion on her spine, but we'll have to wait for the MRI to be certain.'

'Poor Emily,' James said, 'and poor you. Sounds terrifying.' Mandy knew that James knew exactly what she was going through. He'd spent months having to rush his husband Paul in and out of the York Hospital during the last few months of his battle with cancer. 'Would it be okay for me to come in?' James asked.

Mandy felt a rush of affection for her oldest friend. It couldn't be easy for James to go back to hospital visiting, but she knew he loved Emily. 'That will be fine,' she said. 'They'd love to see you.'

She walked back onto the ward. Janice the nurse had set up a drip. 'Your mum's a bit dehydrated,' she told Mandy.

'They need to do some more tests,' Emily said. 'Why don't the two of you get some lunch in the canteen? I can text you when I'm ready.'

'Sounds like a plan,' Adam said. 'See you in a few minutes.'

The restaurant was as bright and clinical as the rest of the hospital. They grabbed some sandwiches from a refrigerated stand, paid, then went and sat down at a white table. Mandy pulled out her phone and sent a text to James. 'Dad and I are in Ellerby's canteen.'

They were just finishing their rather dry sandwiches when James appeared. 'How is she?' he asked.

Adam's mouth tightened. 'Not so good,' he said. 'They're doing more tests, but I don't think they'll know for a few days how things are going to pan out with these latest symptoms.'

Emily was talking to a doctor when they arrived back at her bedside. She smiled at them. 'You've met my husband and daughter before, Dr Dingwall. This is her friend James, who lives in York. James, this is Frances Dingwall.'

Frances reached out her hand and shook James's.

'Good to meet you,' she said. She turned back to Emily. 'Would you like me to go over that again for your family?'

Emily nodded. 'Please,' she said.

Frances gave them a professionally calm smile. 'It's always frightening when something like this happens, but there's a good chance at this stage that there'll be a partial, or maybe even complete, reversal of the loss of sensation. We're starting with methylprednisolone for now, but there are other immune-mediating drugs that might help. Once this crisis is over, we'll reassess the current regimen to see if anything should be adjusted.' She looked at Emily. 'We'll get the physio down as well,' she told her. 'They'll need to do some assessments, once we see how things are going.' She turned back to Adam and Emily. 'Do you have any questions?'

'Nothing I can think of,' Adam said, 'though I'll probably come up with hundreds once you leave.'

Frances nodded. 'Tell them to Emily here and I'll do my best to answer them,' she said. She swept off and the sound of her heels tapping on the floor receded.

Adam pulled one of the visitor's chairs into position beside the bed and dropped into it. He didn't look as pale as Emily, but there were exhausted lines beneath his eyes and round his mouth. James pulled up a chair and sat down as well, and Mandy walked round to the other side of the bed and pulled up a third. There were four other beds in the ward, but only two of them were filled, though the rumpled sheets in one of the others suggested its occupant wasn't too far away.

'I can't stay long,' James said, 'though I thought I could pop back later and bring you some soup, Emily, and maybe a sandwich. The food here's not bad for a hospital, but I reckon I can do better.'

Emily smiled at him. 'That would be very nice,' she said, 'but are you sure you can spare the time? How are things going? Raj and Taresh, how are they?'

James's face lit up. 'They're both very well. Taresh is settling in so fast, it's hard to remember there was a time when he wasn't here.'

'How lovely.' Emily reached out a hand and gave James's a squeeze. 'Maybe in a day or two, I'll be able to meet him.'

'Soon as you're out, we'll come over to Welford,' James promised.

Mandy shuffled to the edge of her seat. 'I'm afraid I'm going to have to go, Mum.'

'Of course, love,' Emily said. 'Thanks for coming.'

A couple of leaflets that were lying on the bedside table fell to the floor as Mandy stood up. She crouched down and picked them up. The top one was about the hospital chaplaincy service. Mandy had come across the service before, when Paul had been in hospital.

But the leaflet underneath was for disability aids. Mandy felt a sense of shock as she looked down at the picture of a smiling woman in a wheelchair. Would this be her mum, when she got out of hospital? She caught

Emily watching her and tried to smile. 'See you soon,' she muttered, leaning over to give her a kiss. Her legs felt strange and heavy as she walked away.

Outside the rain had started again. The air was blissfully cool after the stuffy ward. Mandy sat in her car for a moment. *It's going to be okay.* Emily was in good hands. Even if she had to use crutches or a wheelchair, her life wouldn't be over. Mandy turned on the radio, hoping for something cheery.

'. . . severe gale warning for North Yorkshire.' It was the weather forecast. 'Batten down the hatches, everyone. And now here's a classic. "I'm Still Standing" by Elton John.'

Mandy switched the radio off. She wished she could go home and hug Jimmy, but instead she was going back to an empty house. Tears welled in her eyes, but she blinked them back. If her mum could face the future bravely, she had to as well.

Chapter Four

Helen was in the paddock behind Hope Meadows when Mandy arrived. She was exercising Sky, Jimmy's dogs, and her own dogs Lucy and Isla. All six dogs made a beeline for Mandy and engulfed her in a swirling sea of sniffing noses and wagging tails.

'How's your mum?' Helen asked once the dogs had zoomed off again.

Mandy put her hands in her pockets, gazing after the dogs as they disappeared into the gloom. 'I don't really know,' she admitted. 'She said she couldn't feel her foot and both her legs were weak. The doctor seemed to think the feeling and some of the strength might come back, but the whole thing's so unpredictable.' It was impossible to keep the frustration out of her voice. 'I suppose I'd better crack on,' she said. 'Dad'll need something to eat when he gets home, too.'

Helen turned to look at the cottage and Mandy followed her gaze. To her surprise, warm light was shining from the kitchen window. 'Actually,' Helen said, 'we called your grandparents. I hope that's okay. Dorothy insisted on coming round to sort everything out. Toby and Rachel are managing evening surgery between them, so if you like, I can help with the rescue animals.'

Not for the first time that day, Mandy felt the prickle of tears starting behind her eyes. Earlier, she had been wishing for Jimmy, but he was not the only one who could help. She had friends and family all around her. 'Thanks, Helen,' she managed to say.

They walked inside together, taking the dogs with them. 'I can take Jasper, Olive and Mustard out if you like,' Helen offered.

'That'd be great,' Mandy replied. 'Just keep Jasper on his lead until Mustard's run some of his energy off.'

She went to the cats first. Sixpence hissed at her as she came into the room, but when Mandy opened his cage door, moving very slowly, she managed to stroke his cheek. 'You're a sweet little thing really, aren't you?' she told the wide-eyed tabby. Goodness knows what awful things might have happened to him in his short life in the squat. She closed the cage quietly and headed to the food-prep room. She was about to carry the first of the cat bowls through when the phone on the reception desk rang.

'Hello.' It was a woman's voice on the other end of the line. 'I'm Vicky Beaumont. Roo Dhanjal suggested I get in touch with you. I'm looking to rehome some kittens, if you have any?' She sounded warm and friendly.

'Thanks for ringing,' Mandy replied. 'We actually

have two at the moment. A brother and sister. They're twelve weeks old. Would you like to make an appointment to see them?'

'That'd be great. Is it okay if I bring the children?'

'Of course,' Mandy said. 'How about tomorrow afternoon?'

'After school would be good,' Vicky told her. 'About four?'

'Perfect!' Mandy put down the phone feeling pleased.

'Someone wanting a pet?' Helen asked. She had put the dogs back in their kennels and was standing with her hands on her hips.

'Looking for kittens,' Mandy said. 'She sounded nice.'

'Excellent. What's left to do?'

'Not much,' Mandy told her. 'All the bowls are ready to hand out.'

'In that case, I'll finish up,' Helen said. 'You can go in and see how Dorothy's getting on. Your dad isn't back yet, but he called Rachel to say he wouldn't be long. Evening surgery's finished.'

'Thanks again, Helen,' Mandy said, meaning it. 'We'd be lost without you!'

Though the wind had dropped, there was still rain in the air. It was starting to feel like winter was only just around the corner. Mandy pushed open the door to the cottage and stepped inside. The kitchen was warm and there were pans bubbling on the stove. Whatever Gran was making, it smelled wonderful.

'Hello, love.' Gran turned and smiled. She was

sporting a pair of oven gloves. 'Just making a mushroom casserole. It'll be ready in a few minutes.'

Gran's white hair was wispy and she walked with a stick, but the determined woman who had raised Adam, seen him marry, then welcomed his adoptive daughter into the family, was still very much there behind the clouded blue eyes. 'How are you doing?' Without waiting for an answer, she walked over to Mandy, leaning hard on her stick, then put her arm around Mandy's waist. She was so tiny, it was as if a blue tit had flown over to comfort her, but Mandy felt the warmth of her gran's love flow into her.

'This must be very frightening for you,' she said, 'but the York Hospital staff are lovely.' She knew what she was talking about, Mandy thought. Gran had been in York a few years ago for a hip replacement and she was often over there these days, visiting friends.

'Jenny McFarlane's going to take me over tomorrow to see her,' Gran went on. 'I baked some shortbread this morning and I'll take some for your mum. I don't want her wasting away with the hospital food.'

'She'll be thrilled,' Mandy told her. No chance of her mum starving, with James and Gran both trying to feed her up.

The door to the hallway opened and Tom Hope, Mandy's grandfather, walked in. His face lit up when he saw Mandy. 'Oh good,' he said. 'I wasn't sure if you'd go straight home.' He turned to Dorothy. 'That's the fire lit,' he announced. 'Is there anything else I can do?'

'You could drain the potatoes and broccoli,' Gran told him. 'Now all we need is your dad,' she said to Mandy.

The curtain in the corner of the room twitched and a paw appeared, followed by a furry ginger head. It was Tango. Just as he finished stretching and set off towards the door, Sky stood up and began to bark, quickly joined by Zoe, Simba and Emma. The door opened and Adam stepped inside. He bent to greet the dogs and Tango, then glanced up and beamed.

'Hello, Mum,' he said.

Gran stretched her arms around him and tipped her head back to look up at his face. 'I'm so sorry, love. Poor Emily.'

Tom Hope put a hand on Adam's shoulder. 'She's in good hands,' he said.

Adam took a deep breath and visibly squared his shoulders. 'Whatever you're cooking, Mum, it smells great.' His voice was hearty, but Mandy could see the effort it took. They sat down at the table and Gran served up the casserole and vegetables. Though it tasted great, Mandy didn't have much of an appetite.

Gran patted her shoulder as she cleared away the plates. 'Why don't you go into the sitting room, love? I'll bring you some shortbread.'

Mandy sat at one end of the sofa and lowered her head onto the armrest. She stared at the flames in the grate, feeling her eyelids grow heavy. The door swung open and Adam walked in, followed by Tom Hope with a plate of shortbread. Dorothy Hope peeked out from behind him. 'We're going to head home now,' she said. 'Will you two be okay?'

'We'll be fine, I promise,' Adam said. Mandy heard their footsteps dying away as they walked down the hall, and then the sound of the door closing.

Adam sat down in his chair and picked up his mug of coffee. 'You okay, Mands?'

Mandy nodded. 'Would it be okay if I stayed the night? I know I have all these dogs, but . . .'

Adam let out a gentle laugh. 'We've had more than a few dogs in here,' he pointed out. 'I'm sure Tango will share his kitchen. And you know you're always welcome.'

Mandy had to blink back the tears that jumped into her eyes. It had been a very long day, she thought. It would be so nice to walk up the familiar stairs and lie down in the little bed she had slept in for so many years. And in the morning, she could get up early and make breakfast for both of them. There was so little that she could do to help her mum, but she could keep her dad company.

In front of the fire, Simba lurched upright, staggered a few steps, then lay down again where it would be slightly cooler. One by one, the other dogs followed. Mandy clutched her mug in her hands and buried her toes in the nearest dog's fur. It's all going to be okay, she told herself. It just had to be.

*

Mandy awoke to the gentle light of a late October morning. Outside, a blackbird was singing. She blinked a couple of times, then reached out a hand to pick up her phone from the little table that stood beside the single bed. It was close to seven-thirty. She had meant to get up at seven, but when she checked the alarm function on her phone it was off. She couldn't tell if she'd hit the button while still asleep or had forgotten to set it altogether.

Sky was stirring. The little collie stood up slowly and stretched, walked a few steps, stretched again, then galloped across the room and jumped on Mandy's bed. Despite everything that had happened, it felt like a good start to the day.

'Morning, poppet.' Mandy put her arms round the collie and buried her face in the soft fur of Sky's neck. She smelled of hay and autumn leaves. Mandy breathed in her scent for a moment, then nudged Sky over and swung her legs out of bed. 'Time to get up,' she announced.

Downstairs in the kitchen, Adam was prising a piece of toast from the toaster with a wooden fork. The kettle was boiling and two mugs stood ready on the counter. Mandy felt a pang of guilt. 'Sorry, Dad,' she said. 'I meant to get up and make your breakfast, not the other way round.'

Adam narrowed his eyes. 'Yes,' he said. 'What time do you call this for coming downstairs? Another hour and you'd have been late for work.' Mandy grinned, relieved that his sense of humour had returned after the tension of yesterday.

Adam finished pouring the coffee, handed her a mug and pushed the milk carton in her direction. 'It's good to have you here,' he told her.

The phone in the hallway rang and Adam stood up. 'Hello, love,' he said when he lifted the receiver. Mandy could tell by his tone that it was Emily. She took another piece of toast, half listening to the conversation, half reading a copy of *Dogs Weekly*.

'I'll see you later,' she heard her dad say. He came back into the kitchen and Mandy closed the magazine.

'Your mum's doing well,' Adam announced. 'She sends her love.' He sat down. 'She sounded much better, I must say. I don't think she's in as much pain as she was yesterday.'

'Was she in pain?' Mandy felt a stab of alarm. 'Why didn't she tell me?'

Adam's smile was gentle. 'I think she doesn't want to worry you,' he said. 'She knows how hard this is for all of us and she's trying to make it easier.'

Mandy rubbed at a mark on the table. 'I'd much rather she was honest. I want to help her and I can't do my best for her if she doesn't tell me the truth.'

'I know,' Adam said. 'I wish she'd ask for more help, but she hates to do it. It's hard to watch her struggle, but I honestly think she prefers to battle on her own than feel she can't do things for herself. She can't bear the thought of being useless.'

Mandy wanted to lay her head on the table and howl. Mum was the exact opposite of useless.

Her dad was watching her. 'I know it's difficult,' he said, 'but we just have to carry on giving what support we can. Your mum's an incredible woman. Very much like you, in fact.' He reached across the table and squeezed her hand. 'If you can be on duty tonight, I'll go over to York after afternoon surgery. You can stay here again, if you like. I'll get something to eat while I'm out, but help yourself to anything in the freezer.'

'Thanks, Dad.' Mandy managed to smile. 'We need to show Mum that we're still a good team.'

'Hopes United,' Adam agreed. 'Winners every time!'

Morning clinic was, as Mandy had expected, quite busy. They had to see several of the clients who'd agreed to delay their appointments yesterday. Mandy was happy to have the distraction. She had a quick lunch with her dad before he headed off to York, and Mandy took the rescue dogs for a spin around the orchard. There was a tang of ice on the air, as if the first hard frost was on its way.

Afternoon surgery came and went, and at four o'clock on the dot a blue Volvo pulled up outside. All four doors opened, and a man and woman emerged, along with two small girls. The woman had long brown hair and a friendly face and she was dressed in jeans and a striped sweater. She pulled open the waiting room door, then held it open for the man, who was holding the smaller girl's hand. He was tall with a shaved head and warm brown eyes.

The woman walked across to the desk and spoke to Helen. 'Hi,' she said. 'I'm Vicky Beaumont. I spoke to Amanda Hope yesterday about adopting some kittens?'

'Hello.' Mandy held out her hand. 'I'm Mandy.'

'Good to meet you.' Vicky's handshake was firm, the palm of her hand warm and dry.

Mandy frowned as she turned to the man. 'Have I seen you somewhere before?' she asked. His face seemed familiar, but she couldn't place him.

He grinned. 'Quite possibly,' he said. 'I'm a tree surgeon. I've worked with Jimmy a few times. I'm Ben, by the way. This is Elodie.' He waved a hand at the taller girl, who was standing very close beside Vicky. 'And Connie.' He lifted the small hand that was in his and Connie looked up at him, and then at Mandy. Her brown eyes were wide and solemn.

'How do you know Roo?' Mandy asked Vicky as she led the family out of Animal Ark and down the stone path that ran along the side of Hope Meadows.

'Elodie's in Herbie's class at school. Roo and I first met over playdates, but now she and I are friends as well. I'm a school nurse.'

Mandy led them into the rescue centre with her usual sense of pride at the spectacular reception area, with the floor to ceiling window that looked out to the moors. 'I need to take a few details down, then we can go and meet Goldie and Patchy.' They went through the family details: name and address and a few questions about the house. 'Right,' Mandy said, 'I think that's everything. I'll take you through to the cats. Can you tell me a bit about why you're looking to rehome kittens?' she asked Vicky as she held open the door.

Vicky smiled. 'The girls have wanted kittens for ages,' she admitted. 'Truth be told,' she added, 'I'm more of a dog person. But in this case I'm outnumbered.' Mandy couldn't help but appreciate her honesty. It didn't mean Vicky wouldn't make a good cat owner.

She opened the door to the kittens' cage. Goldie, who had always been the more adventurous of the pair, walked straight out and rubbed herself against Elodie's leg.

'Oh!' Elodie looked transfixed with delight. She bent down and touched the kitten's fur. 'I think she likes me!'

Mandy reached into the cage and stroked Patchy's face, then gently lifted him into Connie's arms. Connie beamed, and Mandy was pleased to see that she didn't grip the kitten too tightly. Patchy started purring and pushed his head against Connie's chin. 'Hello, little cat,' Connie whispered.

'What do you think?' Mandy asked Vicky, raising one eyebrow.

'They're very sweet,' Vicky said. 'And I think it's love at first sight for the girls!'

Mandy watched the whole family as they stroked the

kittens. She noticed that Ben and Vicky were keeping a close eye on the girls, making sure they didn't squash the kittens or hurt them unintentionally.

'Can we take them home now?' Elodie asked, looking up at Mandy.

'Not today, I'm afraid,' Mandy told her.

'Mandy will have to come out to our house first.' Ben was quick to explain. 'She needs to make sure it's safe for the kittens to live with us.'

Elodie nodded. 'We're going to get lots of toys to play with them,' she told Mandy earnestly. 'And we need to get a bowl for water and one for food. Herbie's cats have a green bowl,' she went on, 'but I want a blue one for Patchy.'

'Blue would be a very good colour,' Mandy said. 'What colour bowl do you think Goldie should have?'

Elodie put a finger to her mouth and stood on one leg for a moment with her head on one side. 'Goldie should have a gold bowl,' she announced.

Ben laughed. 'I don't think we can afford a gold bowl,' he said. 'Would yellow do?'

'Yellow would be fine,' Elodie decided.

Mandy smiled. It looked as if this was the start of another successful rehoming.

Chapter Five

Emily improved quickly, to Mandy's relief. She went over to York on Wednesday afternoon and was pleased to find her mum out of bed and sitting in a chair, looking much brighter. Emily phoned Adam on Thursday morning to give him another update.

'She told Dad she should be home by the weekend,' Mandy said to Rachel, leaning on the reception desk in the clinic. 'She'll need to take it easy for a while though,' she added. 'The physio told her she mustn't do too much until the strength comes back properly. Goodness knows how she and Dad will manage, but I'm glad she's coming home.'

Rachel looked at Mandy, her eyes thoughtful. 'I don't know what your parents would say,' she began, 'but I'm looking for a few more hours' work. Brandon and I are saving up for a deposit.' She grinned. 'It's lovely living at the farm, but even though they're easygoing, there's not much privacy when you're living with your in-laws.'

Mandy laughed. 'I can imagine,' she said. David and Maureen Gill were decent enough people, but

Greystones Farmhouse would be a tight fit with two couples living together.

'What sort of help would your mum need?' Rachel asked. 'I'd be happy to come in on the mornings I'm not working here to help with cleaning and laundry. And I could do shopping, or take your mum out to do it, if that's what she'd prefer.'

Mandy felt a wave of gratitude. 'Sounds perfect to me. I'll tell Mum and Dad,' she said.

'Thanks.' Rachel looked at the computer screen, checking the morning's list. 'There's nothing in at the moment,' she said. 'Would you be able to man the phones for a few minutes while I nip to the post office? There are some samples in the fridge.'

'I could, if you like,' Mandy said, 'but if you'd prefer, I can take them.'

Rachel beamed. 'That'd be even better,' she said. 'I need to make a start on the invoices. We're a bit behind this month.' No wonder, Mandy thought, with all the extra work Rachel and Helen had been doing.

Mandy grabbed the packages of samples from the fridge and headed outside. Though it was cloudy, it looked like the rain would hold off for now. She called in at the cottage, whistled to Sky and Simba, and set off down the lane. The hedgerows were looking bare after the storm. There were a few berries on the hawthorn, though the birds had stripped most of them. Tiny yellow-green flowers were appearing among the glossy ivy leaves, reminding Mandy of miniature

Christmas decorations. After the long hot summer, autumn seemed to have come and gone very fast.

Gemma Moss stood behind the counter in the post office. She was wearing her favourite Moody Mare sweatshirt and her blonde hair, which had been cut short in a chic French style, was looking rather fluffy. Mandy had been surprised how much she missed Gemma when she took a long trip through France in the summer with Helen Steer's horse.

Gemma smiled as Mandy handed over the parcels. 'Usual next-day service?' she checked, and Mandy nodded. The man who had worked as relief in the post office over the summer had always made a massive song and dance over the Animal Ark samples. 'Anyone would think we'd smeared anthrax spores all over the outside,' Helen had commented to Mandy after one exchange.

'Did you manage to get your chicken shed fixed?' Gemma asked as she put the second parcel on the scales.

Mandy resisted the urge to laugh. Like Mrs McFarlane who had run the post office before her, Gemma made it her business to keep up with everything that was going on in and around Welford. 'Yup, the feathered ladies are back where they belong,' Mandy assured her.

Gemma stuck stamps on both parcels and slid them into a cubbyhole behind her. 'Is that everything?'

'For today,' Mandy replied.

Gemma straightened the pens on her side of the counter. 'There was a woman in earlier who was looking for you,' she said. 'Did she manage to get in touch?'

Mandy looked at her in surprise. If someone was looking for Hope Meadows, they usually found the information on the internet. 'Not that I know of,' she said. 'What did she want?'

'She was asking about Hope Meadows, if it was open to visitors? She was quite chatty. She'd read an article about you, she said. Seemed interested in seeing your work.'

Mandy frowned. 'She mentioned me by name?'

Gemma laughed when she saw Mandy's serious expression. 'Yes, she mentioned you by name,' she said. 'You're more famous than you realise!'

Gemma seemed to find it amusing, but Mandy couldn't help feeling wary. Two years ago, Mandy had found herself at the centre of a whispering campaign that seemed determined to shut down Hope Meadows. The rumours had started in the post office, with a petition that Gemma had taken down as soon as she realised what was going on.

'Anyway,' Gemma went on, 'I said the rescue centre wasn't open to the public, but that she could find the phone number online if she wanted to visit.'

Mandy pulled herself together. Almost certainly the woman was looking for a dog or something. 'Thanks. Did she tell you her name?'

Gemma shook her head. 'No, but you'll recognise

her if she comes in. She had bright red hair and she was almost as tall as you. I don't think you could miss her.'

The morning passed slowly. Adam and Toby were still out on calls over lunch and neither had returned by two-thirty. Mandy was sitting alone in reception when her phone buzzed. She was pleased to see a text from Jimmy.

'Good Wi-Fi reception in today's camp,' it read. 'Any chance we could Skype now?'

Mandy called Helen through from the stockroom, where she had been counting the injectables. 'Can you take the phones?' she asked. 'Jimmy wants to chat. I'm going into the cottage. Call me if anything urgent comes.'

She rushed inside and grabbed the Animal Ark laptop. Rejecting the kitchen table – she wouldn't have privacy if her dad arrived back – she carried it into the sitting room and opened it on the coffee table. Her heart was thudding and her hands felt clammy. She wanted to see him, of course, but she knew they couldn't ignore the sword of her failed proposal dangling over them. They had so much to talk about, none of it suitable for an unreliable Skype connection when one of them was in the Arctic wilds. And since her conversation with Molly, Mandy couldn't help wondering if one of the postgrads would be hovering in the background, ready to offer a fun distraction.

The connecting tone rang for a moment and then Jimmy's face swam into focus. Despite the distance and the problems that hung over their relationship, Mandy's heart flipped, just as it always did when she saw him. His handsome face was wind-tanned and unshaven, but his green eyes were warm and steady.

'Thanks for calling,' he told her, fuzzily. 'I wanted to chat while I had the time. Everyone else is still asleep, but we're heading out in about an hour.'

'What time is it?' Mandy asked. Even after all these weeks, she still found it difficult to calculate the time difference.

'Just gone 5.30 a.m.'

'What's happening?'

'We're following the bears northwards,' Jimmy explained. 'The weather's turned in the past couple of weeks and the sea's beginning to freeze properly. They're moving out to their winter hunting grounds at last.'

'Will you follow them onto the ice?'

Jimmy shook his head. 'No. We're moving a bit further north today, but we'll be done by the middle of next week. I'm flying into Manchester next Friday. Do you think you could get the afternoon off to meet me?'

Mandy felt as if the breath had been knocked out of her lungs. Jimmy would be home in a week's time. 'I'll have to check with Dad,' she said. 'Mum's not been well. She's been in hospital, but she's coming home for the weekend.'

A shadow passed over Jimmy's face. 'I'm sorry to hear that,' he said. He moved his hands as if he wanted to reach through the screen to touch Mandy. 'It'll be good to see you,' he added.

A voice sounded in the background and Jimmy seemed annoyed for a moment, but he glanced round as Aira loomed up behind him. 'I brought you some coffee,' Aira announced, waving a flask of coffee. He nodded to Mandy. 'Keeping tabs on him?' he asked with a grin. 'You'll be glad to know the only thing keeping this fella warm at night is his sleeping bag.' His eyes gleamed. 'Much to the disappointment of a certain Miss Mackenzie!'

Jimmy frowned, but his cheeks were turning red. 'Don't be an idiot. Mandy, Liz Mackenzie is one of the students I was telling you about. She's a good colleague, that's all.'

'Ah, but doth he protest too much?' Aira teased from behind him.

Mandy tried not to cringe. How was it Belle had described Aira and Jimmy when they were together? A pair of Boy Scouts?

Jimmy was looking at her apologetically. 'I have to go. Have a good week, and I'll see you on Friday, all being well. Bye.'

'Goodbye,' Mandy called, but Jimmy's face had vanished. 'I love you,' she whispered.

★

Mandy had arranged to spend the afternoon at Hope Meadows. She had some paperwork to catch up on, as well as the website to update. Her head was filled with thoughts about Jimmy's imminent return as she took a quick tour round her furry residents. Half of her was beyond excited to see him, but the feeling was tempered with anxiety. The weeks they had spent apart had shown her that without him, her life felt empty. If they split up, the twins would no longer visit and Jimmy's dogs would leave, and Wildacre would be quieter still. But could she bear to go back to how things had been before, knowing that Jimmy didn't want to settle down and start a family with her? Was it even possible to go back? He'd obviously had a great time in Canada, with Aira and the postgrad students. Would he decide that this kind of free, unattached lifestyle suited him better?

Shoving the thoughts aside, she fired up the laptop and opened her emails. Right at the top, there was one from Vicky Beaumont.

'Dear Mandy,' it said. 'Thanks for showing us your wonderful kittens. We would love to be formally considered for their adoption. We have made a few adjustments to the house and you are welcome to visit any time to inspect us.'

Mandy found herself grinning. Vicky Beaumont had an honest directness that she appreciated. 'Glad you liked them,' she wrote in reply. 'Would Sunday afternoon work for you?'

Once she had sent the message, she dealt with the rest of the emails, updated the website with a new picture of Mustard, and then went back into the kennel to put a lead on him. She would take him outside for a solo training session today, she thought. It was good to have a bit of extra time while it was still light.

As she made her way across the reception, she saw a woman passing the window. She frowned for a moment. She wasn't expecting anyone, but the figure that had rounded the corner and disappeared from sight had a mane of scarlet hair. This must be the woman Gemma had mentioned. A second later, she appeared at the door and held up her hand as if to knock, but when she saw Mandy, she smiled and pushed the door open.

She was, as Gemma had said, quite tall. She was quite a bit older than Mandy, though her willowy frame and the vibrant hair made her look younger than the lines around her eyes and mouth suggested.

'What a lovely building!' she exclaimed. She looked at Mandy for a moment. Her eyes were blue and shrewd, as if she was assessing Mandy against some unknown criteria. 'Sorry for just dropping in,' she said. 'I've been wanting to visit for ages. The girl in the post office said I could find a phone number on your website but when I realised how close you were to the village, I thought I'd call in person.'

Mandy felt a stir of unease. Lots of people came to Hope Meadows, but most of them wanted to see the animals and said so straight away. 'Ah yes, Gemma said she spoke to you.'

The woman laughed. 'I'm amazed that got back to you so quickly. It must be quite something to live in a small village.'

Mandy sent her a dry smile. 'It has its benefits,' she commented.

They stood looking at one another for a moment, then the woman held out her hand to Mandy. 'Sorry, I should introduce myself. I'm Geraldine Craven.'

Mandy told herself not to be suspicious. Maybe Geraldine was a journalist who could give Hope Meadows some valuable publicity, or perhaps she wanted to donate some money. She might even be trying to work out if she wanted a new pet. Whoever the woman was, she seemed harmless and friendly.

Mandy took the proffered hand and shook it. 'Mandy Hope,' she replied.

Chapter Six

'I'm afraid I don't have time for a full guided tour at the moment,' Mandy apologised. 'I'm about to do some work with Mustard. You're welcome to watch if you like.'

Geraldine beamed. 'As long as I'm not in the way. Sorry, it must seem rather strange, me just turning up, but I was fascinated when I read about Hope Meadows in my local paper in Manchester. I'm actually on holiday here, and when I realised you were so close, I couldn't resist tracking you down! If it's inconvenient, I can come back another time.'

Mandy shook her head. 'No, it's fine.' She patted Mustard, who was sitting quietly at her feet, and clicked with her tongue to indicate that it was time to concentrate. The little dog jumped up, ears pricked.

Geraldine followed Mandy and Mustard into the orchard. Mandy wondered if she would get in the way, as some overly-invested visitors had in the past, but Geraldine stood well back and watched as Mandy put Mustard through some basic exercises.

'I'm mostly trying to encourage him to give me eye

contact at the moment,' Mandy explained. 'In this exercise, it doesn't really matter if he's sitting down or standing up, I just want him to be paying attention to me.' Mustard looked up at her and she moved a little from side to side until he was distracted. When he looked up at her again, she said 'Good!' in a crisp voice, then reached into her belt for a treat. 'The faster he looks at me, or if he holds eye contact well, the better the treat he gets.' She showed Geraldine the contents of her belt. In addition to kibble, she had small pieces of cheese and some chewy beef-flavoured treats as well as two different tug toys.

'Don't they put on weight?' Geraldine looked down at Mustard, who was, like many of his breed, quite muscular.

Mandy leaned down to unclip Mustard's leash. 'No,' she said, 'though some, like Mustard here, are underweight when they come, and then we feed them up a bit. But I regulate their diets and I allow for the treats when I dish up their main meals. They have to work for quite a lot of their food.'

Mustard padded away from them and began sniffing his way round the roots of a tree, stopping now and then to scrabble in the dirt.

'He seems very sweet,' Geraldine commented as Mustard abandoned the tree roots and rushed over to inspect the fence. 'I've never had a dog,' she admitted. 'It hasn't fitted in with my life. But I do love animals. Now that I've got more time, I've been thinking about finding a pet.'

Mustard was finally looking in her direction. Mandy leaned over, slapped her hands on her legs and called out loudly, 'Come!' To her delight, Mustard came cannoning across the paddock and she pulled one of the tug toys from her belt and wrestled with him until she was breathless.

'Goodness,' Geraldine said as Mandy snapped Mustard's lead back on. 'I never knew dog training was so physical.'

Mandy laughed. 'Having a dog is physical, full stop,' she said. 'Even the little ones need exercise.' She put the toy into her belt and made Mustard sit beside her. 'I'm going to put him away and bring the other two dogs out. I'm not going to do so much with them. One of them has a heart condition and I think the other was dumped; she's very timid, so I'm working on her socialisation. You're welcome to stay though, if you're not bored?'

Geraldine shook her head. 'Definitely not bored. Do you need a hand?'

'No, I won't be a minute.' She took Mustard inside and returned him to his kennel. Jasper was already at the front of his kennel, wagging his tail. 'Hang on, chap. I need to get Olive out first,' Mandy told him, and he looked at her with his head on one side.

Olive wasn't so easy to get out of her cage. She had a tendency to stand and bark, and when Mandy went in, she sometimes growled. Mandy knew that what looked like aggression was due to nervousness, but unless Mandy could help Olive to get over her fear, she would be difficult to rehome.

Mandy entered the cage sideways and slowly managed to get the sliding leash over Olive's head and pull it tight. She turned and walked out of the kennel, careful not to face Olive as that could be seen as a challenge. To her relief, Olive followed her willingly. 'Good girl,' Mandy said. She opened Jasper's cage and the little whippet trotted out. Olive seemed very relaxed around Jasper, but was still tense with the other dogs.

They went outside, and Mandy walked towards Geraldine. 'Please stay still,' Mandy called. She moved a little closer with Olive and told the dog to sit down. Mandy crouched at her head, letting her nibble at a piece of cheese. Once Olive was calm, she spoke again to Geraldine in a quiet voice. 'Can you come towards us slowly? If I hold up my hand, then stop. If not, then keep on until you're beside me.'

To Mandy's delight, Olive seemed quite happy with Geraldine's presence. It had taken her days to get used to Mandy, Helen and Adam. 'You can stroke her if you like,' Mandy told Geraldine. She didn't look away from Olive, but in her peripheral vision, she could see the older woman crouch down, her movements smooth, and reach out a hand to stroke the silky fur on Olive's back.

'That's great,' Mandy said after a moment. She told Geraldine to take a step back, and then she let Olive off the lead to join Jasper, who was pottering around under the trees.

'What's the whippet called?' Geraldine asked. 'He's adorable.'

'Jasper. He's thirteen and has a heart condition.'

'Really?' Geraldine sounded surprised. 'I'd never have guessed. He's so elegant and light-footed.'

Mandy found herself smiling. She was warming to Geraldine more and more. 'Glad you like him,' she said. 'Whippets can be an acquired taste. I love them.' She shrugged. 'Mind you, I've never met a dog I didn't love at first sight, though some of them can be a bit of a challenge.'

'Do you have any dogs yourself?'

'Four,' Mandy confessed. 'Well, three belong to my boyfriend but they all live with us.'

'Yikes! They must keep you busy! Do you all live here?' Geraldine asked, glancing at the cottage.

Mandy shook her head. 'I grew up here, but only Mum and Dad live here now. My boyfriend and I have a house nearby.'

'A family business, then?' Geraldine said. 'How nice for you all.'

The two dogs were still sauntering round the paddock. Mandy glanced down at her watch. Where had the afternoon gone?

'I'm awfully sorry,' she said to Geraldine. 'I'm afraid I have to go. My turn for evening surgery,' she added.

Geraldine smiled. 'No problem,' she said. 'I've probably overstayed my welcome already. Thanks very much for showing me what you do.'

Mandy called the dogs. She slipped Olive's lead around her neck and reached over to clip Jasper's into place. 'You haven't,' she said, looking up with a smile. 'Overstayed your welcome, I mean.'

'I'm glad.' Geraldine sounded genuinely pleased. Mandy led the dogs back to their kennels and closed the doors. Geraldine waited for her in the reception area and when Mandy returned, she was holding out a twenty-pound note. 'Do you take cash donations?'

'Donations are always very welcome,' Mandy said with a smile. They walked outside and Mandy locked the door. 'Thanks for calling in,' she said. 'It was lovely to meet you.'

'You too,' replied Geraldine. Mandy watched as she got into her car and drove away, then headed for the clinic.

Chapter Seven

Mandy was up early for a non-working Saturday. Sky was curled in the passenger seat beside her and the other dogs were in the back. She drew up in front of Animal Ark and pulled on the brake. Today was the day that Emily was due to come home.

She put the dogs in the garden, then opened the kitchen door to find her dad sitting at the table munching a slice of toast. 'Would you like some breakfast?' he asked.

'Just a coffee.' She sat down at the table and Tango weaved around her legs until she reached down and stroked his ears.

'I'll need to head off at about ten-thirty,' Adam said. 'I can give you a hand with the rescues before I go, if you like.'

'That'd be good,' Mandy replied.

Her phone rang two hours later as she was vacuuming the sitting room. James's number was on the screen.

'Hi Mandy. Raj and I are visiting my folks today with Taresh. It'd be great to see you. Are you free?'

'I'd love to see you,' she said. 'Mum's coming home shortly, but I'll be free this afternoon.'

'Excellent! We'll pop over to Animal Ark after lunch.'

As she put the vacuum cleaner back in the hall cupboard, Mandy heard the back door open and close. She walked into the kitchen to find Tom and Dorothy Hope sorting out a pile of things they had dumped on the table. There seemed to be masses of food parcels as well as some neatly folded bed linen. They had insisted on taking it home to wash and iron. 'Emily'll want to come home to a nice, clean bed,' Gran had said, and despite Adam's protests that he could manage, she and Tom had stumped upstairs to strip the beds.

'Do you need any help in the rescue centre?' Tom Hope offered.

Mandy nodded. Though she and Adam had done the feeding and toileting basics, it would be good to get the dogs outside for a bit longer before lunch. 'That'd be great,' she said. 'I really need to look for another assistant. There's too much to do now Nicole has left.'

'Why don't you put up an advert in the post office?' suggested Gran. 'I'm sure there are people who'd love to help out.'

'That's a good idea,' Mandy said.

'If you write it, I'll deliver it for you later,' Grandad offered.

'Deal,' said Mandy with a grin.

*

Emily looked very pale and tired when she arrived home just before lunchtime. It was immediately obvious that she wasn't able to get around as easily as they had all hoped, and she was making heavy use of her crutches every time she took a step. She barely seemed able to put her left foot to the floor. Either the feeling hadn't returned, or she was in a lot more pain than she had admitted.

Mandy settled her mum on the sofa in front of the fire. Tom brought in a tray containing a bowl of home-made soup. He placed it carefully on Emily's lap, twitching the spoon into place to make it easier for Emily to pick up. Dorothy followed with a napkin that she spread on the edge of the tray. Mandy watched her mum's apathy with growing alarm. Usually Emily would be protesting about them all making too much fuss.

Mandy went into the kitchen to find her dad. He was sitting at the table in front of a half full bowl. Another place was set opposite, presumably for Mandy, though she didn't feel hungry.

'Is Mum really well enough to come home?' she asked him.

Adam shrugged. 'It's where she wants to be,' he said. 'I spoke to one of her doctors this morning. It's possible that the feeling won't return fully to her legs, and she's getting a lot of pain in her thigh muscles now.'

Mandy felt tears welling up in her eyes. Why wasn't there anything anyone could do to help her mum? She didn't deserve this!

The door opened and Gran walked in from the hallway, her stick in one hand and a glass in the other. She took one look at Mandy's face, put down the glass, hung the stick over the back of a chair and put her arms round her granddaughter. Despite Mandy being so much taller, Dorothy patted her on the back over and over, just as she had when Mandy was small enough to fit on her lap.

She released Mandy from the hug but hung onto her hands. 'I know it's difficult,' she said quietly, 'but we all have to be strong for your mum.' She squeezed Mandy's fingers. 'I know you,' she said. 'And I know you'll find the strength somewhere.'

Mandy felt strength running into her from the gnarled arthritic hands. She wiped away her tears and managed a smile.

'That's better.' Dorothy patted her arm. 'It's normal to be sad. You're grieving for what your dear mum has lost. We all are. But life goes on. And nobody knows better than you that things aren't always as bad as they seem.' She glanced around the kitchen and saw Mandy's untouched bowl. 'You haven't eaten your soup,' she scolded. 'You have to keep your strength up, you know. And it's your favourite. I made it specially.'

Mandy took her soup in to eat beside Emily on the sofa. Her mum seemed a little more animated, now she'd eaten.

'Tell me what's been going on,' she said. 'How are the kittens?'

71

'I think we might have a home for them,' Mandy said, blowing on her steaming spoon. 'A lovely family, Vicky and Ben Beaumont and their young daughters. I'm doing their house visit tomorrow.'

Emily frowned. 'You won't push yourself too hard, will you?' she said. 'You don't have to do extra work on Sundays.'

Mandy shook her head. It seemed faintly ludicrous that she was the one being told to take it easy. 'Doing a house inspection doesn't really feel like work,' she said. 'I just wander round a bit and make a few notes. It's not like being called out at midnight to a calving.'

Emily folded her napkin and laid it on her tray. 'I guess with Jimmy coming home next week, you're trying to get everything done while you have some free time.'

Mandy felt the familiar twist of worry, but she shoved it down.

'You must have missed him so much,' Emily went on. 'He's a lovely young man, exactly what any mother would want for her daughter.'

Mandy could tell her mum was half-teasing, but only half. Mum and Dad both loved Jimmy. Goodness knows what they'd think if Mandy told them her future with him was far less stable than they had all assumed.

She reached out a hand and squeezed her mum's fingers. 'I have missed him,' she said truthfully, 'and when he's recovered from his journey, I'll bring him round so that he can bore you as well with his polar bear stories.'

Emily laughed, and Mandy felt a layer of anxiety fade away. If her mum got better, everything would be absolutely fine.

Mandy was bending down to put the last of the plates in the dishwasher, when someone knocked on the back door. James and Raj stood outside. James was holding Taresh, and both he and Raj were beaming, though the shadows under their eyes echoed those of all new parents.

'Hi,' James said. He reached out his free arm and gave Mandy a hug. 'Taresh needs some fresh air and a chance to use up some of his energy. Mum and Dad are looking battered already!'

Mandy laughed. She lifted her hand to Taresh and felt a thrill of delight when he gripped her fingers. 'He looks like he's grown already!'

'Must be all the good Yorkshire air,' Raj said. He was looking handsome in a dark green turban that matched the thin stripe in his jacket.

Mandy pulled on her boots and followed them into the garden. Taresh was soon tottering around the lawn, looking adorable in his tiny yellow dungarees. He hugged Raj's leg for a moment, then wobbled towards Mandy. Just as he looked up at her, he tripped over his feet and toppled over. The pack of dogs, who had been zooming round the lawn, made a beeline for him, and for a moment he was lost in a tumble of dogs. Mandy scooped him up.

How soft his little body felt in her arms. She found herself smiling into his gorgeous eyes and he reached up a hand to tug her hair, then laughed at the face she pulled, his chubby cheeks crinkling.

Raj held out his arms to take him. 'Would it be okay if I held him a bit longer?' she asked. Raj nodded, and Mandy held Taresh on her lap as she crouched down to introduce all the dogs.

James was watching her closely. 'When did you learn to like children?' he teased.

'I've got used to having small people around from looking after Abi and Max,' Mandy replied. It was halfway to the truth. She hadn't met Abi and Max until they were eight and the small person she wanted seemed like a pipe dream for now.

The kitchen door opened and Gran stuck her head out. 'Come on in,' she called. 'I've made coffee.'

They trooped inside and sat down at the table. Gran offered Taresh a fresh-baked piece of shortbread and he reached out a chubby hand and stuffed it into his mouth, shedding crumbs.

'He's learning to love British food,' Raj said.

'He had a Yorkshire pudding for lunch today,' James told them. 'There was gravy up to his eyebrows.'

Mandy and Gran laughed. In between bites of short-bread, Taresh babbled cheerfully. When he held out his biscuit to James, he clearly said, 'Dada.'

'We're going with Papa and Daddy,' James explained.

'Sounds sensible,' Mandy replied.

Adam appeared just as they were finishing their coffee. 'Your mum's asleep on the couch,' he told Mandy. 'I've something Taresh might like,' he added. He smiled his lopsided grin and headed outside. He reappeared two minutes later, brandishing a football. 'Anyone fancy a game?'

It was quite the match, with the dogs and Adam careering round the garden, occasionally kicking the football. Taresh was soon in peals of laughter. Mandy felt her heart melting again as she looked at him, lost in a helpless fit of giggles as Adam pretended to miss the ball.

She sat down beside Raj on the bench at the end of the lawn. 'Your dad's really funny,' he said. 'That's how I'd like to be for Taresh.'

'You're doing amazingly already,' Mandy said. 'I can't believe how happy and settled Taresh seems to be.'

Raj grinned. 'We've never been happier,' he admitted. 'Parenthood's a steep learning curve, but James and I couldn't love Taresh more if he was biologically ours.'

Mandy wanted to hug him. It was wonderful to hear that the adoption was working out so well. 'He's yours through and through,' she told him. 'Biology has nothing to do with it.'

Chapter Eight

The visit to the Beaumonts went even better than Mandy had hoped. It wasn't the first time she had carried out an inspection where everything seemed perfect, but when it happened, it was a rare pleasure. They would be able to pick up the kittens in a few days' time.

Vicky's wheelchair-bound mum was visiting, so Vicky arranged to collect the cats the day after she had left. 'Not that Mum's any trouble,' she told Mandy cheerfully, 'but when the kittens come, I want to be able to give them my full attention.'

Mandy noticed a few things that were set up for convenient use with the wheelchair. The bathroom was large and had a rail beside the toilet. The whole bathroom floor was heated and the shower wasn't in a cubicle, but behind glass doors that could be pulled right back. Thinking of the leaflet she had seen at the hospital, Mandy wanted to ask more, but it seemed enough of an imposition that she was inspecting the house already.

Ben took the girls out when Mandy arrived, and

Vicky and Mandy had chatted easily through the inspection and over a coffee afterwards. As well as knowing Roo, Vicky was friends with Susan Collins. Mandy, Helen, Molly and Susan tried to meet up at least once a month for a night out at the Fox and Goose. She decided to invite Vicky along next time. When she left, Vicky gave her a hug, and Mandy returned it warmly. Goldie and Patchy had found a perfect home, and she had made a new friend. Satisfying all round.

Back in her own sitting room, Mandy stretched out her legs, enjoying the heat from the fire. Two of the dogs were beside her on the sofa, snoring gently. The other two were lying on the rug in front of the hearth. The lights were out, but Mandy had lit the wonderful oakmoss-scented candle she had found in the little junk shop beside James's café in York.

Her mobile buzzed with an unknown number. Mandy pressed the answer button without enthusiasm, anticipating yet another scam caller. 'Hello?'

'Hi, is that Mandy Hope?'

Mandy frowned. The voice on the other end sounded familiar, but she couldn't place it. 'Yes, I'm Mandy,' she said.

'Sorry to trouble you on a Sunday evening, but it's Geraldine Craven here. I visited you a couple of days ago.'

'Oh.' Mandy felt her shoulders relax. 'Hi again. What can I do for you?' She leaned back into the sofa and

Sky shuffled a little closer. Mandy put a hand on the collie's head.

'I spotted your advert in the post office this morning. I was in collecting my Sunday paper . . .' Geraldine sounded oddly nervous. She stopped, then gave a half laugh. 'You probably don't need to know that,' she added. 'Sorry, I'm babbling. Anyway, I'd love to be considered for the position, if it's still available.'

Mandy felt an odd sensation. Sympathy? Compassion? She wasn't sure, but Geraldine sounded apprehensive, as if she believed she was applying for a proper paid position. Mandy had expected part-time teenage helpers such as Nicole calling her. Not someone looking for a real job.

'I'm sorry, Geraldine,' she said, searching for a gentle way to break the news. 'I was really looking for someone part-time and I can't afford to pay much. I'm not sure it's suitable . . .'

'Oh no, I understood that completely.' The voice on the other end of the line sounded more positive now. 'Sorry if I wasn't clear. I actually work three days a week in Manchester as a psychotherapist. I've thought for a while I might like to live in the countryside, so I've rented a cottage here for six months. I'm based in Manchester during the week and here at weekends for the moment. When I saw your advert, I thought it would be a perfect way to fill my time when I'm not working. I don't need paying, honestly.'

Mandy's mind was working furiously. Even if

Geraldine was willing to work as a volunteer, it would be better to employ her properly. That way Mandy could ask for specific hours and give her more responsibility. 'I'd feel better if I paid you for your time,' she said.

'Well, I won't argue! When shall I start?' Geraldine sounded as if she was smiling. 'I have to go back to Manchester tomorrow, but I can be with you at 8 a.m. on Thursday; how does that sound?'

Mandy blinked. There didn't seem to be a catch. Having a reliable assistant, even just for weekends, would be an enormous help. 'That sounds great. I'll see you on Thursday.'

She pushed the phone back into her pocket. Could her staffing problem be solved already? It seemed too good to be true. 'Well, Sky,' she said, ruffling her dog's soft fur. 'Maybe our luck has turned!'

The weather turned dramatically colder on Tuesday morning, with thick frost on the tops of Silver Dale. Predictably, Mandy was called out to a farm almost at the top of the narrow valley. She stood outside in the biting wind, tucking her freezing fingers under her arms while the farmer tried to get his recalcitrant bull into the cattle crush.

As she drove back down the winding road afterwards, car heaters on full blast, she decided to call in at Six Oaks. It would be good to see how Marlowe and Bill were. More than that, the temptation to spend half an hour in Molly's warm kitchen before heading back to Animal Ark was too strong to resist.

'Hello!' Molly looked pleased when she opened the door. 'Come on in.' Mandy had brought all the dogs with her today and they too seemed to appreciate the warmth, rushing over and settling quickly beside the Aga alongside Molly's shaggy Jack Russell, Bertie.

'Were you up at High Float?' Molly asked as she put the kettle on.

'I was.' Mandy grimaced. 'I'll be charging extra for the frostbite!'

Molly laughed at Mandy's expression. 'Was there ice around the waterfall yet?'

Silver Force waterfall lay almost at the top of the dale. Back in the mists of time, it was rumoured that a prospector had found silver in the beck. There had certainly been lead mining in the area, and supposedly there had been a tiny village, but now there was only the farm and a disused shepherd's cottage clinging to the fellside.

'It wasn't properly frozen,' Mandy said, 'but there were some icicles.'

Molly put out mugs and warmed milk in the microwave. 'So,' she said as she added boiling water to the mugs and handed one to Mandy, 'Jimmy's back this weekend.' She lowered herself into the armchair on the far side of the stove. 'Have you dug out your best lingerie?'

Mandy could feel her face going red.

Molly leaned forwards. 'You are looking forward to him coming back, aren't you?'

Mandy shrugged, aiming for offhand, though she could see from Molly's face that it wasn't working. 'Things weren't going that well when he left,' she muttered.

Molly patted Mandy's knee. Mandy tried not to grin. She could imagine Molly comforting an unhappy horse in much the same manner. 'Sorry to hear that,' Molly said. 'Some men are arseholes,' she added, 'though I rather think Jimmy isn't one of them. But sometimes it just doesn't work out. If you need someone to talk to, you know I'm here.'

Mandy couldn't help but feel touched. 'Thanks.' She was starting to think she had underestimated Molly. Though she loved to gossip with the best of them, Molly didn't seem inclined to pry into what had gone wrong between Mandy and Jimmy, and right now, a sensitive lack of questions was just what Mandy wanted.

Coffee drunk, Molly pulled on her ancient Barbour and boots and led Mandy into the windy yard. A few leaves flew down from one of the trees that overhung the garden wall and Molly glared at them, as if offended that they were making a mess of her spotless yard. 'All the horses are inside now,' she shouted over the wind. 'Even Bill can't stay out in this.'

They stopped at Marlowe's stable first. Molly held his head as Mandy unwound the bandage. His leg was healing well. The wound was clean, the stitches weren't pulling, and the skin was beginning to knit together. Mandy left Marlowe's stable feeling very relieved. It could be difficult to get wounds to heal so low on the leg, but it looked as though Marlowe would barely have a scar.

'Bill next.' Molly's voice was brisk. 'I'm using shavings to avoid dust but he obviously struggles a bit more.'

Bill looked incredibly cosy, wrapped in an enormous dark blue rug, but he was still finding it harder to breathe than he should.

'I'm afraid he's losing weight,' Molly said, peeling back the blanket.

'I can see he's not as sturdy as he was.' Mandy studied the old horse. His face was looking bony again, as it had been when she had first seen him. 'You're obviously looking after him beautifully.' She ran a hand along his smooth neck. Although his fur was patchy and dull, it was soft and spotlessly clean.

'I make sure I brush him most days,' Molly said. 'He really does love the attention. And there are worse places to be than in here with this wonderful boy.' She walked over and began to pull Bill's rugs back into place. 'I know he hasn't got long,' she said without looking at Mandy. 'You will tell me when it's time, won't you?'

Mandy put her hand on Molly's shoulder and squeezed it gently. 'We can certainly talk about it,' she said, 'but I think you'll know when the time comes.'

Molly looked over her shoulder, her eyes bright with unshed tears. 'You will come yourself, won't you?'

Mandy swallowed. 'Of course. Any time,' she said. 'Day or night.'

Mandy scrambled into her jacket, wishing she had time for a coffee. 'I'm going to have to train you to shove me out of bed,' she told Sky, who was watching her from the foot of the stairs. She'd had a call in the early hours to a foaling. It had gone well at the end, but for a few minutes it had been touch and go. By the time she'd left, the still damp newborn had been struggling to stand on its spindly legs and the grey dawn was edging its way over the top of the fells. There had only been an hour and a half's sleeping time left. Mandy had fallen back into bed and failed to wake up to her alarm, and now she barely had time to get to Animal Ark before Geraldine arrived for her first day.

Icy roads meant she had to drive more slowly than usual and Geraldine was waiting in the car park when Mandy drew up. She was wearing a brand new pair of wellies and a spotless Barbour jacket. The outfit suited her, though the bright scarlet of her hair looked exotic against the wintry trees in the orchard.

'Hi there!' Geraldine greeted her, then bent down to stroke Sky. Mandy watched her beloved collie's eyes close in ecstasy as Geraldine rubbed the soft fur of her neck. Though Sky was generally okay with strangers, she didn't usually relax quite so quickly and it boded well for Geraldine's success with the rescues.

They went inside and Geraldine took off her Barbour to reveal a smart pair of jeans and a carefully ironed white shirt. Mandy couldn't help but feel a little concerned. 'I'm afraid you might get dirty,' she said. 'Especially if you take the dogs out.' After the rain earlier in the week, the paddock was churned up and Mustard still had a habit of planting both front paws squarely on anyone who looked like they might play with him.

Geraldine laughed. 'I'll buy some overalls for next time,' she replied, 'but really, don't worry about anything. It'll be fine.' She sounded so cheerful that Mandy found herself smiling too.

'We'll start with breakfast,' Mandy said. She showed Geraldine the details for each animal's daily care. Every rescue had a sheet attached to the front of its kennel with information about feeding likes and dislikes, personality and handling recommendations and any special care or medicines.

'The dogs don't get much at mealtimes,' Mandy explained when she saw Geraldine frowning at the tiny amount of food she was putting in each of the bowls. 'I use a lot of food for training.'

'Oh.' Light dawned on Geraldine's face. 'I remember you said that the other day. That makes sense.'

'Some positive trainers don't give their dogs any meals in bowls,' Mandy went on. 'They use all food for training. But when it comes to the dogs that arrive here, most are used to having meals at set times. It seems to help them settle, so I give them a little something morning and evening.'

'And I guess it helps them get used to being in the kennel,' Geraldine offered, 'if you feed them there.'

'Exactly,' Mandy said. 'Could you feed Jasper?' She handed Geraldine the bowl with the special cardiac-health food.

'Do I make him wait first?' Geraldine asked.

Mandy nodded. 'Yes, good manners around food are very important. Make sure he's sitting before you open the kennel door.' She looked at the grey-muzzled whippet. As usual, he was already sitting up very straight. 'When you open the door to the kennel, stay well back. If he gets up, just swing the door closed again and wait for him to sit back down. Put the food bowl down slowly. Stay right beside it and be ready to pick it back up if he tries to get to it. Once it's on the floor, take a tiny step back, wait until he looks up at you, then say "Go!"'

'Really?' Geraldine looked fascinated. 'And he'll know what to do?'

Mandy grinned. 'Yup!'

Geraldine stepped forwards and pulled back the bolt on Jasper's kennel. Geraldine put the bowl down, waited for Jasper's eyes to meet hers and cried 'Go!' in a very happy voice. In an instant, Jasper's long nose was in the bowl. Geraldine's eyes widened and before Mandy could stop her, she crouched down and began to stroke

Jasper's head. Though Jasper's ears went back, his only other response was to gulp even faster at his food.

'You should come out now,' Mandy told Geraldine quietly.

Geraldine swung the door closed behind her. 'Did I do something wrong?'

Mandy gave her a small smile. 'Sort of,' she said. 'I'm sorry, I should have told you. You shouldn't ever stroke a strange dog when it's eating. Jasper was okay, but some dogs get very protective over their food. You don't want to upset them or put yourself in danger.'

'Okay.' Geraldine looked crestfallen. 'I'm sorry.'

'It's fine,' Mandy said. 'You weren't to know.'

Geraldine watched as Mandy gave Mustard his bowl, then made sure he had plenty of space to eat it in peace. Olive's routine was different. She was so shy that Mandy often tried to hand feed her with something really tasty. As Olive was becoming more trusting, Mandy had begun to stroke her neck while she was eating. It felt a little ironic, having just told Geraldine off for doing the same to Jasper, but Geraldine seemed interested rather than offended when Mandy tried to explain. 'I want her to learn to associate being stroked with something nice,' she said.

It seemed a bit thin as she explained it, but Geraldine nodded. 'I guess you really get a feel for each of the animals,' she said. 'It's fascinating watching you.'

Mandy could feel her face reddening, but she was pleased. 'I do try,' she said.

Geraldine pulled out her mobile phone from her pocket. 'Would it be okay for me to take notes?'

'Of course.'

Feeding the cats went more smoothly. Though Mandy tried to an extent to train the cats under her care, it was often more important to encourage inter-action rather than make them wait.

To Mandy's relief, Geraldine seemed to get the hang of things quickly. As well as listening carefully, she used her initiative when she saw something that needed doing. She sought out a dustpan and brush to sweep up some spilled rabbit feed and told Mandy they were running out of handsoap in the lavatory. She also suggested Mandy should get some whiteboards and number the cages so she could leave instructions about the animals without having to use so much paper. Having grown up with clinical history and consent forms attached to the kennels in Animal Ark, using them had seemed natural, but if there was a less wasteful way, Mandy was keen to adopt it.

Mandy checked her watch as they finished the feed round. With Geraldine's help, she had managed to catch up on the time she had lost earlier. There was just enough time to give the dogs a run before morning surgery.

'Can you take Jasper's lead?' she asked Geraldine. 'Keep the lead in your right hand and him on your left.' She handed Geraldine a few pieces of food. 'If he looks up at you when you're taking him out, say "Good!" and give him some food. I'll bring Olive.'

She walked behind Geraldine as she led Jasper outside. As they reached the grass, Mandy felt the touch of a wet nose against her hand. Olive's shining eyes were looking up at her. 'Good!' she exclaimed. She reached into her pocket for one of her best treats. Olive didn't often make eye contact. This morning was turning out well.

The sun was properly risen now, and the fellside was bathed in golden sunlight. The bracken had turned rusty brown, like crumpled paper. The trees in the orchard were almost bare, their branches dark against the clear blue sky. Mandy found herself smiling as she watched Olive and Jasper trotting round sniffing at the last of the fallen leaves.

She felt Geraldine walk over and stand beside her. 'What a wonderful place you have here, Mandy,' she murmured. 'And I think you have the best job in the world. Thank you for letting me share it.'

'My pleasure,' said Mandy.

'Why don't I stay on and do some cleaning for you while you're in surgery?' Geraldine offered.

Mandy hesitated. She generally didn't leave people alone in the rescue centre until they knew exactly what they were doing – for their sake as well as the animals'. It wasn't that she didn't trust Geraldine, but she didn't want to rush her into taking on more responsibility than necessary.

Geraldine seemed to guess what Mandy was thinking. 'It's okay, I understand if you'd rather not. I just thought it might be helpful while you're so busy in the clinic.' She looked so anxious that Mandy smiled to reassure her.

'It's a really kind offer,' she said. 'I'd love to take you up on it. But if there are any issues with the animals, come straight over to the clinic, okay?'

'Will do!' Geraldine promised.

89

Chapter Nine

'How's it going with your new assistant?' Helen was sitting at the reception desk in the clinic, preparing client details.

'Fine,' Mandy replied. 'Good, actually.'

'That's great.' Helen looked pleased.

Morning surgery was unexpectedly hectic and Mandy was relieved to know that Geraldine would be taking care of some of the Hope Meadows chores. Toby had to go out on an emergency call and Mandy was needed to assist Adam in theatre with a complicated fracture. She watched admiringly as her father pieced the bone back together, screwing fragments into position until the dog's leg was more or less back to its original anatomy.

Adam looked at her over the neat row of sutures he'd created from the ragged wound with which the dog had arrived. 'Not bad,' he said. He glanced up at the clock on the wall. 'I'm going out in a minute,' he said, 'and I won't be back till mid-afternoon. Would you have time to go and check on your mum and see about getting her something to eat at lunchtime? She didn't have a good night last night. Her leg was hurting and she couldn't sleep. Rachel was in first thing, but she could only stay an hour.' He looked at Mandy with raised eyebrows and a rather worried smile.

'Of course I can,' she replied. 'Is there food in the house, or will I need to get something?'

Adam removed the clips that were holding the drape in place and dropped them on the instrument tray. 'Plenty of salad and cheese in the fridge,' he said. 'Bread in the bread bin. Cans of soup in the usual cupboard.'

Adam stepped back from the operating table, threw the disposable drape into the bin, then stripped off the gloves and gown he'd been wearing. He looked at Helen, who had been monitoring the anaesthetic throughout and was now cleaning up the operation site. 'You can take it from here, can't you?' he said, and Helen nodded.

Mandy cleaned herself up, filled out some notes and headed for the door that led into the cottage. She paused, wondering how Geraldine was getting on. She might have left, if she'd finished the cleaning.

'Has Geraldine been in?' she asked Helen, who was sitting behind the reception desk, catching up on some paperwork.

Helen shook her head. 'Not that I've seen,' she said. 'Didn't see her going through the car park either, though I might have missed her, what with all the rush.'

'I'll pop round and see if she's gone,' Mandy said.

She walked round to Hope Meadows. A high layer of cloud had covered the sun and the scenery looked dull and flat. Mandy pushed open the door of the rescue centre and checked each of the rooms. Geraldine seemed to have done a good job with the cleaning and to Mandy's relief, all the animals seemed undisturbed. She figured Geraldine had slipped away without disturbing anyone in the busy clinic.

She took the long route to the kitchen, through the garden, and pushed open the door. To her astonishment, Geraldine was sitting at the kitchen table, which was set for lunch. Emily was standing at the counter waiting for the kettle to boil.

Mandy frowned. Though Emily seemed to be managing without her crutches, her face was very pale. What on earth was she doing up? And what was Geraldine doing in here?

'Hello, love.' Emily's voice, though warm, sounded weak. 'We're just about to have lunch. Will you join us?' Without waiting for a reply, she shuffled to her left, opened a cupboard and began to pull out an extra bowl.

Mandy made a rush to help when she saw the bowl shaking in Emily's hand. 'I'll get that,' she said. Her voice sounded sharp – more than she had intended, but Emily's unsteadiness was alarming. 'Why don't you sit down?' she added, a little more gently. Mandy noticed a pan of soup bubbling on the stove. She tried not to think about what would have happened if Emily had tried to pour it into the bowls.

To her relief, her mum limped towards the table.

Mandy pulled out a chair and ushered her into it. She couldn't help feeling confused and angry. Mum should be resting. It hadn't crossed Mandy's mind that Geraldine would come over and disturb her.

'Geraldine tells me she's had a lovely time this morning,' Emily said.

'Oh yes?' Mandy said. 'Good.' She gave the soup a stir, then pulled open the drawer to collect a knife. There was a loaf of bread on the side and she carved a few slices. She was trying to keep her frustration down, but the more she thought about it, the angrier she felt.

She had been impressed by Geraldine this morning, but Mandy couldn't believe she'd pushed herself into the cottage and was being waited on by Emily. Couldn't she see that Mum was ill?

Geraldine was very quiet. Mandy had the feeling that before she'd come in, Geraldine and Emily had been chatting comfortably, but now there was an apprehensive look on her face. 'Have I done something wrong?' she asked.

Mandy shook her head very slightly, but then she took a deep breath. Obviously Geraldine didn't know she shouldn't have come into the cottage, but it wasn't okay for her to disturb her mum, who ought to have been resting. If she didn't say something, what was to stop it happening again? 'Not wrong exactly,' Mandy told her. There was a sharp tone in her voice that she felt unable to stop. 'I'm happy for you to work in the rescue centre if you still want to, but I'd prefer it if you kept it professional and stayed over there for lunch. Mum's not been well. She should be resting.'

'Mandy, please don't . . . I'm fine,' Emily objected.

Mandy frowned. 'You're not fine,' she said. 'Dad asked me to come over to make you lunch. He told me you hadn't slept. I'm sorry that you've been disturbed.'

There was a look of distress on Emily's face. 'But I wasn't,' she protested. 'Not really. I was already up and about. I looked out of the window and saw Geraldine there and thought it'd be nice to get to know her a bit, that's all.'

'It's not your mum's fault,' Geraldine said. Her voice was conciliatory. 'If it's anyone's, it's mine. I was in the garden and I shouldn't have been. I'm very sorry.' She pushed out her chair and stood up. 'I apologise, Emily. I didn't know there was a problem. I wouldn't have come in if I'd known.'

'There isn't a problem,' Emily insisted. 'Really, there isn't.'

Geraldine gave a weak smile. 'It's been lovely to meet you, Emily. I hope I can see you again when you're feeling better.' She walked to the door, pulled it open, then turned to look at Mandy. 'May I have a quick word?'

Mandy followed Geraldine out. Her anger had abated a little on Geraldine's genuine-sounding apology. She pulled the door closed behind her and stepped down onto the grass. 'I'm sorry if I sounded sharp. Maybe I should have explained about staying away from the cottage.' She took a deep breath. She was going to have to get used to telling people, however much she hated it. Emily's illness was going to get worse, and like it or not, it would become more visible. 'Mum's not well,' she explained. 'She has MS and she's supposed to be resting.'

Geraldine's eyes widened, then her face filled with sympathy. 'I'm really sorry,' she said. 'I had no idea she was so unwell.'

Mandy shook her head. 'It's not your fault,' she said. Her anger had vanished and she just felt tired. 'I was being overprotective. Will you still come back tomorrow?' It suddenly felt very important to ask. Mandy had got into trouble in the past when she had lost her temper. It would be awful to lose someone who seemed reliable over something so silly.

Geraldine smiled and patted Mandy's arm. 'Of course I will,' she said. 'I'm happy to help wherever I can. I really am sorry. I promise I won't trouble your mum again.' She gave Mandy's arm a squeeze, then walked briskly down the path to the gate that led onto the drive. Mandy watched her for a moment, then went back to the kitchen.

Emily was still sitting at the table. Her head was drooping as Mandy opened the door, but she looked up when Mandy came in. Her green eyes were huge. Her hands were shaking very slightly, but after a moment's hesitation, she held one of them out to Mandy, who took it and sat down in the nearest chair.

'I'm sorry, Mum,' Mandy blurted out. 'I lost my temper.'

Emily smiled. 'Please don't be sorry,' she said. 'You were right to be angry. I should have been resting. But Geraldine didn't know that, and it was nice to have a chance to meet her.' With a pang, Mandy realised she should have introduced Geraldine to her parents at the start of the day, since she was going to be working in the rescue centre. Everything was happening in such a rush at the moment, she could hardly remember what day it was.

'She seems nice,' Emily went on.

'She does,' Mandy agreed. 'And she worked hard this morning. She seemed quite happy to clean and so on. She wasn't just there to cuddle kittens.'

'Is she coming back?'

Mandy couldn't help feeling relieved Geraldine had agreed to return. If she had walked away, it would have been something else for Emily to feel bad about. 'Tomorrow morning,' Mandy assured her. She stood up and put both hands on the back of her chair. 'I don't know about you,' she said, 'but I'm starving. Will the soup still be edible, do you think?'

Emily laughed. 'I'm sure it'll be fine,' she said.

Chapter Ten

Mandy parked her car and walked into Terminal Two in Manchester airport for the second time in less than two weeks. The sight of a huge artificial Christmas tree, glittering with white lights and dotted with shiny presents, reminded her that it was nearly November and festive fever was looming. She felt a million light years away from thinking about it, though.

There were butterflies in her stomach as she made her way to the arrivals area. She had planned to have a cup of tea on the way, but when she pulled into the service station and checked her phone, the flight scanner told her Jimmy's flight was ahead of schedule. Aira was flying straight to London to edit the documentary. When Jimmy arrived, he and Mandy would be alone together for the first time in months.

Mandy joined the rest of the people who were waiting for the Seattle flight. The doors slid open and a weary-looking woman trudged through, dragging a heavy case behind her. The doors closed again, then reopened. Passengers began to trickle past, some perky, others looking exhausted from the overnight flight, and Mandy found herself searching each face.

Her eyes lighted on a handsome, clean-shaven man, and her heart began to beat faster when she realised it was Jimmy. She had expected a wild beard and grown-out hair, but he had obviously used the stopover in Seattle to tidy himself up. He caught sight of Mandy, and his familiar green eyes lit up with a smile. He strode over and wrapped his arms around her, and it was as if the starkness of the airport and the mumble of the crowd faded away. His lips met hers and she was whirling in his embrace as if she was weightless.

He loosened his grip, though his arms still held her close, and looked down at her. The smile spread across his face again, as if she was the most wonderful thing he'd seen in months, and Mandy felt the fluttering in her stomach that she still felt every time he was close. 'Hello,' he said, lifting his hand to touch her cheek. 'I see you missed me as much as I missed you.'

They walked side by side to the car park and Mandy felt almost light-headed. For the moment, the future seemed unimportant. It was just wonderful to have him back, as if something that had been missing had fallen into place. He seemed equally pleased to see her, glancing at her constantly, meeting her eyes and grinning as if the very sight of her lifted him. Mandy wondered how she could have been worried about the postgrad students, when it was so obvious that Jimmy loved her.

He unhitched his massive rucksack and slung it into the back seat. Mandy opened the driver's door and climbed in. Suddenly she felt nervous, as if she was on a first date. She searched for something innocuous to talk about.

'How was the flight?' she asked as she pulled on her seat belt.

Jimmy shrugged. 'Could have been worse. The guy beside me started snoring half an hour into the flight and slept almost all the way. I was ready to smother him with his travel pillow by the time we were over the Atlantic!'

'And how's Aira?' She began to make her way out of the car park.

'He's fine,' Jimmy said, 'though he had a bit of a close shave a couple of nights ago. There'd been reports of one of the bears getting a bit too close to one of the villages. Some of the villagers were fermenting walrus flippers. I told you about that before, remember? They stink and the bears are attracted to them. When Aira went to investigate, there was no sign of the bear. Aira scrambled up the ridge that ran along the side of the houses and there it was, just waiting on the other side. He caught a glimpse of its black nose and it kind of grunted at him and he had to run all the way back down to get enough distance to fire his rifle safely.'

Mandy knew from their previous conversations that the researchers and wardens used a technique they called hazing when the bears got too close: making a loud noise or flashing lights at the bears until they retreated. There was never any intention to harm the animals, which would only be the very last resort, to save a life.

'Even when he fired his rifle over its head, the bear was still coming at him. One of the wardens on the neighbouring station had ended up killing one of the bears a few days earlier and Aira didn't want to end the expedition with something so awful. Luckily he had the mother of all head torches in his jacket pocket. It could light up half the tundra when it was dark. He flashed it right in the big guy's eyes and luckily, it did a swift about-turn and went back up the slope.'

Mandy felt almost breathless, imagining the scene. It must have been amazing and terrifying in equal measure. She had been to Churchill in Manitoba many years ago with her parents to see the bears migrating. Now, with the Arctic ice diminishing, the hungry polar bears were that much more dangerous, coming into the villages to scavenge for food.

She waited for Jimmy to continue but there was silence. Mandy glanced at him. He was fast asleep, looking much younger and eerily like Max. Mandy felt her heart melt, and steered carefully onto the motorway.

Jimmy opened his eyes as Mandy turned onto the steep track that led up to Wildacre. Wind was stirring the trees, clattering the branches together. Jimmy gazed around, then sighed. 'It's good to be back,' he said. 'Trees were the things I missed most on the tundra.'

Mandy laughed. 'Good to know where your priorities lie,' she told him.

Jimmy grinned. 'Well, it was a close run thing,' he said, 'but if you were to push me, I might have to admit . . . I missed the dogs even more.'

Mandy sent him a mock glare. He put his arm around her as they walked up the front path and glanced up at the white-painted weatherboard cottage. 'Home sweet home,' he said.

When Mandy opened the door, they were greeted by an avalanche of excited fur and frantic wagging. She took Jimmy's rucksack from him and carried it into the front room. When she returned to the hallway, he was still crouching with the four dogs, laughing as they licked his face and lashed him with their tails. He looked up at Mandy. 'Thanks for coming to get me,' he said. He stood up and pulled her into his arms and kissed her deeply. 'Shall we take them out?' he asked. 'I want to stretch my legs.'

They went into the garden, followed closely by the dogs. Despite the gusting wind, which normally would have sent them scurrying round in circles, the dogs seemed reluctant to move too far away from Jimmy. Jimmy's eyes seemed to be drinking everything in, from the scudding clouds trailing over the distant fells on the far side of the dale, to the woodland that stretched up the fellside behind the cottage. 'The beech tree looks amazing,' he said. Mandy followed his gaze. The graceful tree that stood on the boundary between the garden and the woods was still clinging to most of its leaves.

Jimmy pointed to a long piece of twisted wood that lay on the grass. 'Is that the branch that damaged the chicken hut?'

Mandy nodded. They crossed the damp grass and looked at the chickens, who were back in their repaired run. Jimmy studied the repair job Mandy had done on the door. 'Good as new,' he said, his voice approving.

They walked round the end of the house to the little yard with its stone trough, and into the barn. 'I was thinking while I was away,' Jimmy said. 'Why don't we build a mezzanine level in here?' He gestured to the strong beams that supported the lofty roof. 'It could be a playroom for Abi and Max. They'll need more space as they get older. And they could play music as loud as they like without it disturbing anyone.'

Mandy felt something jar inside her. Jimmy seemed to be taking their future together for granted. He'd done so much work around Wildacre it had come to seem almost as much his as it was Mandy's. Yet she couldn't help wondering why he was cheerfully planning more changes, when in her head there was still a huge hurdle to be overcome before she could think about the long-term future.

Before Mandy met Jimmy, she would have said she had little interest in having a family. He couldn't have known her feelings would change, and somehow she and Jimmy had never discussed where they thought their relationship would go. But now, as he spoke with such enthusiasm about their future together, Mandy felt as if there was a cold shell around her heart. It wouldn't be tonight, but she would have to talk to him about what she wanted from the rest of her life. Marriage was negotiable, but if he didn't want another child, there was a difficult decision ahead. And it was obvious how much Jimmy had enjoyed being away with Aira – and the students, even if Mandy did trust him absolutely. She didn't want to lose him for several weeks every year because he wanted to pursue far-flung adventures with other people. Was he really ready to limit that part of his life?

They walked a little way up into the woods, soaking the knees of their trousers in the wet undergrowth, then wound their way back to the house. Though it was still above freezing, the wind made it feel chillier than it was, and Mandy was glad to get back to the fire.

'Mum and Dad invited us for dinner,' Mandy told Jimmy, 'but I thought I'd cook for us tonight.'

Jimmy quirked an eyebrow at her. He knew the extent of Mandy's culinary skills.

Mandy opened the fridge and looked at him over her shoulder. 'Abi, Max and I have been practising,' she told him. 'We have a fail-safe recipe for butternut squash filled with mushrooms and rice and flavoured with thyme.'

Jimmy looked impressed as Mandy pulled the squash out of the fridge and held it out to show him. 'Sounds wonderful,' he told her with a grin. 'I'll have to leave you alone with Abi and Max more often.'

He put the kettle on to make tea and Mandy started to cook the dinner, putting the halved squash in the oven to roast while she chopped and fried the mushrooms and set the rice on to boil. Jimmy carried over a mug of tea for her, set it on the shelf just to the right of the range and wrapped his arms around her from behind. 'It smells good already,' he said. He placed a kiss on the side of her neck and a shiver ran down her spine. 'I'm very grateful you let Abi and Max come while I was away,' he murmured, his lips grazing her skin.

'They're part of my family now,' Mandy said, with a familiar twinge of sadness about what lay ahead. The family life which had felt so stable only a few months ago, no longer seemed solid. She pushed the thought away, gave the mushrooms a quick stir, then pulled her phone out of her pocket.

'Look,' she said, showing Jimmy a picture of Taresh in James's arms, staring straight at the camera.

'Wow! What a gorgeous chap. Did they all arrive back safe and sound?'

'They did,' Mandy told him. She scrolled through the photos: Taresh with James, with Raj, with Gran's shortbread, laughing at Adam playing football.

'He's a lovely little boy, isn't he?' Was his voice the tiniest bit wistful, Mandy wondered? Then he laughed. 'I don't envy Raj and James the toddler stage though. I still have nightmares about the twins at two!'

Mandy stopped herself from wincing. She'd asked him to marry her and he'd told her he wanted their lives to stay just as they were. Soon she was going to have to ask him outright whether it was marriage he rejected, or whether he was certain he didn't want to have any more children. And when she knew the answer, then she would have to make her decision and they'd both have to live with it. But now wasn't the time. Now was the time to welcome him home.

She felt proud as she pulled the stuffed squash from the oven, fragrant and slightly caramelised with a bitter-sweet flavour. She had selected a bottle of wine to complement the food and they sat a long time over dinner, chatting comfortably. After loading the dishwasher, they took cups of coffee through to the sofa and sat close together, hemmed in by dogs in the light of the fire.

Jimmy put down his mug and turned to grin at Mandy. 'Well,' he said, 'it's been a long day. Think I could do with an early night.'

Mandy looked innocently at him. 'Of course,' she said. 'You must be worn out from all the travelling. You can go up whenever you want. I'm sure there's something I can watch on TV.'

She pretended to reach for the remote control, but Jimmy caught her hand and held onto it. He raised an eyebrow. 'I wasn't planning to go up on my own,' he said.

Mandy pursed her lips. 'Well, I normally take Sky

up,' she pointed out. 'I'm sure she'll come up with you if you ask her. I don't want you to be lonely.'

Jimmy laughed. 'Thanks very much for the offer, but I confess I would be more honoured if Sky's owner would come up with me instead.' He stood up and offered Mandy a hand. She took it and he pulled her upright until his body was pressed the length of hers.

'Well,' she said, 'I suppose Sky will still go up with you, but since you asked so nicely, Sky's owner could come, too.'

Jimmy grinned wolfishly, and a moment later, he was chasing her up the stairs.

Chapter Eleven

Jimmy groaned as Mandy swung the car up the narrow lane that led to Animal Ark. 'Remind me next time I'm due for a bout of jet lag that I shouldn't drink wine the night I come home,' he muttered. His voice sounded hoarse. Despite the rings under his eyes, he had dragged himself out of bed with Mandy to walk the dogs. Now they were heading to Hope Meadows. 'So as well as the usual duties, we're delivering some kittens to their new home?' he said as she parked.

Mandy had arranged to deliver the kittens to the Beaumonts today. Patchy and Goldie had been renamed Smudge and Tigger by Elodie and Connie, and Mandy was looking forward to seeing them in their new home.

Jimmy seemed to recover quickly once they arrived at Hope Meadows. He instantly took a shine to Jasper and spent several minutes sitting in the old dog's kennel, stroking Jasper's tummy when the old dog uncharacteristically rolled on his back.

Emily and Adam seemed equally pleased to see him when they went over to the cottage for coffee.

'It's lovely to see him again,' Emily whispered when Adam took Jimmy off to see the new bird feeder he'd installed in the garden. 'You must be so relieved to have him back safe and sound. I'm happy for you.' She patted Mandy's arm.

Mandy could see Jimmy through the window. He and Adam seemed to be chatting easily. A few months ago, Mandy would have been delighted, but now the sight of her parents and Jimmy playing happy families left her feeling uneasy.

The relationship she'd had with her parents had always been wonderful, despite the fact that she was adopted. Much as she loved Abi and Max, it wasn't the same. It was all about distance, she realised as she watched Jimmy point out a hawk circling on a current of air over the fell. She might have been adopted, but she couldn't remember a time before she had lived with Emily and Adam. They were her family in every sense of the word. Taresh would be the same; James and Raj would be parents to him in a way that Mandy would never be to Abi and Max. Mandy was with their dad, and she was a stepmum to them . . . a good one, she hoped. But she would never be their mother. They already had one of those.

She thought again about her childhood. They had been a tight-knit unit. Mandy, her mum and her dad. That was what she wanted, she thought, with a sudden fierce longing. A committed partner for life and a family all of her own. If Jimmy was the one, then Abi and

Max would be an integral part of it, but without a child of her own, it would seem incomplete.

Emily took Mandy's hand, making her jump. She'd been so caught up in her thoughts, she'd forgotten her mum was standing right beside her. 'I'm so glad you have Jimmy,' Emily murmured. 'It's such a relief to know that whatever happens to me, you have someone to look after you.'

Mandy felt as if she'd swallowed something hot. There was a burning sensation inside, but she bit back the words that tried to escape. What was the point in telling Emily that she didn't know how much of a future she had with Jimmy? She needed to talk to him first. 'He's very kind,' she said quietly and was relieved when Emily seemed to take her agreement at face value.

Adam and Jimmy came inside, chatting about pink-footed geese migration. Mandy looked at the clock on the wall. 'We have to go,' she told Emily and Adam. 'We're due at the Beaumonts' house in twenty minutes.'

'Kitten delivery!' Jimmy announced with a broad grin. 'Best job in the world!'

The whole of the Beaumont family were waiting for them when they arrived.

'Good to see you back, mate.' Ben shook hands with Jimmy and a few moments later, they were deep in conversation about some forestry work to be done at Running Wild.

Mandy brought the kittens in. She put the cage down on the kitchen floor and opened the door. For about thirty seconds, the two kittens stood very still, peering out at the kitchen with huge, wide eyes, and then first Goldie, who was now Tigger, and then Patchy – Smudge – crept onto the kitchen tiles and began to explore.

Vicky put the kettle on and invited Mandy to sit down at the kitchen table. Elodie and Connie seemed utterly entranced as they watched the kittens exploring. Mandy had told them to sit quietly on the floor and wait for the kittens to come to them, and within a few minutes, the four of them were playing together with some of the toys the Beaumonts had bought.

'When can Herbie come over?' Elodie asked as Tigger climbed onto her lap.

'Soon,' Vicky promised. She lifted her mug, took a sip, then set it back on the table. 'I bet you're pleased to have Jimmy home,' she said to Mandy. 'Ben was forever off on wild expeditions when we were younger. He'd disappear with his bike and a tent and I wouldn't know when he was coming back. Luckily once the girls came along, he settled down a bit.' She glanced at the doorway, listening to Ben's voice with an uncomplicated smile. 'Nowadays I have to chase him out on his bike when he's getting under my feet.'

The two men appeared, still discussing the work that Ben was going to do. Vicky leaned towards Mandy. 'Top tip for marriage,' she said with a grin, 'make sure he keeps his hobbies!'

Just for an instant, Mandy wanted to blurt out that they wouldn't be getting married, but this was hardly the time or place. She managed a smile. 'I'm sure Jimmy'll never tire of adventuring,' she admitted.

As if he had heard, Jimmy turned his head to look at Mandy. He smiled when he caught her eye, then looked away again.

Vicky sent a roguish look at Mandy. 'I can see he's smitten,' she said. 'That much is obvious.'

Mandy picked up her drink and buried her face in the mug. 'He's a great guy,' she mumbled. Suddenly Tigger, apparently wanting a better view of the kitchen than she could get from Elodie's lap, ran up Vicky's leg and scrabbled up to her left shoulder. Vicky let out a squeak and gently disentangled Tigger's tiny claws from her sweater. To Mandy's relief, the conversation moved on.

It felt good on Monday morning to wave off Jimmy with his three dogs and head down to Animal Ark with only Sky in tow. Sky seemed equally pleased to have Mandy to herself again. Much as Mandy liked being surrounded by animals, she loved the closeness of her partnership with Sky.

Geraldine arrived on time. She was wearing a practical pair of dark blue dungarees over a thick fleece, with a handkerchief to tie her scarlet hair back out of the way. Mandy had felt a little nervous the day after her run-in with Geraldine and Emily, but Geraldine had been so cheery and professional on the Friday morning that there had been no difficulty at all. She was starting to pick up the Hope Meadows routines already. For the first time in a while, Mandy found herself relaxing properly. There had been so much tension recently with Jimmy's return and Emily's illness that the uncomplicated chat with Geraldine felt like balm.

'You look happy.' Geraldine studied Mandy with her head on one side. They were outside in the paddock, working with Mustard. 'Did your boyfriend get back safely?' Mandy had told Geraldine about Jimmy on Friday. Not in any great detail, but she knew he'd been away for quite a while. 'Did he have a good trip?'

Mandy nodded.

'Was he somewhere exciting?' Geraldine asked. 'If it's okay for me to ask,' she added. 'Do tell me if I overstep the mark.'

'He's been in the Arctic tracking polar bears,' Mandy told her.

'Really?' Geraldine sounded surprised and impressed. 'What an interesting thing to do. Didn't you want to go with him?' She glanced around. 'Though I guess it's not easy to get away with all this going on. Have you been together long?'

Mandy bent down to pick up Mustard's ball, then straightened up and smiled at Geraldine. 'It would have been interesting to go with him,' she agreed, keeping her voice light. 'But there's no way I could get away, as you said. Anyway, I'm not sure he'd have wanted me there, cramping his style.' It came out sounding a little more bitter than Mandy had intended. 'We've been together just over two years,' she added quickly, hoping Geraldine wouldn't pick up on her tone. 'I thought he was a terrible townie when I first met him. He's an Outward Bound instructor and I was sure he was going to ruin the local woodland with his fancy ropes course! But it turned out he's almost as animal-mad as I am.' She threw the ball and Mustard scampered after it, bounding through the fallen leaves that crunched under his feet.

'It all sounds very romantic,' Geraldine commented.

Mandy took her eyes off Mustard and glanced down at Geraldine's hand. There was no wedding ring, and no sign there ever had been one. Then again, not everyone wore a ring, and lots of people had long-term partners now without marrying. It seemed a little intrusive to ask, though it crossed Mandy's mind just how little she knew about Geraldine. Then again, how much did anybody really know about anybody else? And ultimately, it didn't matter. Geraldine was here to do a job and she was doing it well. If she wanted Mandy to know about her private life, she'd no doubt offer the information herself. There was no rush.

Mustard rushed back up to Mandy, dropped his ball on her foot and sat gazing up at her, his face expectant. 'Do you want to have a go?' Mandy offered, holding out the ball to Geraldine. 'See if he'll bring it back for you too.'

★

113

Susan Collins came over at lunchtime, bringing her five-year-old son Jack. Susan worked in the nursery which stood near the church in the centre of Welford. 'We brought you these,' she announced, as she stepped inside into the sunny reception area and held up two large carrier bags filled with tins of cat and dog food. 'More in the car,' she added. 'We'll be doing another collection before Christmas.'

Mandy had been friends with Susan for many years before Mandy had gone away to university to train as a vet. Now Welford was her home again, she was very glad she and Susan had rekindled their friendship. Susan and Jack often helped out at Hope Meadows, and the nursery had turned out to be excellent at fundraising and collecting donated food and pet toys. Mandy liked to socialise the animals in the centre with as many different people as she could persuade to come in. Jack had been playing with the kittens since the time they had opened their eyes, getting them used to children. He loved coming to see the animals and asked a never-ending stream of questions that left Mandy half-convinced he knew as much as she did!

Geraldine kept out of the way as Mandy took Jack's hand and led him off to see the animals.

'How's Jasper?' he asked as they walked into the dog kennels. Mandy had explained to him about Jasper's heart, and though she hadn't known how much of her explanation he had understood, he was aware that Jasper was more fragile than some of the other residents.

'He's doing well,' Mandy told him. 'His cough has mostly gone now. Would you like to take him out?'

'Yes, please.' Jack's brown eyes sparkled as he followed Mandy to get the lead. He always wanted to help any animal that was weak or unwell.

'How's Frostflake?' Mandy asked as she unhooked Jasper's lead. Susan and Jack had adopted a deaf kitten from Hope Meadows almost a year ago. Frostflake had grown into a handsome white tomcat with very blue eyes.

Jack grinned up at her. 'Brilliant,' he said. 'It's his birthday next week. Mum took me to the shop in Walton and we chose him some toys. Mum said she'd make cakes too. One for us and one out of things that cats can eat.'

'Sounds great,' Mandy told him with a smile. 'He's a very lucky cat.'

Jack beamed.

'You should tell Mandy what we've been teaching Frostflake,' Susan prompted. They were outside now, walking round with Jack firmly clutching Jasper's lead. He was such a good dog, and seemed to know it was important never to pull on his lead when Jack was with him.

Jack's chest swelled with pride. 'We've been teaching Frostflake hand signals,' he announced. 'When you point at a place on the ground, he comes over to it and when you hold your hand out to him, he touches his nose on your fingers. We're trying to teach him to sit, but he doesn't seem to want to do it. Mummy says I just have to be very patient.'

Mandy found herself smiling. 'You'll be an awesome animal trainer one day,' she told Jack and he sighed, as if that would be the most wonderful thing in the world.

'What a lovely young woman,' Geraldine said, once Susan and Jack had headed back to the nursery. 'Lovely little boy, too.'

Mandy was cleaning out the guinea pigs. She had taken off the lid of their cage and was scrubbing the base, while Geraldine was at the sink, washing up some of the morning's food and water bowls.

'Isn't he!' Mandy exclaimed. Susan had been one of the first of her friends to have children and at first Mandy had been almost afraid of Jack, which seemed like madness now.

'You were very kind to him,' Geraldine went on. 'Do you want to have children of your own?'

Mandy wasn't sure what to say. She definitely did, but with the situation still up in the air with Jimmy, she didn't want to admit too much. 'I have two step-children,' she told Geraldine. 'Jimmy has twins, a boy and a girl. I'd like to have children of my own one day, though.'

Geraldine smiled at her. 'I think you'd be a lovely mum,' she said. 'Nothing's more important than family.'

'How about you?' Mandy asked. 'Do you have children?'

The porcelain bowl that held the guinea pigs' water fell from Geraldine's fingers and crashed to the floor, smashing into a million pieces. 'Oh!' Geraldine gasped. She stared at Mandy, who almost laughed at Geraldine's stricken expression.

'Don't worry about it,' Mandy assured her. 'Happens all the time.'

Geraldine shook her head. 'Silly me,' she said in a tight voice. She crouched down and began to pick up the pieces. Mandy watched her for a moment, then went back to scrubbing the base of the guinea pig cage. Just before the bowl fell, Mandy had caught a glimpse of something in the older woman's eyes. Had it been sadness? Perhaps Geraldine had wanted children but hadn't had the chance. Or maybe she'd lost a child. If Geraldine was grieving, the last thing Mandy wanted to do was to stir up any unwanted emotions. If Geraldine wanted to keep her private life private, that was up to her.

Chapter Twelve

Mandy drew up outside Wildacre. The house looked the same as it had since she and Jimmy had finished working on it eighteen months ago. The weatherboarding was clean and white, the slate roof low and cosy. Yet it no longer felt like coming home. She and Jimmy had been so tightly connected, but whatever had been holding them there had cracked apart. Unlike Mandy, Jimmy seemed perfectly content. He had returned from Canada and fallen back into his life as if he'd never been away. But for Mandy, everything had changed.

She had felt a swell of mortification at the Beaumonts' house last weekend. Quite unsolicited, Vicky had given them marriage advice. Advice they would never need, Mandy had thought. Vicky had looked at them and assumed the future: a future Mandy herself had hoped for and lost.

Then there had been the conversation at Hope Meadows. Geraldine's voice came back to her. 'I think you'd be a lovely mum.' Mandy felt sadder still. If she stayed with Jimmy, perhaps she would never get the chance.

Beyond the windscreen, the trees were bending before the gale. In a matter of hours, they would be stripped bare of their last remaining leaves. The wind buffeted the side of the car. Mandy knew she was going to have to say something. She had never been one for holding back. She thought about Jimmy again. He had looked so happy to see her. The last thing she wanted to do was hurt him. And yet . . .

He hurt me. The memory of his reaction to her proposal flooded over her. He hadn't meant to hurt her, but he had. She had built herself up to the moment: strengthened her resolve. *He should have said yes.*

She glanced again at the cottage. There was smoke coming from the chimney, though the wind was snatching it away. Jimmy was in there, waiting for her. He loved her and she loved him. It would be so easy to let things drift on. They had each other, and Abi and Max and the dogs and their jobs. If she threw it all away, there was no guarantee that the future would be better.

She pushed open the car door and felt the wind rush in. There was no point delaying the conversation. It would only be wasting both their time. She jumped down, telling Sky to wait, and closed the car door with a hand that was shaking slightly. A few minutes, she told herself. A few minutes of angst, and then she would know. *For better or worse.*

Jimmy was standing at the stove when she walked in. Before he went away he had taken to cooking the dinner most nights, and on his return he had taken up the task again. He looked round and smiled as she walked in. 'Veggie chilli!' he announced, and he sounded so cheerful that for a moment Mandy's heart quailed. How much easier would it be just to drop into a chair and eat the chilli, sit down for a cosy evening in front of the fire, and then up to bed together?

She swallowed hard. 'Sounds good,' she said, 'but there's something I want to talk about first. Would you mind turning it down for a few minutes?'

Jimmy turned to her, his face open, eyebrows raised. 'Yes, of course,' he replied. He adjusted the control and left the pan simmering gently.

Mandy felt the adrenaline rush through her body as she walked through to the sitting room and sat down on the sofa. Jimmy had lit the fire too. Everything was ready for her to come home, to the place where she was loved. *But it's not enough.*

Jimmy sat down in one of the armchairs and looked expectantly at her. Mandy took a deep breath. 'We need to talk about the future,' she began. 'Our future.' She stopped, already feeling breathless. 'I had a lot of time to think when you were in Canada,' she ploughed on. 'About the discussion we had around marriage.' She couldn't call it a proposal, she would feel humiliated beyond measure. 'When I asked you to marry me, it wasn't all about having a wedding.' She could feel heat in her face, but she lifted her head to look at him more squarely. 'It was about the future . . . about what I want from life.'

Jimmy looked a little wary. 'And what would that be?'

Mandy paused for a moment. How to express the intense feeling that had invaded her? 'I want us to be a family,' she said finally. 'A real family. I want to be married: a sense of stability. And I want a child. I love Abi and Max. So much so that it hurts to think I might lose them. But they have a mother of their own. I want to join myself to you. And be a mum, with you as the father. I know how wonderful you are as a dad and I want that for my own child.'

She stopped. There was a lump in her throat that was choking her. She could feel heat from the fire on the side of her face, adding to the blush she felt rising from her neck.

Jimmy gazed steadily at her, unseen thoughts flashing behind his eyes. His hands rested on his knees, very still.

Say something. Please.

Jimmy rubbed his palm over his face. 'I think you know what I'm going to say,' he said. How steady his voice was compared to hers. 'Oh, Mandy. Part of me wants to give you what you want. I really do love you very much and I only ever want you to be happy.' He swallowed, and for the first time, his mouth twitched as if he was also fighting back tears. 'But I've been married before. And I've had children. And wonderful as they are, I'm not sure I want to start all over again. I may in the future, but I'm not ready right now. If I was going to, then you would be the ideal person. For what it's worth, I think you'd be a wonderful mum. What we've had these last two years has been amazing. I love you, and Abi and Max do too. I think I could be happy with you forever. But it seems to me that we're at a crossroads.'

He paused and rubbed awkwardly at a worn patch on his jeans. Mandy couldn't speak. The room around her blurred and suddenly felt far too hot.

'I know what you're asking, and I'd love to say yes,' Jimmy said quietly, 'but I won't lie to you and I won't make promises I can't keep. I can only say how sorry I am.'

He sounded like he meant it. But there was a stabbing sensation in Mandy's chest and for a moment she thought her heart was going to explode.

'I don't want to lose you, but I'll respect your choice,' Jimmy went on, 'whatever it is.'

Mandy felt strangely empty. There didn't seem to be anything else to say. After a few awkward minutes, Jimmy stood up and went to finish off the chilli. He served it on trays and they sat beside one another on the sofa, yet the distance between them stretched as far as the chilly Arctic. By the time they walked up the narrow staircase to the bedroom, Jimmy might as well have been on the moon.

He fell asleep as soon as his head hit the pillow. He always did, yet tonight it seemed almost indecent. Mandy listened to his steady breathing. She could see the outline of his face against the pillow. The conversation kept echoing through her mind.

I want you to be happy . . . but I'm not sure I want to start all over again. I may in the future, but I'm not ready right now.

Was it true, she wondered? Had being with Aira reminded him of how much fun he could have on his own, meeting new people and exploring faraway places?

Or is it me he doesn't want?

A friend at university had been strung along for years by one of the junior staff. He loved her, he'd said. He just didn't believe in marriage and never wanted children. She'd left him eventually and within the year he was engaged to another girl. Another year and they had married and had a baby. Mandy's friend had been devastated.

She looked again at Jimmy's sleeping face. *He wouldn't do that. Not Jimmy. He's too honest.*

But was he?

Do you ever really know anyone?

Mandy sighed and Jimmy stirred a little and turned towards her. She had to stop herself from reaching out and stroking his face.

The truth was staring at her, bright as a Christmas star. If Jimmy didn't want to marry her, they would have to separate for a while. Mandy wasn't sure yet what she would decide in the long run. Maybe with a bit of distance, it would be easier to tell whether what he was offering was enough. She was thirty years old.

Still young enough to meet someone else and have children. But if she waited with Jimmy, hoping for a change of heart, and then found out years down the line that he still felt the same, then the chances of having a family would drop away.

For a moment, she wanted to wake him up and tell him. *I've made my decision.* But it could wait for the morning. For now, he may as well sleep. A tear trickled down Mandy's cheek onto the pillow.

She would move out, she decided. It would be easier that way. Mistletoe Cottage, where Jimmy had lived before, had a new tenant. With Abi and Max and three dogs, it wouldn't be easy to find somewhere straight away. Wildacre was Mandy's, but for now she could move back into Animal Ark. She could help her mum and keep her dad company. Sad as it was to move out, at least she had somewhere safe and comfortable to go. She wiped away the salty tear that was itching on her cheek. Exhaustion was dragging her down. Two minutes later, she had fallen into an uneasy sleep.

By the time she woke up, Jimmy was downstairs. Mandy walked slowly down the narrow staircase and into the kitchen.

'The dogs've been out,' Jimmy told her, looking up from his cereal bowl. 'There's plenty of porridge if you'd like.' He waved his spoon at the pan on the stove.

He sounded the same as ever, but Mandy felt strangely weightless and empty, as if she wasn't really there. 'Thanks,' she said. She pulled out a chair opposite him and sat down.

He smiled across the table at her. 'Sleep okay?'

Mandy shook her head. 'I've made a decision,' she said.

Jimmy's eyes flickered, a fleeting reaction she couldn't read, but then his face was calm again. 'What did you decide?'

'I need some space,' she said. 'You were kind enough to be honest with me, and I need to be equally honest with myself.'

Jimmy looked sad now, but he made no attempt to argue. 'Fair enough,' he said. 'I'll look round for somewhere to stay. I could ask Jared if I could lodge with him until I get something sorted.' Jared Boone was the farm manager at Upper Welford Hall, where Running Wild was situated.

Mandy raised her hand to stop him. 'It'll be easier if I move out,' she said. 'Sky and I can move back to Animal Ark. Mum and Dad won't mind.'

Jimmy frowned. 'Wildacre's yours,' he pointed out. 'It shouldn't be you who moves out.'

Mandy managed a smile, though it was an effort. 'I know Wildacre is mine,' she said, 'but it's easier for me to go. Not so easy for you with the dogs. And if you're here, Abi and Max will have more continuity. I can still come over and see them . . . and you,' she added.

Jimmy looked troubled for a moment and she thought he was going to refuse.

'It makes more sense that way,' she persisted.

'I can see you've made up your mind.' He pushed his chair back and stood up. 'But if at any time you want your home back,' he went on, 'I'll be straight out the door. Okay?' He lifted his empty bowl from the table and stood for a moment, his eyebrows raised.

'Okay,' Mandy agreed. She turned to leave the kitchen.

'Won't you have some breakfast before you go?'

Mandy shook her head. 'Not hungry,' she muttered. She had to pack a bag as well. If she was going to leave, she wanted to get it over with.

Sky seemed to know there was something wrong as soon as they were in the car. She lay in the passenger seat with her ears flat against her head, glancing now and then in Mandy's direction. There were tears in Mandy's eyes as she drove down the track. Half her brain was screaming that she should turn round and go back. Tell Jimmy it would all be fine. Accept the half-life that he was offering. But that wouldn't solve anything. If she returned, she had to accept that the dream of marriage and children could be beyond her reach forever. And she knew she couldn't do that.

In the rearview mirror, she caught sight of the hurriedly packed holdall on the back seat. Should she tell her parents what was happening, she wondered? Mum's illness had turned everything upside down.

Mandy stroked Sky's soft head as she pulled into the car park at Animal Ark. 'Probably better not to tell them for now,' she said aloud. She could tell them when and if she decided to make the split permanent. Until then, she would say she was moving back in to help Emily.

She parked the car, then took her overnight bag into the house. Better get it over with. Emily was sitting in one of the comfortable chairs they had installed near the stove. Despite the mildness of the day, the stove was lit.

'Hello, love.' Adam smiled at Mandy, then turned to take another mug out of the cupboard.

Emily looked round with a smile, until her eyes lit on the bag Mandy was carrying. 'What've you got there?'

Mandy could feel her face going red. 'It's an overnight bag,' she said. 'I've come to stay for a few days. If you'll have me, of course.'

Emily looked up at Mandy. 'There's nothing wrong, is there? With you and Jimmy, I mean?' There was alarm in her voice.

Mandy's cheeks were burning, but she shook her head. 'Why would you think that?' She swallowed hard. It wasn't easy to speak, but she forced herself to go on. 'I wanted to move back in to give you a hand,' she said. 'I should have come as soon as you got out of hospital.'

Emily sent her a gentle smile and patted the arm of the seat beside her. Mandy felt another stab of anguish. A few years ago, Emily would have jumped up out of her chair. That she hadn't tried to get up was very telling. Mandy swallowed down the pain, forced a smile onto her face and perched on the arm of the chair.

Emily lifted her hand and placed it on Mandy's cheek. 'You're a dear, precious girl,' she said. 'But you have your own life now. You've more than enough to keep yourself busy. The last thing I want is for you to give up your life for me.'

Mandy breathed in and out. She pressed her fingernails into the palms of her hands, willing herself not to cry.

Adam came over and put a mug of coffee into Mandy's hand. 'Your mum's right,' he told her. 'You've got too much going on with Jimmy and the twins and Wildacre and Hope Meadows. There are only twenty-four hours in a day, love. You have to take care of yourself before everyone else, remember.'

Mandy felt as if she'd been kicked in the stomach. That they would turn down her offer hadn't even crossed her mind. The tears that had threatened before rose into her eyes and she blinked them away angrily.

Emily was watching her with a slight frown. 'Are you sure there's nothing wrong?'

Mandy shook her head. 'I'm fine,' she lied. 'I just want to help you,' she added. 'Really.'

Adam patted her on the shoulder. 'I know you do,' he said. 'And we appreciate it. We'd never turn you away if there was a problem. If you need to come home, you're welcome any time, day or night. But your mum and I have been talking about this. It's challenging, the way things are changing, but we have to learn to cope with it ourselves. I promise we'll ask if we need anything, but for now, we need some time to find our way. So long as you're all right, it's better for you to stay at Wildacre. It's not as if you won't see us every day!'

Emily nodded. 'I know it's difficult for all of us,' she said, 'but you can't drop everything every time I have a crisis. Other people need you, even now, and in the future maybe more . . .'

Mandy felt sick. Was Emily talking about the idea of Mandy having a family of her own? If only she knew how far from reality that was.

Emily heaved herself out of the chair and Mandy stood up to help her. How tiny she seemed. Mandy could remember reaching her arms up to wrap around Emily's waist. Now her mum had to reach up to hug Mandy. 'You really are the best daughter anyone could wish for,' she said. 'But it's time for you to put yourself first now. Whatever happens, you will do that for me, won't you?'

Mandy buried her face in Emily's shoulder. Her mother felt frail and bony, yet so much strength and love flowed out of her. For a moment, she wanted to break down, cry herself out as she would have done years ago and pour out all her problems. Instead she took a breath, straightened up and looked directly into Emily's eyes.

'I'll do my best,' she promised.

Chapter Thirteen

Mandy felt sick as she shoved her overnight bag back into the car. She had no idea what to do next. The idea of traipsing back up to Wildacre this evening and telling Jimmy what had happened was awful, but where else could she go? She didn't want to beg Helen or Susan for space. Neither of them had the room. Nor could she ask Gran and Grandad to have her. The information would go right back to her parents. She sighed. Whatever else had happened, she had work to do. Hope Meadows had to be opened up, then she needed to be in the clinic for morning surgery.

'Good morning!'

Mandy was surprised to see Geraldine standing outside the rescue centre. She'd forgotten that Geraldine had offered to work this Tuesday as well.

'Oh . . . hi,' she replied. She unlocked the door to the rescue centre and held it open. Geraldine walked in ahead of her, then turned and studied Mandy's face. 'Is everything okay?' she asked.

Mandy felt hot as she glanced at her watch. 'I'm running late. Morning surgery starts in ten minutes.'

Geraldine gave her a reassuring smile. 'Why don't you leave me to get started here? I'll take the dogs out first, then clean the kennels and get the feeding done and you can pop back when you have a moment.'

Mandy felt an urge to hug her. 'That would be fabulous,' she said. 'Thank you so much.' As she made her way to the door, she heard the single bark that Olive gave every morning when someone entered the kennel, and Geraldine's calm voice greeting each of the dogs in turn.

She walked back over to the rescue centre at eleven o'clock to see how Geraldine had got on. Mandy had brought her a coffee from the percolator in the clinic, and they sat down together in the reception area.

'Did everything go okay?' Mandy asked.

Geraldine grinned. 'It was fine. Jasper took his tablets in cheese spread. And Mustard walked all the way round the orchard without pulling on his lead.'

Mandy was impressed. 'Crikey,' she said. 'You must be a miracle worker if you managed that.'

Geraldine looked pleased. 'I took the tube of cheese with me,' she said. 'A few bungs of squeezy deliciousness and he didn't take his eyes off me!'

Mandy laughed. 'Brilliant!' she said. 'I've used that cheese before for training, but I hadn't tried Mustard on it. Good to know which bribe works best.'

'Other than that,' Geraldine went on, 'the cats are fine, as are the guinea pigs. And I cleaned out the fridge too. Not that it was dirty.'

'I can't believe how much you've done! It's really good to have you here,' Mandy said, meaning it. 'I'll be having lunch at the cottage in a couple of hours with my parents. Why don't you join us?' It would be quite helpful for Geraldine to be there, she thought. Not only to avoid another conversation about this morning, but to smooth over any awkwardness about the last time Geraldine had been in the cottage.

Geraldine paused. 'I'm afraid I can't,' she said. 'I need to pop into Walton for some shopping when I'm done here. I've brought my car in today.'

'Oh,' Mandy said. 'Would it be too cheeky to ask for a lift into town, please? There's a couple of things I need to get.' She had forgotten to bring any toiletries. If she wasn't staying at Animal Ark, she couldn't borrow from her parents.

'Of course,' Geraldine said. 'Just let me know when you're finished and we can go together.'

Mandy felt a little more cheerful as she walked back to Animal Ark. She was starting to enjoy Geraldine's company, as well as appreciate her help. Whatever happened, she decided she wasn't going back to Wildacre that night. Even if she had to get a hotel or a bed and breakfast for a night or two. She had been out so rarely during the time Jimmy had been away that she had plenty of money saved. She might as well make the most of it. Better than trying to kip on someone's couch.

★

Though it had been easy to chat to Geraldine in Hope Meadows where there was plenty to discuss about the rescues, it wasn't so easy to chat in the car. Mandy's head was full of conflicting thoughts about where she should go. She had glanced through Airbnb's website, hoping for a bargain, but the only property available at such short notice was a six-bed mansion with a swimming pool. Lovely as it looked, it was hardly suitable. There was a local guest house with a spare room, but it had a shared bathroom. Mandy wasn't squeamish, but after a long day at work, she wanted the freedom to shower at leisure. The idea of scuttling in and out of a bathroom a stranger might need was not very enticing.

They parked behind the supermarket. 'Can you get what you need here?' Geraldine asked.

'This is perfect,' Mandy said.

Geraldine grabbed a basket and disappeared. Mandy headed to the aisle with the toothbrushes and toothpaste. A silly thing to forget, but she had been in a hurry this morning. And it hadn't been the easiest thing ever, walking away from Jimmy.

She bumped into Geraldine again in the shampoo aisle. Geraldine was lifting down a bottle of Rhubarb Crumble Balsam. She caught Mandy's eye as Mandy went to grab another bottle of the same shampoo. 'Oh, do you use that as well?' Geraldine asked. 'I knew you were a woman of taste!'

Mandy laughed. 'Either that, or a weirdo who likes food-scented hair product,' she countered.

Geraldine grinned. 'Well, who doesn't like rhubarb crumble?' She put the bottle in her basket. 'Speaking of crumble,' she said, 'I hear Sheep from the Goats has a great apple crumble on their specials menu at the moment. How about I treat you to lunch in celebration of my new job at Hope Meadows?'

Sheep from the Goats was an upmarket bar not far from the supermarket. If they went now, there would just be enough time for lunch before she had to be back. 'That's very generous,' Mandy said.

'Great.' Geraldine sounded pleased. 'I'll just go and pay for these and meet you outside.'

A few minutes later, Mandy pulled open the door of the bar and let Geraldine through. She had met Susan, Helen and Molly here a few times. They always sat at the same table near the window, but it wasn't available today. Instead, the waiter led them to the other end of the room to a quiet table in the corner. 'I'll sit you here, if that's okay?' he said. 'We've got a big party coming in and it'll be more peaceful back here.'

'Perfect!' Geraldine said.

Mandy pulled out the curved white leather chair and sat down. The waiter handed her a menu. Mandy found herself looking through it without enthusiasm. She didn't feel all that hungry, she realised. But Geraldine was looking so happy that Mandy felt she couldn't let her down. When the waiter returned, she ordered tomato and basil soup and the apple crumble, making her voice as cheerful as she could.

'You seem very quiet today,' Geraldine said, adjusting her dessert fork so that it lined up with the spoon. 'Is everything all right?'

Her eyes were so kind that Mandy suddenly felt tears prickling at the back of her eyelids. Geraldine was a therapist, she remembered. She must be good at picking up on people's feelings, however well they tried to hide them. She swallowed hard, then took a breath. 'Not really,' she admitted.

'Want to tell me about it?' Geraldine prompted. 'Whatever it is, you can tell me. It won't go any further.'

'I've moved out of Wildacre,' Mandy admitted, the words spilling out of her like cold water.

'Have you and Jimmy fallen out?'

There was so much sympathy in Geraldine's voice that Mandy found she couldn't stop talking. About the disastrous proposal and its aftermath. Jimmy's absence and the lack of a resolution, and what a great time he seemed to have with Aira, then their discussion last night. 'It feels so strange,' Mandy finished. 'I didn't realise how much I would want to have a family of my own. I was so lucky when I was growing up, having such fantastic parents. I want to see if I can be as good for my own children. I was sure Jimmy was the one, but he doesn't seem to want me.'

She broke off. Her voice was starting to shake.

Geraldine reached across the table and touched

Mandy's clenched fist. 'It doesn't sound to me as if he doesn't want you,' she murmured. 'It sounds like he does, very much, but that you want different things. I suppose he's at a different stage of life from you in many ways. But I'm sure he does love you.'

Mandy closed her eyes for a moment, breathing in and out. She opened her eyes and looked at Geraldine and tried to smile. 'You're right,' she admitted. 'He does love me. But that makes it almost worse, don't you think? I hated to choose, but that's what I had to do.'

The waiter arrived with her soup and Geraldine's goat's cheese tart and Geraldine waited until he left before she began again. 'For what it's worth,' she said, picking up her knife and fork, 'I think it's the right thing you're doing. Giving yourself time, that is.'

Mandy scooped up some soup. 'It ought to be,' she said, watching steam rise from her spoon, 'but even that seems to have gone wrong. I was going to stay with Mum and Dad, but I didn't tell them why. They thought I was only going to help Mum and they turned me down, saying I need to keep on with my own life. I don't even know where I'm going to sleep tonight.' She put the soup back into her bowl and felt her eyes prick again.

Geraldine was looking at her thoughtfully. 'Is it just you and Sky?' she asked. 'If it is, the two of you are welcome to stay at the cottage I've rented. There's a spare bedroom you can have.'

Mandy felt her face going red. 'That's very kind,'

she said, 'but I wasn't angling for shelter. I'm sorry if it sounded that way.'

Geraldine smiled and shook her head. 'Don't worry. It didn't sound like that at all. But there is a spare bedroom and the cottage is empty half the week. It would be no trouble at all for you and Sky to stay for a few weeks until you're feeling a bit more settled.'

Mandy didn't know what to say. Surprising as it was, the idea of moving in with Geraldine was very tempting: easier in some ways than with someone who knew her better, or with a complete stranger.

'Tell you what,' Geraldine said. 'You don't have to tell me right now. Come over this evening and have a look around. And if you like it, you can move right in. Winter's just round the corner. I've already noticed the house is a bit damp when I come back from Manchester. It'd do no harm to keep the place occupied and warm. And I promise I don't bite!'

Mandy hesitated. What would it be like to live with Geraldine and work with her at the same time? But then she'd lived with Adam and Emily all these years and worked with them, too. It had never come close to feeling like a problem. And if it didn't work out, she would at least have time to find somewhere else.

She took a deep breath. 'Thank you very much,' she said. 'I'll come over later, after work.'

Geraldine looked pleased. 'I'm looking forward to it already,' she said.

★

It was starting to get dark by the time afternoon surgery finished. Mandy couldn't help feeling a little uneasy as she walked out to her car. She hoped Geraldine's cottage would be suitable. If not, it was getting quite late to find somewhere else. And what if Geraldine had changed her mind?

The cottage was halfway up the fell on the far side of Kimbleton. There would be a wonderful view in the morning, Mandy thought, but for now, all she could see were the lights of the houses in the valley. When she got out of the car, the cold air stung her lungs. November was well underway, she realised. Winter and Christmas were just around the corner.

Will I be spending Christmas alone?

She walked across the stone flags of the path and knocked on the door. Barn End Cottage was part of a modern barn conversion. Mandy could vaguely remember the low sturdy building when it was used for animals. In the last year, it had been cleaned up and made into a row of three stylish holiday cottages, but the only lights were in Geraldine's.

The door swung open. 'Hello, dear,' Geraldine said, beaming. Mandy found herself smiling back, though thoughts of Jimmy kept trickling into her head.

The scent of baking engulfed Mandy as she walked into the warm kitchen.

'I put some scones in the oven,' Geraldine confessed. Now Mandy was in her space, Geraldine seemed almost shy, but Mandy was already starting to relax. The kitchen was surprisingly homely for a holiday let. Fresh flowers stood in a vase on the mahogany table. Quiet music was playing from speakers suspended in the corners of the ceiling. 'I'll show you the bedroom and you can decide if you'd like to stay.'

She led Mandy up a narrow wooden staircase that led off the kitchen. The little bedroom was charming, with beams and a sloping roof over a single bed dressed with a flowery quilt. More flowers stood on the little bedside table. 'It's lovely,' Mandy said. 'Just what I need.'

She followed Geraldine back downstairs and watched as she bent to check the oven, then opened it and took out the fragrant scones. Geraldine reached into a cupboard, took out a cooling rack and slid the scones onto it, before turning back to Mandy. 'It's a delightful place, don't you think?' Her blue eyes shone and her cheeks were flushed from the heat of the oven.

Lovely as the cottage was, Mandy was finding it hard to feel joyful. Jimmy would be home at Wildacre by now. Zoe and the other dogs would be sniffing round, wondering where she and Sky had gone.

'I've got a blanket that Sky can lie on,' Geraldine added, as if sensing Mandy's distress. 'She'll sleep in your bedroom, won't she?'

Mandy pulled herself together. She reached over and picked up the key that was lying on the kitchen table. 'Is this for me?' she asked, and Geraldine nodded.

I'm not leaving Wildacre forever, Mandy reminded

herself. *This is only to give me space to think*. She forced herself to smile, though she couldn't help wondering whether Geraldine could see through her effort. 'I'd love to stay, thank you,' she said.

Geraldine opened her arms and Mandy leaned into her embrace. The hug was a little awkward and Mandy found herself wondering for a moment whether Geraldine was unused to physical contact, but she couldn't help feeling relieved to have found somewhere so instantly comfortable and welcoming to stay.

'It's all going to be okay,' Geraldine murmured, her breath warm against Mandy's hair. 'Thank you for coming, Mandy.'

Chapter Fourteen

Steely grey light was edging under the blinds when Mandy woke. The bed was comfortable, but firmer than the one at Wildacre and a lot more narrow and for a moment, she thought she was at Animal Ark. But she opened her eyes to beams and the sloping ceiling and yesterday's events came flooding back with a rush of self-pity. She had left Jimmy. She was alone in the world, sleeping in the house of a stranger.

Sky stirred. She was lying on the bed, curled into the space behind Mandy's knees, and when she saw Mandy was awake, her tail thumped on the quilt. She shuffled round into a more comfortable position and lay back down with a contented sigh. Mandy watched her for a moment. How wonderful to be Sky, with her uncomplicated life. She normally didn't get to sleep on the bed, but Mandy was glad she was there. Painful as it was to be here without Jimmy, Mandy felt a sad sense of peace. She had followed what her conscience had told her was the right thing to do. *You'll get over this*, she told herself. *Give it time.*

She heard the sound of a door opening and closing

downstairs. In contrast to her own quiet sadness, Geraldine sounded happy. She was humming and Mandy could hear the cheerful clatter of the table being set.

Pulling herself upright, bending so as not to hit her head on the low ceiling, Mandy crept into the little bathroom that had been constructed in a niche under the eaves. It was lovely to have an en suite, tiny as it was. Then with Sky at her heels, Mandy descended the steep staircase and stepped into the kitchen.

'Good morning.' Geraldine smiled at her. 'How did you sleep?'

'Well, thanks,' Mandy replied. Unusually well, she realised.

Sky ran across to greet Geraldine, wagging her tail. Mandy found it reassuring. Sky usually had good taste in people. Geraldine bent to stroke Sky, but she lifted her head to look at Mandy. 'I didn't know whether to leave the heating on overnight,' she said. 'Were you warm enough?'

'Definitely. Sky was on the bed. I hope that's okay.'

'Of course it is.' Geraldine ran her hand over Sky's domed head. 'The room is yours for as long as you want it, so make yourself at home. What would you like for breakfast?'

'A cup of tea and a slice of toast would be perfect,' Mandy said.

Once the toast was ready, they sat down together.

'I do love it here,' Geraldine said, leaning back in

her chair to see out of the window. The green shoulder of the fell loomed above them and the sky behind was a startling shade of pewter. 'It's so beautiful. It brings out the frustrated artist in me.'

'Frustrated artist?' Mandy echoed. 'Do you mean you draw and the results frustrate you, or that you don't get to draw as much as you'd like?'

Geraldine laughed. 'When I was young, I always imagined I'd be a famous artist, but here I am, part-time therapist and part-time kennel assistant, who draws in her spare time. Not that I don't love that, of course, but life hasn't exactly turned out as I'd expected it.'

'Do you have any of your drawings you can show me?' Mandy asked.

Geraldine stood up and went to a briefcase in the corner of the room. She pulled out a sketchbook with a marbled gold and dove-grey cover and brought it over to the table.

'These are amazing,' Mandy said. The book was filled with exquisite pencil drawings of local scenery. There was the rocky outcrop of Axwith Tor and a wonderful view of the Beacon. Geraldine must have spent a few days exploring Silver Dale. There was Silver Force in full spate and there were several studies of some of the rock formations around the upper end of the valley. The last picture in the book was a sketch of a hawk. Unlike most of the other pencil drawings, this was in colour. It was anatomically perfect, and so beautiful it took Mandy's breath away.

She stared at Geraldine with newfound admiration. 'It must be wonderful to be able to draw like that,' she said. 'You're so lucky. I'm hopeless at art. Even my stick men look fat!'

Geraldine smiled. 'Drawing makes me happy,' she said, 'though I don't think my skill is so unusual. The dreams of being well-known are long behind me.'

'Well, I'm glad I've seen some of your work,' Mandy said. 'I think you're incredible.'

Geraldine wasn't due at the rescue centre that day. She had told Mandy when she started that she would have to go back to Manchester on odd days. 'But I'll be back this evening,' Geraldine assured her.

Mandy drove towards Animal Ark on her own in the car. She couldn't help comparing today, after a good night's sleep under Geraldine's roof, with yesterday, when everything had been up in the air. Things could have turned out much worse, she thought.

Her phone rang just as she arrived. She pulled it out of her pocket and sat staring at the screen for a long moment. It was Jimmy. A surge of hope rushed through her. Maybe he was ringing to tell her it had all been a big mistake. She could come home and they would get married . . . She squashed the feeling down, let out a sigh and clicked to accept the call.

'Hello. I was just ringing to see if you were getting on okay?'

Despite trying to prepare herself, Mandy felt a physical shock when she heard his voice. She sat in the driver's seat of the RAV4 almost unable to breathe. *I want to come home.* The words were screaming in her head.

'It's fine,' she said. 'I'm fine . . . Thank you for asking.' She could hear how flat her voice sounded.

'And was everything okay with your parents?' Though it was Jimmy's voice, Mandy felt as if she was having a polite discussion with a stranger.

'They're both fine,' Mandy said, deliberately pretending to misunderstand.

'That's good,' he said.

'Yes,' Mandy replied. She looked out through the car window. A car had drawn up on the far side of the gravel. It must be nearly time for morning surgery. 'I'd better go,' she said. 'Work,' she added briefly. She felt, if anything, even more empty than before. Such a brief, impersonal phone call. She wanted to call him back, do something – anything – to get back to their comfortable life together, but unless one of them changed their mind, that life was gone.

Adam appeared as Mandy was walking to the rescue centre. He held out his arms for a hug, and Mandy put her arms round him. For a moment, she clung to him, then she let go, hoping he hadn't been able to sense how insecure and confused she was feeling. 'I just wanted a quick word,' he said. 'I wanted to make sure you didn't take it personally that we thought it was better you stayed at home.' He stood back, gazing at her. 'I know I tell you this often,' he told her, 'but we're very proud of you, and we love you as much as we always have done. But we want you to live your own life! It's important to us that you don't feel you have to look after us. We have to manage for ourselves.'

Mandy felt a wave of guilt rise up inside her, along with the urge to tell him the truth. He thought she had made a selfless offer to help her mum, yet the real reason she'd wanted to stay was anything but selfless. But the idea of telling him she was staying with Geraldine, and not at home, seemed impossible. She didn't want to talk about leaving Jimmy. Not until she knew for sure what was happening. What would happen, she wondered, when people started to notice she wasn't going back to Wildacre at night? She could only hope nobody would mention it to her parents, or at least not before the situation was resolved. *What a mess*, she thought. *I never liked secrets.*

'I'll have to go now,' Helen said, glancing at her watch. She had been helping Mandy with the midday feeds. 'Seb's bringing our sandwiches in two minutes.'

'Thanks for your help,' Mandy said. She had told Helen quietly what had happened and where she was staying, and to her relief, Helen had taken everything in her stride.

'See you after lunch,' Helen called as she let herself out.

Mandy began wiping down the counters in the food prep room.

'How are you, love?' She turned at the sound of Emily's voice. 'I thought I'd come out and see the dogs,' Emily said.

'I'm fine, Mum.' Mandy noticed with a pang that Emily was using her crutches. She studied her mum's face for signs of pain, but although Emily was pale, she looked peaceful. 'I'm going to take the dogs out to the orchard,' she said. 'Can you manage on the grass?'

'Oh, I'm getting very nimble on my sticks,' Emily said, waving a crutch in the air. 'Lead on!'

They stood side by side at the edge of the paddock, watching as Mustard, Olive and Jasper trotted round the trees, sometimes running together, but more often separating out to sniff at the leaf-strewn ground.

'Jasper's looking well,' Emily commented. 'Does he still cough in the mornings?'

'Hardly at all,' Mandy replied. 'I think we can advertise him for a gentle and understanding home soon.'

'Emily?' Rachel's voice rang in the still air and a moment later, she appeared at the gate. 'I've made a toasted sandwich for your lunch,' she said. 'The washing's finished and I've folded it up and put it on the beds.'

Mandy felt a jab of dismay. Though helping Emily hadn't been her primary reason for moving back to Animal Ark, it would have been nice to be the one who was helping. Emily reached out and squeezed her arm, as if sensing Mandy's regret. 'Why don't you come in and make yourself a toastie? I'd love to have some company while I'm eating. Speaking of which, I know it didn't go too well last time, but please can you invite Geraldine over for dinner one day next week? I know we didn't get off to the best start, but I really would like to get to know her better.'

'For dinner?' Geraldine said. 'Are you sure?' She looked across the table at Mandy. Geraldine had bought a frozen vegetable lasagne from the farm shop at Upper Welford Hall and they were sitting in the comfortable kitchen at Barn End Cottage. Mandy was feeling quite relaxed after a glass of rosé wine.

'Yes, for dinner,' Mandy repeated. She lifted her glass and took another sip of the wine. 'My parents don't bite,' she added with a grin.

'I'm sure they don't.' Geraldine still sounded reluctant.

'How would it be if I promised not to bite either?' Mandy offered, remembering how unreasonable she had been the last time Geraldine had tried to have a meal in the cottage.

'That would help a bit.' Geraldine met Mandy's grin with one of her own. 'So they actually invited me?'

'Definitely. Though just to make things more complicated, I haven't told Mum and Dad I'm living here. They think I went back to Wildacre.'

'Haven't you told them about Jimmy?'

Mandy shook her head. 'It's too difficult,' she said. 'Mum thinks Jimmy's wonderful and that I'm lucky to have him.' She paused, feeling suddenly gloomy. 'Of course, I could have all those things, if I just accepted that he doesn't want the same things as I do.'

Geraldine rested her hand on Mandy's arm. 'No, you couldn't,' she said. 'Not really. It wouldn't work.' She patted Mandy's sleeve. 'I can tell you're someone who gives a lot of yourself. You'd always be there if there was an animal or a person in need.' She took a sip of wine, then set it back on the table, her eyes not leaving Mandy's face. 'But you have too much integrity to do something when you know it's not right. It's unusual in someone so young, but it's something I really admire.' She took in a deep breath, as if something had stirred in her own memories. 'And don't worry,' she added. 'I can have dinner with your parents without telling them anything. You moving in here can be our secret. I won't give you away.'

Mandy sat back in her chair, telling herself this was exactly what she'd asked for. But she couldn't help feeling niggled by what Geraldine had just said. It didn't feel good, knowing that she was keeping such a huge secret from her mum and dad. On the other hand, she trusted Geraldine. If she thought Mandy was doing the right thing, then she probably was, however uncomfortable it made her feel.

It felt rather nice to drive in together to Hope Meadows on Saturday morning. They discussed the day's tasks and planned various training exercises for each of the dogs. Though Mandy missed Jimmy with an intensity that sometimes took her breath away, Geraldine was turning out to be an excellent housemate. Mandy had made breakfast that morning, and Geraldine had seemed delighted even though Mandy overcooked the scrambled eggs.

As they took the dogs into the orchard, Mandy could hear cars coming and going in the car park. Dad must be having a busy morning in the clinic, she thought, feeling very fortunate to be out in the fresh air. It was windy again, as it was so often when winter arrived, but though the sky was grey, there was no sign of rain. Olive and Jasper were exploring slowly, their ears ruffled by the breeze. Geraldine was standing ready with the tube of cheese to reward signs of good behaviour.

'Hello?' Mandy heard a voice calling. She turned to see a young woman with black curly hair and a tall young man with a shaven head walking towards them. Both were wearing matching overcoats. 'I hope it's okay just to call in,' the woman said once they were near enough to chat easily. 'I know it's rather sudden, but we were looking at your website and we saw a lovely little crossbreed dog. Her name was Olive. Would it be possible for us to meet her, please?'

Mandy felt a little flustered. She usually tried to set up appointments with people on the phone, with a list of questions to run through first.

Geraldine seemed to sense that Mandy was struggling. 'Mandy, why don't you take Mr and Mrs . . . ?' She looked at the couple with a raised eyebrow.

'Anderson,' the young man supplied. 'Richie and Bridget.'

'. . . Mr and Mrs Anderson into reception,' Geraldine continued, 'and I'll bring the dogs in a few minutes.'

'Thanks,' Mandy said, grateful to Geraldine for taking charge. She looked at Bridget Anderson. 'Come this way, please.'

By the time Geraldine came in with Jasper and Olive, Mandy felt as if everything was under control. Though the young couple seemed pleasant, she was starting to think that they weren't ready to rehome a dog. Neither of them had owned a pet before, and Mandy wasn't sure they'd given enough thought about whether a dog would suit their lifestyle.

'Anyway,' Mandy said as Geraldine walked in, 'this is Olive here, if you'd still like to meet her?'

'That would be a real treat,' Richie said.

'She's quite shy,' Geraldine warned. She looked at Mandy. 'Have you explained how to greet her?'

Mandy nodded. 'I have,' she said. 'Do you want to lead the introduction?'

'Love to,' Geraldine replied, looking pleased. Mandy found herself watching with interest. She had given Geraldine lots of instructions about how to introduce potential owners to the dogs, and Geraldine had watched once or twice as Mandy had brought some clients in. It would be good to see how she fared with doing the introduction herself.

Everything went smoothly, but Mandy still wasn't convinced she had found Olive's new owners. She told Geraldine her concerns when the couple had left.

'Really?' Geraldine said. 'They seemed lovely to me. Bridget has a very kind face.'

'True,' Mandy admitted. She thought for a moment. Though her instincts were to be wary, maybe Geraldine's mind was steadier than hers at the moment. And Geraldine had done the introduction. Maybe she had seen more than Mandy, whose attention had been mostly on Geraldine herself. 'What else makes you think they would be a good match, then?' she pressed. 'A kind face isn't really enough.'

Geraldine narrowed her eyes, thinking. 'Okay then, not just a kind face,' she said. 'She seemed very fond of her husband,' she said slowly, 'and he seemed to feel the same. It looked like a nice, stable relationship. And it wasn't as if they'd just decided on a whim that they wanted a dog. They might have only just seen Olive, but they knew they wanted a crossbreed.' She put her head to one side. 'Not only that,' she went on, 'but I could tell that they listened to you very carefully. They didn't lean over Olive or get in her face. They waited for her to come to them. And when Bridget saw Olive's ears go back, she spoke to her really softly, as if she knew Olive might be afraid.'

Mandy's mind suddenly felt easier. Geraldine's

observations deserved to carry some weight, and everything she said made the Andersons seem entirely positive. In fact, the things she'd mentioned were things Mandy would normally have picked up herself. Was she letting her problems with Jimmy interfere with her judgement?

'I think you're right,' she said. She beamed at Geraldine. 'Thanks for the analysis! I bet you're a brilliant therapist.'

Geraldine grinned back at her. 'I try,' she said. 'It's not easy to get everything right the first time in life, but we all have to keep battling on. And sometimes things turn out much better than we could ever have hoped.'

Mandy nodded. 'They really do,' she said. 'I'll give the Andersons a ring in the morning to see if they'd like to arrange a home visit.'

Chapter Fifteen

Mandy walked out of the barn and round the outer wall of the yard at Upper Welford Hall. She peered in through the archway that led onto the cobbled space that had once been the heart of the farm. It was now filled with artisanal shops and local farming outlets. In a week or so, the shops would be filled with Christmas gifts and decorations, but today there was just a sprinkling of warm white lights decorating the potted trees that were scattered around the yard.

She headed slowly back to her car, looking in the shop windows. She had been out to see a sick cow and she was due back at Animal Ark shortly, but it was almost coffee time. Tossing the bottle of Dex back into the boot, she turned to look across the landscape. Running Wild, Jimmy's Outward Bound centre, was just out of sight in a hollow below the farm. It would only take a minute to get there in the car.

Temptation got the better of her. It wasn't as if she had left him altogether, Mandy told herself. She had moved out to give herself time to think. Maybe if she saw him, it would help her make up her mind one way or the other. Two minutes later, she had pulled into the car park beside the wooden building.

Jimmy was standing outside the portacabin office, addressing a circle of men and women. It looked like one of his corporate country courses and the delegates were all listening intently as Jimmy talked them through the day's events. Mandy found herself watching him hungrily. He always looked so serious when he was presenting. His short brown hair was slicked to the side. His green eyes flicked around the clearing, lighting on Mandy, and for a moment there was a flash of uncomplicated happiness before his face became grave again.

'That's all I have to say about the ropes course,' he announced. 'Now I'll hand you over to Kim Davey, my assistant manager, for some details on quad-bike safety.'

He walked towards Mandy and for a moment, she thought he was going to kiss her, but he stopped short and gave her a rather guarded smile. 'It's nice to see you,' he said. 'We've missed you at home, me and the dogs.'

Mandy managed to smile back. 'Sorry to disturb you at work,' she said. 'I was at Upper Welford looking at a cow.'

'Do you have time for a coffee?' Jimmy asked. 'We can go to the portacabin if you like. It's warmer in there.'

He took her into what Mandy had teasingly named

Running Wild HQ. It was an intensely practical space: three plastic chairs were grouped around a table, there was a small shelf containing maps and leaflets, and a kettle stood on another small shelf with a jar of instant coffee and a jar of coffee creamer.

Jimmy put the kettle on, spooned some coffee and creamer into two mugs and sat down opposite Mandy. Now Mandy could see him more closely, she thought he looked tired. Though he was smiling, she could see the tiny crinkles that formed in the corners of his eyes when he hadn't had enough sleep.

'How have you been?' he asked.

'Not too bad,' Mandy answered. 'You?'

Jimmy sent her that polite smile again. 'We're all doing fine,' he said. He looked at her for a moment, as if considering what to say next. 'Have you thought any more about coming home? Or whether you'd like me to move out?' There was a pained look in his eyes. Mandy couldn't tell whether he was upset about their relationship, or that he found the conversation difficult. He had never found it easy to talk about personal things.

She felt a wave of weariness at going over old, sad ground, but what had she expected him to talk about? They could hardly discuss the weather.

'I'm still not sure,' she admitted. 'I know what I want and I know you want something different.' She let out a painful sigh. 'I don't want to lose you,' she said, though even as she said it, she felt a pain as if she had lost him already.

'Would you give me a hug?' Jimmy asked. Mandy looked at him in surprise. Not that he didn't like hugging, but normally it was she who opened her arms for him.

'Of course,' she said, standing up and going over to him. He wrapped his arms around her and for a long moment, he held her close, resting his head against hers. Mandy breathed in his scent and tried not to cry.

When they broke apart, she felt more empty than ever.

'I'm sorry,' Jimmy said. 'I have to get back to work. Will you be okay?'

Mandy nodded.

'Call any time,' Jimmy said as she walked down the portacabin steps. 'I know it's not easy, but I'm here or at home any time you need me.'

Tears began to run down Mandy's face as she drove towards Welford. She was going to have to make her mind up. Jimmy couldn't always be there for her. Not unless she chose to go back to him on his terms. But the longer they were apart, the less she felt that was what she wanted. Yet she couldn't imagine a future with anyone else but Jimmy. The thoughts went round and round until she wanted to scream.

'Can you hold that, please?' Toby asked. He and Mandy were scrubbed up for surgery to stabilise a labrador's knee joint. Mandy had been reminded of Blackie, James's childhood pet, when the big black dog had limped into the clinic that morning. He had big brown eyes and a rather rolling gait, due to a ruptured ligament in his left knee.

Mandy took the handles of the artery forceps and held them out of Toby's way. He was a great surgeon. It was always interesting to help him operate.

'Almost done,' Toby muttered. He straightened up, waiting for Helen to fetch more of the vicryl suture material he was using to stitch up. Once Helen was out of the room, he turned to Mandy with a more serious look. 'Just a heads up,' he said. 'I was in the Fox and Goose last night and I heard you'd moved out of Wildacre.'

Mandy felt as if she'd been dunked into cold water. She wanted to ask who told him, but it didn't really matter. She nodded, her mouth set in a hard line.

'I'm not going to pry,' Toby told her. 'Just wanted you to know that it's out there.'

Mandy's fingers gripped the artery forceps. If Toby knew, how long would it take for Adam and Emily to find out?

'The person I overheard lives near Wildacre,' Toby went on. 'I told them you wanted to be round for your mum and dad while your mum isn't well. I know you're not staying here, but I thought it might shut them up for now.'

'Thank you.' Mandy felt a little faint. A web of secrets

and lies seemed to be expanding around her, trapping her like a fly.

'I don't know what's going on,' Toby said kindly, 'but I hope you can sort it out. Jimmy's a good bloke.'

Anger rose in Mandy's throat. 'I know he is,' she said. 'But that isn't the be all and end all!' She stopped, biting her tongue. 'Sorry,' she said to Toby. 'Things are a bit complicated.'

Toby shot her a sympathetic smile. 'Give it a bit of time,' he said. 'Things have a habit of sorting themselves out in the end.'

Mandy couldn't manage to return his smile. She couldn't imagine any way this was going to sort itself out.

The door clicked and Helen walked back into the room with a pack of suture material. 'Thanks, Helen,' Toby said.

'Always a pleasure to work with you.' Helen smiled. She sat down beside the anaesthetic machine again, and Toby nodded at Mandy, as if in silent reassurance.

Mandy felt a strange stab of relief as she walked across the car park that evening with Geraldine. They had finished at the rescue centre and were on their way to supper with Adam and Emily. At least if anyone was watching they would see her going into the cottage after work. By the time they went back to Barn End Cottage, it would be well and truly dark. *Not that there's anyone spying on me*, Mandy told herself hastily. She really wasn't that newsworthy, even by Welford standards!

Geraldine had insisted on bringing a chocolate cake for dessert. She seemed determined to make things easier for Emily and she joined in with clearing the table, helped Adam to make the coffee afterwards and then insisted on going home early, leaving Mandy behind to spend the evening with her mum and dad.

'She seems very nice,' Adam commented as he helped Emily through into the sitting room. The fire was lit and it was very cosy.

'She was indeed,' Emily agreed, 'but am I the only one who feels as if I've been grilled by a journalist?'

Adam laughed. 'It was a bit that way.'

Geraldine had certainly asked a lot of questions. She had asked how they had met and all about their career highlights. She had been rather gushing about Mandy, too, how gifted she was with the animals and how well-run the rescue centre was. Mandy had been half pleased, half embarrassed. Once or twice, she had wondered whether it would slip out that she was staying with Geraldine, but somehow each time Geraldine had guided the conversation back onto safer topics.

Mandy tried to relax and enjoy the heat of the fire, but being here with her mum and dad wasn't as relaxing as it normally was. She hated keeping secrets from them, and was dreading them asking if Jimmy was expecting her back at Wildacre. By nine o'clock, she was relieved to make her excuses and leave. It was surprisingly comforting to return to Barn End Cottage. Geraldine had waited up for her and there was a steaming pan of milk on the stove.

'Hot chocolate before bed?' Geraldine offered. 'It's a bit of a weakness of mine, I'm afraid.'

'Me too!' Mandy confessed. 'Mum and Dad can't believe I still like a cup of cocoa. I think they were hoping I'd grow out of it!'

'You're never too old for cocoa,' Geraldine declared, pouring hot milk onto flakes of real chocolate in a pair of mugs. Mandy took hers gratefully and wrapped her hands around it. Despite the sense of distance she was feeling from both her parents and Jimmy, Barn End Cottage and Geraldine were feeling more and more like home.

As the days went by, the feeling that Barn End Cottage was a haven from all the unhappiness in Mandy's life continued. During the week, Mandy had only herself and Sky to please. The cottage itself was charming. She loved her little bedroom under the eaves and as the weather grew chillier, she appreciated the way the oil-fired range kept the whole cottage cosy.

When Geraldine was there during the weekends, it seemed better still. She was good company, consistently cheerful and generous without being overpowering. Like Mandy, she was happy in her own company and didn't insist on accompanying Mandy every time she took Sky for a walk or wanted to read in peace.

Mandy rose early on Saturday and pushed back the blind on the roof window. Bright sun glittered on the frost-traced glass, and the clear blue sky arched over dark green winter heather. The patchy grass was frosty pale. Mandy thrust open the window and put her head outside. The red tiles of the rooftop were white with feathery hoar frost and the air was clean and fresh. Mandy felt a stir of pleasure as the sound of church bells drifted on the cold, still air.

She pulled her head inside and closed the window. After showering and getting dressed in several layers of clothes, she headed downstairs with Sky. She was pleased to find she had beaten Geraldine down for once. Geraldine still did more than her fair share of the cooking, so it would be nice to treat her for a change.

Mandy slipped a batch of home-made muffins into the oven. Geraldine had made the dough last night. They were filled with sultanas and raisins and smelled deliciously of cinnamon and mixed spice. Mandy felt the first stirring of festive excitement. She loved winter and despite having a few worries about how she would spend Christmas Day, she was looking forward to the build-up and all the seasonal frivolity.

She switched on the coffee percolator when she heard Geraldine begin to move about. By the time she arrived in the kitchen, Mandy had the table set and was sliding the muffins out of the oven.

She was rewarded by the look of delight on Geraldine's face. 'Oh, you lovely girl!'

They helped themselves to warm muffins and Mandy poured them each a mug of coffee, topped up with cream for a treat. 'I'm beginning to love weekend mornings,' Geraldine declared. 'That was a real treat, thank you.'

Mandy smiled. 'It should be me thanking you,' she said. 'You're a wonderful baker.'

Geraldine's face lit up. 'That's nice to hear,' she said. 'I can teach you if you like. I'd love to do something together this afternoon – after we've been to Hope Meadows, of course.'

Mandy felt pleased. It was Toby's weekend on duty and she had been wondering how to fill her day. 'How about a walk before it gets dark?' she suggested. 'Maybe we could walk up Silver Dale to the Force?'

'Sounds perfect,' Geraldine said. 'That way we'll be hungry for whatever we cook up!'

They blasted through the rescue centre chores in double quick time. 'Shall we take some of the dogs with us?' Geraldine asked as they stood in the kennels.

'Good idea. Let's take Jasper and Olive,' Mandy said. She had been out to the Andersons' house during the week, and if everything went well, Olive would be leaving in a week's time. Geraldine's instincts had proved right, and though young and inexperienced,

Mandy was confident the couple would give Olive an excellent home. A long walk today would give Olive some valuable experience on the lead, and help her gain confidence in unfamiliar surroundings.

Adam and Emily came out as they were loading the dogs into the car. Mandy was pleased to see that her mum was managing without crutches, though she was leaning heavily on Adam as they made their way down the two steps from the kitchen door.

'Taking them out for a spin?' Adam asked as Mandy helped Jasper into the back of the car and strapped him in.

'How's Olive doing?' Emily asked. Mandy was pleased to see that she directed her question to Geraldine. Though both sides seemed willing to get to know each other better, there was still some tension between the two women. Mandy regretted the way she had intervened when they had first met.

Geraldine and Emily were still talking about Olive when Mandy felt her mobile vibrate in her pocket. She pulled it out. It was a text from Jimmy.

'Hope you're having a good weekend.' She felt a slight pang. He was trying so hard to be friendly, to keep in touch. Mandy didn't quite know what to do. He was still living in Wildacre, and though she wondered whether she should ask him to move out, it was so pleasant living in Barn End Cottage that she didn't feel in any hurry.

'Off for a hike with G + dogs! Wrapped up warm!'

she wrote and clicked send before she had time to think any more about it. She was glad when Emily and Adam went back inside and they could set off on the short drive to Six Oaks where they would park.

Molly was in the yard when they stopped the car. Mandy waved at her and she waved back and a few minutes later, she and Geraldine were striding up the track that followed the river up the length of the dale.

'I know you've been here before from your sketch-book,' Mandy said to Geraldine, who was walking beside her, matching her stride for stride, 'but do you know much about the dale itself?'

Geraldine shook her head. 'I found it more or less by accident,' she admitted.

Mandy pointed almost straight ahead to the biggest of the hills that closed off the end of the narrow valley. 'That over there, with the long ridge at the top, is called Lang Crag,' she said. 'And that one there,' she pointed up the steep slope to their left, 'is Guldale Peak. They use that as one of the summits for the annual Welford Hill Race. And over there is Silver Tor.' She pointed at the most distinctive of the fells. There was a long line of scree stretching almost from top to bottom and a rocky crag at the top, where Silver Force poured out its peaty brown water.

'Why is it called Silver Dale?' Geraldine asked.

They had left the broad track and were weaving their

way up a narrow path through the heather. Frost still clung to the grass wherever there was shade. Mandy could hear the water rushing down through the rocky gully a little way to their left. Olive ran on ahead and Jasper pottered beside them. The air was fresh against Mandy's cheeks and she found herself smiling as she answered. 'The river that runs through the dale is called the Silver Beck. I used to come here with my grandparents when I was very young. Gran told me it wasn't called Silver Beck because of its colour, but because years ago prospectors looking for lead found nuggets of silver ore in the river.'

Geraldine smiled. 'It's lovely to hear you talk about the hills,' she said. 'You obviously belong here.'

'You're so right,' Mandy agreed. 'My roots run deep in Welford. I had to go away to university, of course, and then I lived in Leeds for a while, but I ended up right back where I started.'

'What else do you remember about growing up?'

Mandy was more than happy to talk about her days growing up in Animal Ark. 'You haven't met my friend James yet,' she told Geraldine, 'but he and I were inseparable when we were younger. It was great living next door to Mum and Dad's clinic. James was just as animal-mad as I was. We used to take his dog Blackie for day-long walks up the fells. There was always plenty to do in the practice and in between helping out, we used to get up to all sorts, rescuing wildlife and generally making a nuisance of ourselves!'

'I bet you were never a nuisance,' Geraldine said. 'It sounds like a blissful childhood.'

Mandy nodded. 'It was. I had the best childhood in the world!' She found herself wondering where Geraldine grew up. She knew almost nothing about her past. 'How about you?' she prompted. The path had narrowed a little and she had to turn her head and glance over her shoulder. 'What did you get up to as a child?'

Geraldine shrugged. 'There was nothing exciting about my childhood. I grew up in suburban Manchester and the only animal adventures there involved scrapping neighbourhood cats that kept me awake at night.'

They finally reached Silver Force, breathless from the steep climb near the top. Mandy let the roar of the waterfall fill her ears. The beck dropped straight down for hundreds of feet, thundering into a pool which was surrounded by a flat area of grass where families came to paddle in the summer. After feasting their eyes on the view, they headed back down the hill, reaching Six Oaks as the sun was beginning to set. Olive still had plenty of energy, though Jasper seemed tired. They would both sleep well tonight, Mandy thought.

'Would you mind if we made a quick call into the stables?' Mandy asked Geraldine as they arrived back at the yard. 'One of my old rescues lives here and he's not been well lately.'

'Of course not,' Geraldine said. 'I'd love to meet the horses.'

Molly seemed pleased to see them. 'Come and see the Biscuit Twins,' she told Geraldine. She introduced Geraldine to Bourbon and Party Ring, both of whom were as lively and adorable as before. As they walked back up the track from the two Welsh geldings, Mandy could hear Olive barking in the car.

'I'd better go and see what's up,' she told Molly. 'I'll come back in a minute to have a look at Bill.'

'I'll go,' Geraldine told her. 'I don't mind sitting in the car while you check him.'

'Are you sure?' Mandy asked and Geraldine nodded firmly.

'I'll be fine,' she said and trotted off in the direction of the RAV4.

'Bill's looking much better,' Molly said as she led Mandy across the yard. Sure enough, Mandy was relieved to see that his breathing had eased considerably. 'He seemed to improve when the weather got colder,' Molly added.

Mandy pulled her stethoscope from the pocket of her jacket. Though there was still some rattling in Bill's chest, he did seem to have stabilised. 'Maybe some kind of autumn pollen was bothering him,' she suggested.

'Or leaf mould or something,' Molly agreed. She pulled Bill's blanket back into place and buckled up the straps, then turned to Mandy with a frown. 'I know it's not really my business,' she said, 'but is it true you've left Jimmy?'

Mandy could feel her face going red. 'Am I really

that interesting?' she countered. 'Who's been gossiping now?'

Molly looked slightly abashed. 'I didn't realise it was a secret,' she said. 'It seemed like everyone knew.'

Mandy sighed. 'Sorry if I was a bit sharp. I'm just a bit sick of not being able to do anything without someone chattering about it in the Fox and Goose.'

Molly laughed. 'You should do what I do,' she said. 'Give 'em something proper to talk about. I'm off to a speed dating night in York next week. Why don't you join me?'

'Not quite my scene,' Mandy said.

Molly put her hands on her hips. 'But how will you ever know if you don't give it a whirl?' she demanded. 'Give it a day or two. You might change your mind!'

Mandy shook her head. 'Unlike you,' she said, 'I'm strictly a veggie. I'll leave the man-eating to you.'

Molly shrugged. 'Ah well,' she said. 'It's your loss. Don't blame me if you end up an old maid.'

Chapter Sixteen

The days had dragged when Mandy had first left Jimmy, but they suddenly seemed to be racing by. As she drove in to Animal Ark on Tuesday morning, she realised with a shock that it was exactly three weeks since she had moved out of Wildacre. She knew she couldn't expect to feel better at once, but there were days when she felt as bewildered and lost as she had done the day she left. Maybe she should join Molly next time she went speed dating, Mandy thought, then found herself smiling at the idea. Speed dating wouldn't ever be for her, even if she was uncomplicatedly free.

She walked to the door and was surprised to see that the light in the waiting room hadn't been switched on. When she tried the door, it was still locked. An unoccupied car stood in the car park, one Mandy didn't recognise.

It was her dad's day to open up. Was he already inside, seeing to a client? It was possible he'd locked the door until Helen arrived, but when Mandy banged on the glass door, there was no reply. She could feel panic starting to rise. She made her way round to the kitchen door. To her relief, it opened when she pushed it, and she walked into the kitchen, but it too was empty. Mandy opened the door that led into the hallway. 'Mum?' she called. 'Dad?'

There was a loud creaking from upstairs, then footsteps on the floor above. 'Mandy?' It was Adam's voice, sounding tense and worried. Mandy felt her panic rise another notch. She set off up the stairs two at a time and Adam met her on the landing.

'What's wrong?'

'Your mum's not well,' he told her. 'Dr Grace is here, but you can go in.'

Mandy walked into the bedroom. Emily was lying in bed. Her face was damp with sweat and deathly pale. When she saw Mandy, she tried to smile and push herself upright, but fell back onto her pillow.

'Take it easy,' murmured the doctor, who was sitting on the end of the bed, holding Emily's wrist to check her pulse. 'The morphine will kick in soon, but the gabapentin will take a bit longer.' She looked calm and unruffled, her brown hair neatly brushed and her white shirt crisp.

Mandy watched in horror as her mother struggled to breathe through the pain of the spasm that wracked her body. Emily held out her hand to Mandy. 'I'm sorry,' she whispered. 'I didn't want you to see me like this.'

Tears filled Mandy's eyes. 'Oh, my mummy.' She wanted to tell Emily there was no need to apologise, but the words wouldn't come. She sat down beside her mum and carefully held her hand. It felt as fragile as a bird's wing in her fingers.

Dr Grace left to see another patient, though she urged Adam to call her back if Emily didn't improve. Adam sat on the other side of the bed and pressed a cold flannel to Emily's forehead. Downstairs, Mandy heard Helen and Toby opening up the clinic. Her dad had messaged them to explain where they were, and as usual they had everything under control.

Gradually Emily's breathing slowed and the pain faded from her eyes. 'Better now,' she said. 'Shouldn't you two be at morning surgery?' Her voice was starting to slur from the painkillers.

'We're not leaving you on your own,' Mandy argued softly, and Adam stroked Emily's hair. His eyes were shadowed with concern and Mandy wondered if he'd got any sleep.

Light footsteps sounded on the staircase and Rachel popped her head round the door. 'Helen called me,' she said. 'I can stay with Emily,' she told Adam and Mandy. 'Is that okay with you, Emily?'

Emily nodded. Her eyes were losing focus, as if she was exhausted and spaced out in equal measure.

'Call me the second anything changes,' Adam ordered, and Rachel smiled.

'Of course.'

Once they were in the kitchen, Adam rubbed his face with his hands, pressing his fingers into his temples as if to relieve a headache. 'The doctor says she thinks it's something called central pain, related to the nerve damage,' he explained to Mandy. 'God, she was in agony. Even the weight of the duvet was too much. Hopefully the gabapentin tablets will ease the muscle spasms. Dr Grace doesn't want her on long-term morphine yet.'

'Was she okay at the weekend?' Mandy asked, feeling a stab of guilt that she'd been having a great time with Geraldine when her mum might have needed her.

'She was fine until last night,' Adam said. 'I would have called you otherwise.'

'Thanks,' Mandy said. 'I want to be there for you both, you know that.'

Adam leaned down and kissed the top of her head. 'I know you do. We're so very lucky to have you. Now, white coats on, let's go and treat the four-legged sick!'

Mandy found it difficult to concentrate on her cases and was relieved when Vicky Beaumont appeared in the door to her consulting room. 'I've brought Smudge and Tigger in for a check-up,' she announced.

'How are they doing?'

'Absolutely brilliant! They've climbed up the lounge curtains and ripped a whole toilet roll to shreds on the living room floor, but they're already part of the family. The girls love them, and I might even be warming to them myself.' She winked.

Mandy tried to smile.

Vicky frowned. 'Is everything okay?'

'Sorry.' Mandy picked up Smudge, holding the little

black and white body near her cheek. He nuzzled her face and began to purr. 'Mum had a bad night, that's all. I know it's selfish, but I hate seeing her like that.'

Vicky rested her hand on Mandy's shoulder, squeezing gently. 'I'm sorry to hear that,' she said. 'I haven't met your mum, but she sounds like a very special woman.'

'She is.'

'MS is so difficult,' Vicky said. 'I've nursed a few patients with it. It's so difficult, not knowing what's coming next.' She took a step forwards and put her arms around Mandy, hugging her tightly. Mandy felt truly comforted, and resisted the urge to sob on Vicky's shoulder. 'It's never easy to cross the point when your parents stop looking after you and it's your turn to look after them,' Vicky murmured.

Mandy remembered Vicky's house with its disability aids. At what age had Vicky begun caring for her mum, she wondered? 'Just be honest with each other about what you're going through, and love will get you the rest of the way,' Vicky said. 'You've plenty of that in your family, I can tell.'

Mandy sniffed, and pushed her hair behind her ears. 'Thank you,' she said.

'Any time,' Vicky said with a gentle smile.

Mandy slept surprisingly well at Barn End Cottage that night. She had half expected to lie awake, worrying about her mum. But when she woke, anxiety sat like a cold stone in her belly. It was only seven o'clock, too early to phone her parents in case they were sleeping in.

If only Jimmy were here. He would make everything feel better, she thought. She looked at her phone, half hoping for a message, but there was nothing. Should she text him about Emily, she wondered? She had held off yesterday, but now, lying here, she felt the urge to talk to him. Wouldn't he want to know, after all? She started to type. She didn't want to sound too dramatic, but Emily's attack had been so frightening it was difficult to sound calm. She clicked send, then lay there feeling uncomfortable. She and Jimmy were still friends, but it was early to send such a charged message.

Throwing off the quilt, she climbed out of bed and headed into the little bathroom. She was just about to get in the shower when her phone rang.

'Are you okay?' Jimmy said at once.

Mandy sat down on the bed, feeling shaky. 'I'm okay,' she croaked. She cleared her throat. 'Mum was a bit better yesterday evening, but it was awful to see her in so much pain.'

'It must have been terrifying for all of you,' Jimmy said. 'Can you give them my love, please, when you see them?'

'I will.' Mandy suddenly realised that her parents might wonder why Jimmy hadn't come himself.

'Let me know if there's anything I can do,' Jimmy went on. 'Just call me, day or night.'

Mandy could feel tears prickling behind her eyes. How could he be so generous and loving, yet so determined not to marry her? Would he do the same for anyone in need? His voice had seemed filled with love and understanding of what she was going through. *I love you*. She wanted to scream it out loud, but those words were forbidden. He wants a different future, she reminded herself. He could have all the love in the world, but if she wanted marriage and children, then he wasn't for her.

Mandy dropped the treacherous telephone on the bed and trudged back into the bathroom. She turned on the shower and stood for a long time under the stream of hot water. When she finally emerged, Sky was waiting outside the door. Though they'd been in the cottage for nearly four weeks, Sky hadn't settled as well as Mandy had hoped she would at the beginning, and didn't like letting Mandy out of her sight. She must miss all her doggie friends, Mandy thought.

They headed down to breakfast together. Geraldine greeted Mandy with a kind smile. 'Did you sleep okay?' Geraldine asked.

'Better than I expected.'

Geraldine put the coffee pot on the table. 'You know what day it is?'

Mandy shook her head.

'It's the day we need to start thinking about Christmas!' Geraldine told her. 'We're already a week into December, and I don't know about you, but I haven't even thought about Christmas shopping.' She sat down at the table and poured coffee into two mugs. 'I know it's a tough time for you,' she said, 'but I thought maybe we could take your mind off it. I'd like to do something to celebrate the start of our personal Advent! If you're up to it, why don't we go Christmas shopping in York this weekend?'

To Mandy's surprise, the idea seemed tempting. She had no plans for Saturday, and York was lovely at any time of year. Anything that distracted her from Jimmy had to be good, and she knew her dad would ring if anything changed with her mum.

By ten o'clock on Saturday morning, they had left Sky with Rachel at Animal Ark after seeing to the rescue animals. Mandy had popped in to see her mum and was relieved to find her sitting up in bed, tucking into some muesli. She seemed pleased that Mandy was going out for the day, and asked her to pick up a box of Christmas cards.

As they drove through Welford, Geraldine seemed intent on pointing out every piece of evidence that Christmas was on its way. Strings of gold and green foil stars hung in the post office window. The Fox and Goose pub had been decorated with garlands of evergreen over every window and door, striking and tasteful against the ancient black and white building. And when they passed the church, Mandy caught a glimpse of two men manoeuvring a huge Christmas tree into the church through the big wooden doors.

The journey passed quickly through the wintry countryside. 'Would you mind if I get in touch with James?' Mandy asked Geraldine as they pulled into the Park & Ride car park. 'We could meet him and his partner Raj for lunch, if that's okay with you?'

Geraldine looked delighted. 'I'd love to meet them!'

Mandy fired off a text to James. He instantly invited them to lunch at his café. Mandy had told him that she was staying with Geraldine, and she knew he was dying to meet her new housemate.

As they reached the twisting lanes in the centre of the town, crammed with little shops and street performers, Geraldine seemed to have enough festive excitement for both of them – and Mandy found her spirits lifting, too. Geraldine pointed out all sorts of charming and elegant gifts as they perused the windows. Mandy laughed when she pointed out yet another stylish dress, which she said would suit Mandy perfectly.

'I wish I had your sense of style,' she said. 'I've never progressed beyond my childhood preference for jeans and boots.'

'They're very practical for your job,' Geraldine said. 'And actually, I think you're probably very stylish, but you haven't been given the chance to express that side of you. No wonder, growing up with animals around you day and night.'

Mandy bristled. Geraldine's comment sounded close

to being critical of the way she had been raised. She was about to defend her parents when Geraldine stopped and grabbed Mandy's arm.

'Look at that pendant!' she gasped, pointing at the window of an elegant gift shop. A thin gold chain held an exquisitely made horseshoe of white gold, with sapphires in the places where the nails should go. 'It'd look wonderful on you,' Geraldine said. She looked at it more closely, then she straightened up and sent Mandy a mischievous smile. 'I'm going to buy it,' she announced. 'I'd love to see you wearing it. The sapphires would bring out the blue of your eyes.'

Mandy gulped. Lovely as the pendant was, she didn't wear jewellery very often and though she and Geraldine were having a great time, their friendship was very new. It didn't seem an appropriate gift at all. She felt herself grow hot. 'Please don't,' she said. 'It's far too expensive.'

Geraldine waved her hand at Mandy. 'Not a problem,' she said. 'Anyway, I really want to get it for you. This is the first time I've made an effort for Christmas in years and I'm determined to enjoy it.' Without waiting for a reply, she opened the shop door and strode inside.

Mandy tried not to watch as the pendant was taken from the window display, placed in a box and wrapped in purple and silver tissue paper. Would Geraldine expect Mandy to buy something equally extravagant for her? Mandy hadn't the faintest idea what she would like, even if she did feel the need to buy something. Up until now, it hadn't crossed her mind that she would.

She'd assumed that Geraldine would come to the annual Animal Ark New Year dinner at the Fox and Goose, which acted as a present for all the staff, in addition to their bonuses. But this was a significant gift, far more than a three-course meal with half a bottle of wine.

By the time they turned into the lane that led to James's café, Mandy had begun to relax again. Encouraged by Geraldine's enthusiasm, she had bought a few stocking fillers for Abi and Max and picked up an attractively packaged basket of Lily of the Valley-scented bath products for her mum. Would Emily think it was too boring, she wondered? It was the kind of thing you might buy for elderly ladies who didn't get out much. But her mum had taken to having long, warmish baths in the evening. She couldn't have the water hot as it exacerbated her symptoms, but she did enjoy relaxing in the tub.

As they reached the door of the café-cum-bookshop that James owned, they heard a shout behind them. Mandy turned to see James and Raj jogging up the pavement towards them. Raj was pushing Taresh in his buggy. To Mandy's delight, Taresh was leaning forwards, his little hands clinging to the bars at the sides of his buggy and shouting, 'Faster, faster!'

Mandy grinned at Raj. 'Good to see his English is coming on!'

Raj imitated a squeal of brakes as he stopped the buggy beside Mandy and wrapped her in a bear hug.

James juggled carrier bags and did the same. Mandy was aware of Geraldine hanging back, and she quickly introduced her to the men and Taresh.

James greeted her warmly. 'You've been a lifesaver for Mandy, thank you! I don't know how she keeps on top of two full-time jobs!'

Geraldine smiled. 'It's an absolute pleasure to be around her. I'm learning so much!'

James's manager Sherrie was standing behind the counter when they went in. 'Hello,' she called. She came out and crouched down to bump fists with Taresh. 'Hello, gorgeous! Have you been impressing the ladies today?'

James grinned at Mandy. 'He's a magnet, he really is!'

They sat down at a table near the window. Raj dragged over a high chair for Taresh. 'I'm starting to appreciate cafés that supply decent high chairs,' James told Mandy.

Sherrie came over to the table with a notepad. 'Is there anything in particular you'd like?' she asked. 'Or shall I bring you a selection of festive specials?'

'That sounds great,' Mandy said.

Sherrie put her notepad away and disappeared into the kitchen. She returned a few minutes later with several turkey and cranberry paninis. 'Herby stuffing version for you, Mandy,' she added, putting a loaded sandwich in front of her.

She brought Taresh a little pot of turkey pieces,

stuffing and apple sauce. For a moment, Mandy wondered if she should have warned Geraldine about James's non-traditional family. But Geraldine seemed perfectly relaxed, although she sat quietly as the others chatted and Taresh babbled over his lunch.

'You're going to James's parents for Christmas, aren't you?' Mandy said to Raj. 'First Christmas with the in-laws. You'd better be on your best behaviour.'

Raj rolled his eyes. 'I think the only thing I have to worry about is whether we'll be able to fit all Taresh's presents in the car on the way home.'

'It's not my parents who are in danger of spoiling our son,' James put in. 'I really hope you know that Taresh doesn't need a bicycle yet.'

Raj pretended to look shocked. 'Everybody knows all children want a bicycle for Christmas!'

Sherrie brought Taresh a cookie, and Raj took out his phone to snap a picture of him demolishing it.

Geraldine spoke for almost the first time. 'You're very lucky, having the chance to take so many photos,' she said. 'Babyhood flies by so fast.' She sighed, and for a second Mandy caught a fleeting sense of some emotion she couldn't read. 'You have a beautiful son,' she said to James and Raj. 'Treasure him with all your heart.'

Taresh looked from James to Raj, and then, with his eyes still on Raj, he hurled the remainder of his cookie onto the floor and burst into laughter.

James shrugged. 'So much for my festive baking. I'll

fetch a dustpan.' He pushed his chair out. 'Mandy, do you think your parents would like some mince pies? I've tried a new recipe with lemon and cranberry, a bit lighter than the usual sort.' He headed into the kitchen. Mandy stood up and followed him in.

The kitchen felt calm and quiet after the busy café. James pulled out a box and began to pile mince pies into it. 'It's really interesting to meet Geraldine at last,' he said. 'You obviously get on very well, which is great.'

'Yes?' Mandy prompted, sensing a 'but'.

James wiped up some pastry crumbs with a cloth. 'There's something about her,' he said. 'Nothing bad, but I get the feeling she's terribly sad. Every time she looks at Taresh, something flashes in her eyes. I'm sure I'm not imagining it. Has she told you anything about herself?'

'Not a lot,' Mandy admitted. 'She's a psychotherapist. She works in Manchester and she enjoys drawing.' It seemed very little as she said it. 'I think she's quite a private person.'

'I wondered if she'd lost a baby, perhaps?' James suggested. 'She's never talked about having children?'

Mandy shook her head. 'She told me she thought I'd make a great mum,' she said. 'I really haven't noticed her trying to avoid any subjects like that. She's a great worker and a good friend.' She felt herself becoming defensive, as if James was implying she had missed something glaringly obvious.

But James just sealed the lid on the box of pies and

picked up a dustpan to take into the café. When they reached the table, Geraldine was sitting beside Taresh, telling him a story using the salt and pepper pots. Mandy watched her with a sense of relief. There was no problem with Geraldine and children. James must have imagined it.

Chapter Seventeen

Mandy was mucking out the field shelter behind Hope Meadows on Monday morning when she caught a movement in the corner of her eye. The calf Adam had hospitalised after an operation on its leg had just been taken home and Mandy was preparing the shelter in case any livestock arrived in a hurry. She turned to see Emily, still on crutches, but looking much stronger as she made her way with determination towards the barn.

'Morning, love!'

'Hi, Mum.' Mandy laid her jacket on the wooden bench that stood beside the shelter. 'Have a seat,' she suggested.

'Thanks,' Emily said, easing herself down. 'It's so lovely to get some fresh air at last.' She tipped her face up to the cool light behind the clouds.

Mandy emptied the wheelbarrow and fetched a new bale of straw. She put it at the side of the shelter, ready to spread out if an animal arrived, and joined her mum on the bench.

'How are you, sweetheart?' Emily asked, turning to face her. 'Is there anything you want to tell me?'

Mandy blinked. 'What makes you say that?' she stalled.

Emily gave her a gentle smile. 'I know you're not living at home,' she said. 'You're staying with Geraldine, and that's fine. She seems like a very nice person, and she obviously thinks the world of you. But if you want to talk to me about anything, I'll always be here for you.' She tapped the end of one crutch on the ground. 'I may be falling apart at the seams,' she added, 'but I'm still your mum.'

Mandy felt a wash of guilt that she had kept her new address secret from her parents. 'I should have told you where I was staying,' she said. 'I'm sorry. I just didn't want you to worry. And you'll always be my mum,' she added fiercely. She sighed. 'Jimmy and I are taking some time apart.' She swallowed hard. Tears prickled in her eyes, but she was determined not to cry on her mum. 'He . . . he wants different things from me. It's not easy, but we're trying to be realistic about the future, that's all.'

Emily frowned. 'Wildacre is still your home,' she reminded Mandy. 'Why have you moved out and not Jimmy?'

Mandy pressed her fingers into the surface of the cold bench. 'When I moved out, it was to give me time to think,' she said. 'It seemed easier for me to leave. I don't need somewhere with space for Abi and Max and all the dogs.'

Emily patted Mandy's leg. 'I'm not going to fire

questions at you,' she said. 'I know whatever's going on, you'll find a way forward. It's always a good idea to take some time to know what you really want. You only get one life.'

She opened her arms and Mandy leaned into her hug. Despite all her effort, Mandy's face was wet by the time they sat up. 'I know I'm doing the right thing,' she croaked, 'but I miss Jimmy so much.'

'Oh, sweet girl. It's hardly surprising. The two of you were so close. But I'm proud of you. You can't force him to want the same things as you do, and there are times when you have to put your own needs first.' She regarded Mandy for a moment, her head on one side. 'I'm only sorry you didn't feel you could talk to me and your dad sooner. I know you don't want to worry us, but you can't change that! We're your parents! Why don't you come over tonight, let your dad cook us dinner, and we'll have a lovely evening together?'

Mandy wiped her cheeks and forced herself to smile. Somehow, now her mum knew, it felt as if everything had become just a tiny bit easier. 'Thanks, Mum,' she said. 'I'd love that.'

Mandy stepped out of the shower. She had gone back to Barn End Cottage after work to get changed before dinner with her mum and dad. She was surprised to hear a quiet knock on her bedroom door. Geraldine almost never disturbed her. 'Come in,' she called.

Geraldine's cheeks looked a little pink as she stuck her head into the room. 'I know I haven't checked,' she said, 'but I hope you don't have any plans for tonight!' She held out a pair of tickets. 'I've bought tickets to a Christmas concert in Walton! Happy Advent!'

Mandy frowned. 'Aren't you going back to Manchester tonight?' Geraldine usually headed off early on Monday evening.

Geraldine shook her head. 'I've arranged to see my clients tomorrow afternoon. I can drive over to Manchester in the morning. I really wanted to treat you.'

Mandy smiled in a way she hoped was sympathetic. 'I was actually going to see Mum and Dad tonight.'

Geraldine's face dropped. 'Oh, I'm sorry,' she said, sounding flustered. 'I should have told you what I was planning.' She stepped into the room, folding the tickets into a tiny square with her hands. 'Oh well, I guess I could go alone.'

Mandy couldn't bear to see her looking so disappointed. 'No, no.' She reached out a hand to touch Geraldine's elbow. 'Don't do that,' she said. 'It was only a casual supper, they'll understand! It was very kind of you to think of me.'

Geraldine brightened up. 'Well, if you're sure,' she said. 'I do think the concert will be worth it!'

Mandy sat on her bed and dialled her dad's number. Adam was very understanding when he heard about the concert. 'You know we're always here,' he said, 'but it's important you have friends too. Anyway,' he went on, and now there was laughter in his voice, 'I can always cook another night.' He paused and added, 'That's a threat, you know, not a promise!'

Mandy smiled. 'I love you, Dad.'

'Love you too, precious girl. Have a great time.'

The concert was dreadful, so bad that it was almost funny. Mandy would cheerfully admit that she couldn't carry a tune if you gave her a bucket to put it in, but even to her ears, the orchestra sounded as if they'd only just met each other. The singing was off-key, but seemed determined to put this right by volume alone. Mandy was sure she'd noticed a couple of other audience members push tissue into their ears. To her astonishment, Geraldine seemed to love every moment. She hummed along and clapped enthusiastically for each song.

Mandy couldn't help feeling relieved when the concert came to an end. As they filed out of the hall, Geraldine clasped Mandy's arm. 'Thank you so much for coming! What a fun evening.' She sighed as if she had genuinely been moved by the experience. When they reached the pavement, Geraldine turned to Mandy, her eyes shining. 'It's your turn to plan the next Advent treat!'

She kept hold of Mandy's arm all the way to the car. Mandy started to feel a bit uneasy. First the necklace, now concert tickets. Mandy's parents were both only children, but she wondered if this was what it felt like to have an overly fond aunt. Much as Mandy liked Geraldine, this evening had been a little too much. For the first time, she began to wonder whether it was time to think about moving out of Barn End. Maybe it would be better if they weren't working and living together. It was all starting to feel a little too intense.

Mandy pulled the big glass door at Hope Meadows closed and locked it. She had just seen Olive off to her new home with the Andersons. She felt the usual satisfaction at seeing a rescue animal leave, tinged with hope that the young couple would be open to Mandy checking how they were getting on.

She had her head down, searching in her bag for her keys, as she walked to the car park. She stopped dead when she looked up. Jimmy's Land Rover was pulling into the drive. Beside her, Sky began to bark, and three familiar furry shapes launched themselves at the rear windows, shouting back. Jimmy parked, opened the back door and a moment later, Mandy was engulfed in a whirlpool of enthusiastic dogs.

In contrast, Jimmy seemed a little awkward. He kept his hands in his pockets, making it clear that he wasn't going to greet Mandy with a hug. Instead, he shot her a rather lopsided smile. 'I was just passing,' he muttered. 'Have you had lunch? I thought we could go to the Fox and Goose.'

Mandy blinked. Did he have something he needed to say to her? Maybe he was going to tell her he was moving out of Wildacre. She felt her stomach lurch. Though she was no longer feeling settled at Geraldine's, the idea of him moving out of the home they had once shared seemed horribly final. She looked at his face, trying to read his expression, but he was looking down at the dogs.

There was only one way to find out what he wanted. 'Lunch would be great,' she said.

It felt very strange to walk down the lane with him at her side. The dogs seemed overjoyed to be back together, but the conversation with Jimmy was oddly stilted.

'How's your mum getting on?' he asked.

'Not too bad, thanks.'

'And what's it like living back at home?'

Mandy winced. 'I didn't actually move back,' she admitted. 'I've been staying with Geraldine Craven, my new part-timer at Hope Meadows.'

Jimmy raised an eyebrow. 'Why aren't you at Animal Ark?'

Mandy felt a flash of annoyance. Was he that stupid? 'Because I didn't want to tell them about us,' she snapped. 'That's the last thing Mum needs right now.'

'I'm sorry,' Jimmy said. 'It must be tough, keeping it from them.'

'Oh, they know now,' Mandy told him. 'You know what the grapevine's like round here.'

Jimmy grimaced. 'I do.'

They reached the pub and ducked through the door into the bar. Mandy gulped as her eyeballs were assailed from all directions. She had forgotten just how over the top Bev and Gary Parsons were with their Christmas decorations. A fire blazed, which felt festive enough, but above the mantelpiece, and all round the low ceiling, hung wreaths and tassels and yards and yards of greenery, dotted with twinkling, coloured fairy lights.

'It looks like Santa's grotto exploded,' Jimmy murmured in Mandy's ear, and she tried not to giggle.

Bev looked surprised when she saw them, though she quickly smiled. 'What can I get you, my dears?'

'We're here for lunch,' Jimmy said.

Bev handed them a menu each. 'I recommend the pumpkin and coriander soup. Gary made it this morning and it's selling fast.'

'Sounds perfect,' Mandy said, putting the menu down.

'And for me,' said Jimmy.

They sat down at a little table in the corner by the fire. At least they wouldn't be easily overheard here. There was a Christmas tree just behind Mandy's head. Smothered with tinsel, it would cut their conversation away from flapping ears in the rest of the bar. The dogs squeezed under the table, and Sky flopped weightily on Mandy's feet. She reached down and buried her fingers in the soft fur. It was always comforting to have her there.

The soup came and Mandy forced herself to eat. They chatted about inconsequential things until Jimmy dropped his spoon into his empty bowl and gazed across the table. 'I suppose I'd better get to the point,' he said. 'I wanted to talk to you face to face, rather than over the phone.' Mandy could feel her heart beating faster. 'I just wanted to know if you'd made up your mind yet?' he said. 'When you moved out, I'll be honest, I thought you might come straight back. But if you're not going to, then I need to think about moving out of Wildacre. It's your house, much as I love living there.'

Mandy stared at him, a lump rising in her throat. There was no way she could move back while Jimmy was there. That would tell him she was happy to stay as they were, without marriage, without children, without a plan for their future. But the idea of telling him that it was over – completely and unequivocally over – was overwhelmingly sad. She couldn't bring herself to make it real by putting it into words.

'I'm really sorry,' she said, her voice thick with the effort of not crying. 'I know it's stupid, but I need more time. I don't know what I want.' It was only a half truth. She knew exactly what she wanted. She just couldn't have it.

Jimmy gave her a sad smile. 'It's not stupid. If you want more time, you can have it. But we can't live in limbo forever. That's not fair on either of us.' He glanced at his watch. 'I'm really sorry,' he said, 'but I have to go.' He pushed back his chair and clicked his fingers to his dogs.

Mandy wanted to beg him to sit back down. Surely if they talked about this, really discussed it, they could sort something out?

Jimmy bent down and kissed her cheek and she caught the scent of his aftershave. She pressed her fingernails into the palms of her hands. She wasn't going to cry in front of him. 'Do you want me to see you home?' he offered. He had left his car at Animal Ark, she remembered.

The idea of walking back together seemed suddenly unbearable. 'No, thanks,' she said, and to her relief, her voice was steady. 'I think I'll have a coffee before I go back.'

'Fair enough,' Jimmy said, though he looked uneasy. This must be difficult for him too, Mandy reminded herself. He was a decent and kind man. It wouldn't sit easily with him to stay in Wildacre while she was living with a near-stranger. He walked out of the door and she watched his back as he retreated down the road. Behind her, the lights on the Christmas tree flashed on and off, mocking her with their festive exuberance.

Chapter Eighteen

Wednesday morning dawned, dry, clear and frosty cold. With the kittens and Olive now gone, Mandy felt she had a bit more space in the rescue centre. Her phone rang as she walked out of the cat room.

'Hi, Mandy.' She was pleased to hear James's voice. Maybe he could help her decide what to do about Geraldine and Jimmy and all the stuff that was pulling her in different directions. 'Raj is off to meet a friend in Lancaster,' he said. 'I was wondering if it would be okay to bring Taresh over today?'

Mandy felt her spirits lift. 'That would be lovely,' she said. 'I have the afternoon off. You could bring him for lunch at Geraldine's cottage, if you like?' She gave him directions to get to Barn End and rang off, feeling pleased.

Morning surgery was busy with several brand new clients, and Mandy had to hurry to get back to Geraldine's cottage half an hour before James was due. She just had time to wash and change before putting some veggie sausage rolls into the oven to warm.

The sitting room beside the kitchen was a little chilly so Mandy lit the wood-burning stove and propped a fireguard around it to keep Taresh safe. The flames flickered brightly through the glass door, making the room feel instantly warmer. Geraldine had decorated the windowsill and corner shelves with candles that she'd bought in York. Their cinnamon scent filled the room and there was a tiny Christmas tree on the coffee table, with teeny baubles in green, scarlet and gold. The room looked cosy and welcoming, and Mandy felt a twinge of excitement about helping Taresh celebrate his first British Christmas.

There was a knock on the door as Mandy was adjusting the miniature angel on top of the tree. When she opened it, James was standing on the doorstep and to Mandy's delight, Taresh was standing beside him, looking very pleased with himself. He was a bit wobbly and clung to James's hand, but when he looked up at Mandy and grinned, Mandy found herself grinning back.

'He definitely knows who you are,' James said.

'Of course he does,' Mandy said. 'I'm his favourite aunt!'

Sky looked wary as Taresh toddled into the kitchen. 'Shall we go through into the sitting room?' Mandy suggested. 'I've lit the fire.'

They ate the sausage rolls sitting on the carpet, where it was easier to clear up Taresh's pastry crumbs. Mandy cleared the plates away as soon as they had finished, and put the kettle on to make coffee for herself and

James. She returned to the sitting room while it was coming to the boil.

James had brought a backpack of toys for Taresh, but he seemed more fascinated with the Christmas tree on the table. He stood beside it, rocking on his feet, speaking to one of the baubles that was shaped like a penguin.

Mandy listened, but she couldn't make out what he was saying. 'Is he speaking Punjabi?' she asked James.

James, who was looking very comfortable in one of the brown leather armchairs, shook his head. 'Raj says not,' he told her. 'It's just toddler talk, apparently.'

Taresh pushed off from the coffee table and tottered towards the door that led to the hall. James stood up and followed him.

'The kitchen door is closed,' Mandy said, as he disappeared into the tiny hall. 'Apart from that, there's only Geraldine's bedroom and she keeps the door locked.'

James reappeared a moment later. 'Seems pretty safe,' he said. He sat down and asked Mandy about the animals currently at Hope Meadows.

She was just updating him on Jasper's heart condition when there was a crash from the hallway and more alarmingly, a squawk from Taresh. Mandy and James sprang up and rushed into the hall. To Mandy's dismay, Geraldine's bedroom door was standing open. She followed James in and was relieved to see Taresh standing in the middle of the room, quite unharmed, but with a look of shock in his eyes. Beside him, the contents of a small bookcase were scattered on the floor and the bookshelf was lying on its side.

'Is he okay?' Mandy asked James, who had scooped Taresh up.

'He's fine,' James said. He blew out a long breath. He looked down at the scattered books and papers on the carpet. 'Will you hang onto him, please? I'll tidy up.'

Mandy lifted Taresh from his arms and carried him to the window. 'Can you see any sheep?' she asked him. 'Look, there's a bird!' She glanced over her shoulder. 'Geraldine must have forgotten to lock her door,' she said to James. 'At least nothing is broken.'

James was on his knees, staring down at a large scrapbook that lay open in front of him. He looked as if he had frozen to the spot.

'James?' Mandy said. 'Is something wrong?'

Slowly, James picked up the scrapbook. 'It's . . . it's all about you!' he said, sounding strangled. He reached out to open another identical album. 'And this one. Look.' He held out the first book towards her and began to flip through the pages so Mandy could see them.

The room seemed to start spinning as Mandy stared. Every single page was filled with clippings about her. There was her graduation photo from the *Walton Gazette*. Next, an article about the opening of Hope Meadows. Mandy felt a rising sense of horror when she recognised an article about Stuart Mortimore and his arrest. Was Geraldine connected to the man who had attacked her and Hope Meadows?

James looked up at her, his eyes serious. 'I think Geraldine is stalking you!'

'I don't understand,' Mandy said weakly. 'Geraldine knew who I was when she came to Hope Meadows! Why didn't she say?'

James stood up. 'Surely the real question is, why is she so interested in you?'

Mandy sat down heavily on Geraldine's bed. Taresh began to squirm, so she put him down on the floor and he ran to James. James put a protective arm around him as he continued stacking the files on the bookcase with his other hand.

'I don't understand,' Mandy said again. 'Why would Geraldine do this? She seemed so nice to start with!'

James finished piling the books back on the shelves, lifted Taresh onto his hip and held out a hand to Mandy. 'We should get out of her room,' he said.

Mandy took his hand and let him lead her back to the sitting room.

'You said she was nice at the start. Has something happened that wasn't so good?' James prompted. Without taking his eyes off Mandy, he sat down and pulled some coloured blocks out of the rucksack for Taresh to play with.

Mandy shook her head. 'She was lovely when I first moved in,' she said. 'She's still lovely,' she added, 'but it's begun to feel a bit . . . well, overpowering.'

'In what way?'

'Nothing very concrete,' Mandy admitted. 'When we were in York, she bought me a present that seemed a bit too much, and then she bought tickets to a concert and wanted me to go with her.'

James rubbed his hand through his hair. 'Nothing nasty, then. But it's very strange. I know it's awkward, but you're going to have to talk to her.'

Mandy gave a hollow laugh. 'That'll be an easy conversation!'

'Tell her the truth,' James said. 'Frankly, you're not the one who has some explaining to do.'

Mandy's hands were shaking. 'I can't stay here any more,' she said, fighting down a surge of panic.

James put a green block onto a blue block and watched Taresh dismantle them. 'I don't think Geraldine's an axe murderer,' he said, 'but you're right. Your mum and dad will have you, surely?'

Mandy bit her lip. 'I don't think I can,' she said. 'They'll want to know why, and they're already worried enough about me because of Jimmy.' The phone in her pocket rang. She jumped but to her relief, it was Molly Future.

'I'm sorry to trouble you. I know it's your afternoon off but would you mind coming out to see Bill?'

'Of course,' Mandy replied. 'Give me . . . hmm . . . half an hour.'

'Is there something wrong?' Molly asked. 'You sound weird. What's going on?'

Mandy let out a high-pitched laugh, feeling herself on the verge of hysteria. 'Nothing important,' she said. 'Just looking for a new place to live, that's all.'

'Come here,' Molly said instantly. 'I'd love the company, and there's bags of room. You'd be doing me a favour, honestly. You can keep an eye on the horses while I do the speed dating!'

Her voice was so calm that Mandy felt herself relaxing a tiny bit, like a startled horse. 'Thank you,' she said. 'It won't be for long, I promise.'

Molly was still in practical mode. 'Stay as long as you like,' she replied. 'Well, unless I score a really hot date,' she added. She was laughing as she rang off.

Mandy felt dazed, as though the world had tilted off its axis. 'Looks like I'm moving to Six Oaks,' she said.

James looked relieved. 'Good,' he said. He stood up. 'Come on, I'll help you pack.'

Mandy nodded. She would have to talk to Geraldine at some point, but it could wait. She rushed around the bedroom stuffing her things into her holdall and cleared her toiletries from the bathroom.

'I need to get this one down for a nap,' James said, cradling Taresh. The little boy had snuggled his head under James's chin and was chewing the corner of his yellow blankie. 'Will you be okay if I leave?'

'Of course I will.' Mandy put her arms around them both and gave them a gentle squeeze. 'Sorry it hasn't been the most fun visit ever.'

'Try not to worry,' James said. 'There's probably a

very dull explanation for Geraldine and her scrapbooks. We had enough adventures when we were children. We don't need any more!'

Mandy tried to smile. This didn't feel like an adventure. More like a creepy parallel universe. 'Geraldine's not back for a few days,' she told him. 'I'll stay at Molly's until then, and figure out exactly what to say to her.'

'Good plan.' He carried Taresh to the front door and opened it with his free hand. 'Ring me any time,' he urged and Mandy nodded.

She waved until they had driven out of sight, then went upstairs to strip her bed. She was loading the washing machine when she heard a car draw up outside. James must have forgotten something. She went into the hall and opened the door. To her dismay, Geraldine was climbing up the steps. She was clutching a white polar bear toy under one arm and a rolled-up piece of fabric under the other.

'Look what I got!' she announced, walking past Mandy into the sitting room. She put the polar bear on the coffee table and unfurled the cloth. It was a large embroidered picture of a snowy scene with fallow deer. 'I thought it would look good on the wall,' she said. She folded the cloth and laid it over the back of the sofa. 'I bought extra tinsel, too! Oh,' she said, sounding pleased. 'You've lit the fire.'

Mandy stood in the doorway, unable to speak. She felt as if she was moving through wet cement.

Geraldine looked closely at Mandy. 'What's wrong? Is it your mum? One of the animals?' She glanced past Mandy and frowned. Mandy's packed bags were standing beside the front door. 'What's going on?'

Mandy could feel her heart pounding. 'I'm moving out,' she said. 'I . . . I'm sorry for not telling you,' she added.

'You were just going to leave?' Geraldine said. 'Why? Have I done something wrong?'

Mandy took a deep breath. 'I saw the scrapbooks,' she said in a rush. 'The ones in your bedroom. I wasn't snooping. Taresh got into your room and knocked over the bookcase . . .' She trailed off. Geraldine had turned white and her eyes were huge. She reached out blindly with a hand and lowered herself into an armchair.

'You don't have to tell me what they're about,' Mandy said quickly, alarmed by the look of horror on Geraldine's face. 'Not if you don't want to. Honestly, I'll just give you some space, and we can talk another time.' Geraldine looked as if she was going to pass out. 'Can I get you some water?' Mandy offered. 'Then I'll get out of your way.' She was starting to feel guilty about making Geraldine so distressed. *What on earth was she doing with those bloody scrapbooks?*

But Geraldine held up her hand. 'Please don't go,' she said. Her voice was ragged. 'You can't go, not now. Not after I looked for you for so long . . .'

Mandy turned cold. Sky pressed against her leg and whined. Mandy reached down to rest her fingers on top of the dog's head. 'I really think I should go,' she said, and her words sounded hoarse and twisted.

Geraldine gazed at her with an emotion that was scarily close to hunger. 'You can't go,' she whispered. 'Are you afraid of me? Please don't be. I only want to talk to you.'

Mandy shook her head. 'Whatever this is about, I don't want to know. This . . . this isn't the right time.' She had to force herself to stand still. Every bone in her body was screaming at her to get out of the cottage.

Geraldine looked down at her hands. 'There will never be a right time,' she said quietly. 'I'm starting to realise that.' She stared up at Mandy with so much desperation that Mandy flinched. 'There's no easy way to put this,' Geraldine said. 'I can only tell you and hope for the best. I'm your mother, Mandy.'

Chapter Nineteen

Mandy sat down with a thud on the sofa. The room was spinning and she was dimly aware of Sky putting a paw on her knee with a fretful whine.

'You can't be,' she whispered. 'My mother's dead.'

Geraldine's eyes filled with compassion now and were deadly serious. 'I'm your mother, Mandy,' she said again. 'I gave birth to you.'

Mandy shook her head. 'That's impossible.' Her voice was stronger this time. 'There's been a terrible misunderstanding. I'm adopted, yes, but my parents died in a car accident when I was three months old.' She felt a stab of pity for the woman sitting opposite her, who was still deathly pale. 'I'm really sorry,' she said, 'but I'm not your daughter.'

Geraldine looked as if the breath had been knocked out of her. 'No, no, that isn't right. We didn't die in a car accident. We were both alive when you were taken away from us.' She paused, twisting her hands in her lap. 'I know this must seem incredible. I've been trying to think how I can prove it to you. I'll do a DNA test, of course.'

Mandy blinked. *A DNA test?* Had she fallen into a soap opera, she wondered dimly? 'I . . . I . . .' she began, but Geraldine interrupted her.

'The family freckle!' she exclaimed.

'The family *what*?'

Geraldine stared at her. 'You have a freckle near your tummy button, don't you? Very small, light brown, with squarish edges? I saw it when you were born. I looked for it especially. I have one too, and so did my father.'

How could she possibly know about that freckle? Mandy nodded. 'Yes, I do. But . . .' This wasn't about a freckle. If Geraldine was telling the truth, that meant something far, far worse had to be confronted. 'Mum and Dad must have known you didn't die in an accident,' she whispered. 'And that means . . .'

Geraldine gazed sympathetically at her. 'It means they lied to you, Mandy. I'm so sorry.'

No no no no no no . . .

Mandy suddenly realised she was speaking out loud and someone was sitting beside her on the sofa. It was Geraldine, holding Mandy's hands as if she was never going to let go.

'I don't blame Adam and Emily.' Geraldine was moving her thumb over the back of Mandy's hand, round and round, just as Emily did when she wanted to comfort her. 'They were protecting you from the truth, that's all. I'm sure they've been good to you. They were, weren't they?'

Mandy couldn't take her eyes off that slowly circling

thumb. She could feel herself disintegrating: shattering like a thousand pieces of glass. If she moved, fragments would spill all over the carpet and she would never be whole again.

A tear fell onto her hand. Mandy looked up and saw that Geraldine was trying not to cry, her face twisted with the effort. 'Your father and I . . .' She rubbed Mandy's hand harder, but Mandy felt unable to pull it away. 'We were so young when you were born. We weren't ready for a baby; I wasn't ready. But I still wanted you! I loved you so much!'

'Why did you give me up?' Mandy whispered.

'I . . . we . . . weren't given a choice. There was a bit of a problem . . . with drugs.' For the first time there was shame in her eyes. 'Heroin.' She took a deep breath. 'We were addicts, your father and I, and when you were born . . . well, you were addicted, too.'

The walls closed in around Mandy and the room suddenly felt unbearably stuffy. She had read about babies being born with all the symptoms of addiction from exposure to hard drugs in the womb. They needed instant methadone treatment to go through the long and agonising process of withdrawal. It took months, and there was no way of explaining to a tiny baby that the terrible way they felt was the road to recovery.

Had Adam and Emily been through that with her?

'I was so happy the day you were born,' Geraldine said. 'I'd never been happier in my life. I called you Briony. I was so sure I could quit for you. I knew how much you deserved it.' She smiled, but Mandy wanted to put her hands over her ears. *I don't want to hear this*, she thought, but Geraldine was too intent on telling her story. 'They took you from me the next day,' she said. 'I wasn't well enough to care for you then, I know that. We didn't even have a home. But I could have got better! If someone had given me a chance, given me treatment to get off the drugs.' She stopped and for the first time, she seemed to notice the horror etched on Mandy's face. 'People can be so, so addicted but they can still turn their lives around with the right help. They just have to want it enough, and I know I did.' There was a note of pleading in her voice that made Mandy want to recoil. 'But I didn't get that help, so I lost you. My baby, my precious, beautiful daughter. Briony.'

Mandy could feel Sky shivering against her leg. 'What about my father?' she whispered.

Geraldine sighed. 'His name was Paddy. He was beautiful, too. You look a lot like him when you smile.'

'Where is he? Does he know you're here?'

Geraldine let out a sad little sound. 'Mandy, my love. Paddy died from an overdose,' her forehead wrinkled, 'maybe three, four years after you were born? I wasn't really in touch with him by then. He'd have been so proud of you, though. I know he would.'

You don't, Mandy thought. Had he even known he had a daughter, she wondered? She pulled her hands away and put them down beside her, gripping the edge of the sofa cushion. She felt as if she was trying to anchor herself to something real. This wasn't a past she wanted. Not this terrible, hideous story of a couple of drug addicts and an accidental baby.

'But I did get better.' Geraldine pushed her hair over her shoulders and gazed at Mandy. 'Not at once, not for a long time. But I got tired of being homeless, tired of spending everything I had on the next fix. I got onto a recovery programme, found a job and a flat in Manchester, did an Open University degree in psychology so I could help people who were where I had once been. I never thought I could manage all that, but I did.'

She sounded proud, but Mandy felt chilled to the bone. Was she supposed to feel happy for Geraldine? Impressed? The whole story felt distant and strange. Something that had happened to someone else.

'I've been clean for eighteen years,' Geraldine went on. 'I've got a great job – and I'm really good at it, I know I am. I've got my own flat, friends, a social life! The only thing that was missing was you, so I started to look for you.'

There was a faint buzzing in Mandy's head. 'How did you find me?' She knew that adoption agencies would never give out details without contacting the other person involved for their consent.

Geraldine went red. 'I overheard a social worker talking to one of the nurses just after you were born. She said they had a couple already in mind for you, and the fact that they were vets made it more likely they'd be able to help you through the withdrawal. I . . . I waited until she was out of my room and looked in her bag. I found the name Hope and an address with the word Yorkshire in it, but I heard her coming back before I could see any more. It turned out I had enough information to find the people who took you pretty easily, once I started looking.'

Mandy couldn't speak. Geraldine could have found her years ago. What stopped her?

'I didn't even mean to get in contact when I first found you,' Geraldine went on. 'I just wanted to know that you were okay. For ages, I watched, read about you online, followed all the stories of the animals you rehomed. And I knew you were exactly the daughter I'd dreamed of having. It felt as if you were pulling me towards you like a magnet! I knew I had to meet you, and when I came to Hope Meadows, you were everything I'd imagined and more. I'd spent years waiting, and there you were.'

She looked Mandy straight in the eye. 'I know I should have told you straight away,' she said, 'but I was afraid of what you would think of me. But I'm glad you know now. I just hope it isn't too late to start over. I want to rebuild my life, Mandy. And I want you at the centre of it, as you always should have been.'

Despite the familiarity of the road, Mandy almost missed the sharp turn that would lead her down into

Welford. She put her foot hard on the brake and winced as she saw Sky slipping forwards on the seat behind her. 'Sorry, sweetheart,' she whispered, trying not to look at the frightened eyes in the rearview mirror.

She managed the turn, then tried to keep one eye on the speedometer as she drove up the narrow lane. She could barely remember leaving Barn End. The whole thing still seemed impossible. There was no way Adam and Emily would have lied to her like that. It must be a mistake. It had to be.

Though Geraldine had been in tears when she left, Mandy's eyes were dry. She felt completely numb, as if the wet cement had risen up through her feet and filled her entire body.

She flashed into Welford and made herself slow down again. She paused as she reached the lane that led towards Animal Ark. Should she go home, she wondered for a moment? But Geraldine's revelation was still there, taking up more headspace than she could spare. Had Adam and Emily really lied to her? If they had, they had done so over and over, for years and years. There was no way Mandy could face them. Not right now.

Though it was only a short drive, Mandy was exhausted by the time she arrived at Six Oaks Stables. Her headlights pierced the gathering darkness, picking out the stone walls on either side of the road as the car climbed the last steep rise. She pulled up in the cobbled yard and switched off the engine. It took a huge amount of willpower to haul herself out and she stood on the wet cobbles, gathering strength before she let Sky out and picked up her holdall.

The kitchen was empty, though the front door was unlocked. Molly had said to make herself at home, but Mandy still remembered the sense of urgency she had heard in Molly's voice when she had called in the first place. There was something wrong with Bill. Molly wouldn't have called her otherwise.

Leaving her bags in the kitchen, Mandy made her way back out into the yard. There was a light in Bill's stable. She picked her way across the slippery cobbles and looked over the door. Molly was at Bill's head, speaking quietly and running her hands over his velvety nose. It was glaringly obvious that Bill had taken a turn for the worse. Even from the doorway, Mandy could see his flanks lift and fall in the characteristic double-breath of COPD. His nostrils were flared in a vain attempt to allow more air into his broken lungs. Worse still, he had lost weight and condition. His eyes had sunken into his head and his rump was bony underneath the padded blanket.

Bill's head was resting on Molly's shoulder, his eyes half-closed, listening to her voice. He may have been in pain and struggling to breathe but he was at peace, knowing he was with someone who loved him. Mandy had barely known Molly when she had offered a final home to Bill, but she could have looked for a million years without finding a better place for him.

Molly turned, as if sensing that someone was there.

She looked momentarily flustered, but then she grinned. 'Oops,' she said, her eyes crinkling. 'Caught me having a private moment with the big chap!' She raised her eyebrows. 'Are you okay? It sounded like things were a bit fraught when I called.'

Mandy shrugged. There was no way she wanted to talk about anything that had happened that afternoon. 'A bit tired, that's all,' she said, rubbing her hand over her face.

For the first time since she had seen the scrapbook, she started to feel as if she was back in her real life. How familiar it all seemed: the scent of horse, the heat of Bill's great body, diminished as it was. She ran her hands over the gelding, feeling peace flowing into her. This was who she was, after all.

'I'm afraid he's gone downhill.' Molly was the first to speak. 'I don't want him to suffer,' she added softly.

'I promise I won't let that happen,' Mandy told her. 'And I know you won't either.'

'I've tried to give him the best few years I could,' Molly said. She sounded both proud and sombre at the same time.

'I know you did.' Mandy's voice shook. 'And when the time comes, I'll make it as easy as I can.' To her shock, she realised her face was wet.

Molly put a hand on her shoulder, her face sympathetic. 'Don't worry,' she said. 'He's still eating and getting up on his own. I think he's got a bit of time left. We don't have to let him go just yet.'

Mandy swallowed hard and wiped her hand over her face again, smearing the tears. 'I'm sorry,' she said. 'I know it's not time yet.'

Molly checked Bill's water, switched off his light, then steered Mandy indoors without saying a word. Mandy had never felt more grateful. Even if she had wanted to talk, Mandy wouldn't have known where to begin.

'I've made up the room with the double bed,' Molly told her. Mandy hoisted her holdall and followed Molly up the stairs. It was an old house, and as she followed Molly along a dimly lit corridor, she had to duck her head to pass under an arched doorway. 'Take care,' Molly warned. 'The house isn't made for anyone as tall as you!'

An image of Geraldine's willowy figure flashed into Mandy's mind. Tall like my mum. She squashed the thought down. Geraldine wasn't her mum.

She dumped her holdall down beside the bed. 'Bathroom's here,' Molly told her, leading her to another doorway along the corridor. 'I'm afraid the shower's a bit feeble.' She looked apologetic. 'But the water's usually hot.'

Mandy followed Molly back down to the kitchen and slumped in one of the armchairs by the range. Molly put a frozen pizza in the oven, then swept a load of tack off the table. She tidied a stack of horse show schedules and swept some spilled dog biscuits into the palm of her hand. Mandy couldn't resist smiling. Outside in the yard, everything was in perfect order. Molly's office was immaculate and she paid her vet bills ahead of time. But her home had always been a little more chaotic, and Mandy realised the cosy disorder was exactly what she needed to distract her.

Molly's fat ginger cat Whiskers began to weave around Mandy's feet. Reaching down, she lifted him onto her lap and started to stroke him. He had the most wonderful rumbling purr. Sky was curled up at her feet, her nose tucked under her tail. Mandy was amazed she was managing to sleep, unsettled as she had been by the move and by Mandy's emotional state.

Molly continued to bustle around. She phoned one of her liveries about a farrier's visit, then grabbed some plates and served the pizza. She chatted as they ate, talking about Bourbon and Party Ring and her plans to revamp the outdoor school. She seemed unfazed by the fact that Mandy failed to respond to most of her comments. Mandy was reminded of the way Molly had talked to Bill in the stable, filling his ears with words that didn't need to make sense. It was peaceful, in its way.

After they had eaten, Molly led Mandy to the sitting room. She lit the fire, cheerfully using the bellows until the room was half-filled with smoke, then to Mandy's surprise, fell asleep as soon as she sat down on the hairy sofa with Bertie the Jack Russell snoring beside her.

Mandy sat for a few minutes just staring into the flames. She should probably text James, she thought; let him know what Geraldine said about the scrapbooks. But her phone was in her bedroom and she felt too weary to contemplate the stairs. At least Mum and Dad weren't wondering where she was; as far as they knew, she was still cosily living at Barn End with Geraldine. Mandy found herself wondering what she would say to Adam and Emily when she saw them again. She shoved the thoughts aside. Tomorrow would be soon enough.

She awoke in the unfamiliar bedroom with a start. It was still dark beyond the thick velvet curtains at the window. Her head was thumping. *I'm at Molly's*, she remembered, and all the awfulness from yesterday came flooding back. The bedroom was chilly. Only a few weeks ago, she had woken up in her own bedroom in Wildacre. A pang of homesickness hit her for the first time. How much easier would all this have been if she'd had her own home to go to? A thought swam clearly into Mandy's head, crisp and determined, a decision made: Jimmy was going to have to move out. Much as she loved him, she couldn't hold out any longer. She wanted to go home.

She still didn't feel able to talk to anyone about Geraldine and Adam and Emily, but this was something she could deal with. Pulling out her mobile, she began to type. 'We need to sort this out, don't we?' she wrote. 'Can we talk soon?' Mandy took a deep breath and added, 'I don't want to be away from Wildacre forever.'

Chapter Twenty

Mandy got out of bed and creaked along the landing to the shower. Molly hadn't been kidding about its temperamental nature. She had three minutes of freezing water trickling on her head, and then a feeble jet that seemed hot enough to make a pot of tea. Hoping she'd rinsed off most of the soap, she pulled on her clothes and made her way outside. Molly was mucking out with the help of a silent lad called Paul. He seemed gruff and awkward to Mandy, refusing to meet her eyes when she said good morning, but once he was out of hearing, Molly assured her that he was great with the horses. 'Especially the Biscuit Twins,' she said.

Mandy watched as he led the little ponies out to their winter paddock. Molly was right. Paul handled them with gentle authority, teaching them good manners as they walked beside him. Mandy opened the gate for him and he nodded. 'Thanks,' he said in a rather gravelly voice. The little ponies looked sturdy and fluffy in their winter coats and Mandy found herself feeling pleased that Molly hadn't rugged them. They'd be far happier in their own thick fur. Native ponies had been bred to be outside, even through the Yorkshire winter, and this pair had enough fat stores to protect them against the worst of the weather.

'I'm sorry for being such poor company last night,' Molly said as she munched on a slice of toast and marmalade at the table. 'Terrible host, falling asleep on you.'

'It's fine,' Mandy assured her. 'I wasn't feeling sociable anyway.'

Molly studied her for a moment, then went back to her coffee. Difficult as it would be, Mandy found herself for the first time wishing that Molly would ask. She was going to have to face Adam and Emily soon, whether she liked it or not. It might help to get a fresh perspective, but Molly finished her toast, wiped her hands on her jodhpurs and jumped out of her chair.

'See you later,' she said, heading for the door.

With a sigh, Mandy picked up her plate and put it in the dishwasher. She was feeling sick with nerves, and the toast hadn't helped. But she couldn't put it off any longer. She still worked at Animal Ark, and she had to face her parents.

She felt the knot of anxiety grow in her stomach as she drove down the hill. Was she really going to have this conversation with Adam and Emily today? There was no way she could just come out and tell them who Geraldine was. And tempting as it was to pretend it had never happened, Geraldine could hardly disappear without comment.

Her head felt light when she entered the clinic. In one way it felt utterly familiar, and in another, everything had changed. It felt as if she was looking down the wrong end of a telescope; everyone and everything seemed very far away. Rachel and Helen were putting up Christmas decorations and for a moment, that seemed as preposterous as anything else.

Rachel saw Mandy watching. She blushed, obviously mistaking Mandy's confusion for disapproval. 'I know it's only the first week of December,' she said, 'but we couldn't resist!' She propped a wobbly star on top of the artificial Christmas tree. 'I love this time of year!'

Helen stopped in the middle of winding a piece of tinsel around the branches. 'Are you okay?' She peered at Mandy. 'Not coming down with a winter bug or anything?'

'I'm fine,' Mandy lied.

'I'll be back at eleven for coffee.' Mandy heard Adam's voice calling to Emily as he came through the interconnecting door. A wave of breathless panic washed over her. She didn't want to see him, not yet. She pulled open the door and ducked through it with Sky at her heels.

She strode across the car park to the rescue centre, only stopping to draw breath when she was inside. To her, Hope Meadows was home as much as Wildacre. Mandy found herself able to focus again and after a few moments to catch her breath, she started the familiar morning routine, taking comfort in feeding and cleaning and all the tasks that made the animals' lives that little bit better.

By the time she was finished, she felt much calmer. Then a text arrived from Geraldine. Mandy made herself take three deep breaths before she read it. It was very short and to the point. 'Can we talk?'

Mandy hesitated. She still needed time to get her head together. Geraldine was going to have to wait. 'Soon but not yet,' she typed, then looking at the message, she added, 'Sorry,' before she pressed send. Though her head was feeling clearer, her throat was dry and sore. It wouldn't be easy to deal with a morning full of clients, and for a moment she wondered whether she could get away with going home sick. But it would be worse sitting at Molly's on her own, with everything still churning in her head.

She felt strange again as soon as she walked into the clinic. Adam was humming a Christmas carol and Emily was sitting at the desk, opening some Christmas cards. 'Some people are super organised,' she commented. 'Oh well, they're going to have to put up with ours being late this year.' She smiled when she saw Mandy. 'Hello, love. How are you?'

Mandy managed to keep her expression neutral. 'Fine, thanks.' She felt a frisson of discomfort as the lie rolled from her mouth again. Maybe if she lied often enough, she would get used to it, she thought. Maybe lies began to feel like truth if you told them often enough. Was that what Emily and Adam had found?

She checked the appointment schedule. She was busy all morning but fortunately she was down for all the farm calls, rather than stuck inside. Maybe when she was out and about, she would start to feel more normal. She still had the strangest feeling, as if she was in the audience watching a play rather than an integral part of the scene. Adam was singing 'The Holly and the Ivy' as he checked the operating list. Toby had arrived and Rachel was showing him a photograph of the Christmas tree she and Brandon had put up together. Helen had put a pair of baubles over her ears like earrings and Emily was laughing at her.

Though the room was crowded, Mandy felt impossibly alone. For the first time ever, she began to wish that she had never come back to Welford.

Chapter Twenty-one

Mandy took a cup of tea over to Hope Meadows at lunchtime. She had made an excuse to avoid going into the cottage for lunch and she had felt Helen's eyes on her again, but she didn't care. The rescue centre was the closest thing she had to a sanctuary right now. The soft grey December light filtered in through the huge windows, bringing with it a sense of calm. Mandy gazed out at the fells in the distance and they offered her comfort as well.

She switched on the computer and began to write her annual advice column on the Hope Meadows website about not giving animals as Christmas presents. The centre's Facebook page was already swamped with requests to visit the current residents. How many of them would be looking for Christmas gifts, she wondered?

She stopped writing after a few minutes and began to read over what she had said. It struck her that she sounded distinctly Scrooge-like and for a moment, she wanted to laugh.

'Bah, humbug!' she said out loud. She scrolled back

through her writing and changed 'You should never give animals as Christmas presents' to 'It's important to think carefully about whether an animal will be a suitable gift'. After that, she warned people to check if the person actually wanted and was ready for a pet before throwing them in at the deep end.

She read through the page again. Though it was designed to discourage all but the most determined from seeing pets as gifts, it no longer sounded as if she hated all of humanity. She pasted in a sprig of holly for good measure and started to upload the article to the website.

A bang on the window made her jump. James and Raj were standing on the stone path that led down the side of the orchard. Raj was carrying Taresh, who was dressed in an adorable bright green elf costume. Raj was wearing a Santa hat perched on his turban and James was bravely clad in a sweater dotted with Christmas trees.

'Hey,' James said, pushing open the back door. 'We were wondering if you'd like to join your festive nephew at the nursery's Christmas party?'

'Susan's invited us all,' Raj told Mandy. Taresh reached out and tugged the white pom-pom on the end of Raj's Santa hat. Raj, with seemingly infinite patience, took the pom-pom, tossed it over his shoulder and pulled the hat back into place, all with only one hand. It looked to Mandy as if this game had been going on for a while.

Mandy felt very slightly angry with James. It might have been more tactful for him to come on his own after what had happened yesterday. Not that he knew everything, of course, but surely he had seen enough to guess that something significant was going on? 'I'm not sure I'm in the mood for a party,' she said.

James regarded her for a moment, then moved closer. Raj had turned away to show Taresh the view. 'Sorry,' James murmured, sensing Mandy's tension. 'We can try to find a quiet corner, then you can tell me what excuse Geraldine came up with for the scrapbooks.'

Mandy could feel a muscle twitching in her jaw. James looked sympathetic. 'If you really can't face the party,' he said, 'we can talk later.'

Mandy sighed. Little as she wanted to go to a nursery party, it would be better than staying here with only the animals to watch her going slowly mad. 'I can probably get a couple of hours off,' she said.

James sent her a grateful smile. 'That's better,' he said.

It was impossible for Mandy and James to talk as they walked up to the nursery on the village green. Taresh wanted to get down and toddle. Though Raj could probably have managed on his own, James seemed unable to take his eyes off the little boy. They kept finding interesting things in the hedge and each time they did, Taresh wanted to show Mandy. Despite everything that was going on, Mandy found herself entranced as he earnestly showed her a brown acorn and a shrivelled rosehip. She held out her arms. 'There's more up here,' she told him and was pleased when he allowed her to scoop him up and find some rosehips higher on the hedge. It felt so very right to be holding him. His little body curved into hers, and his weight felt warm and steady on her hip. Mandy almost smiled at the memory of just how certain she used to be that she'd never want children. If Taresh had been willing, she thought she could have been happy to keep him in her arms forever.

When they reached the village green, Taresh wriggled to get down. They walked around the edge of the grass to the large Victorian house which held the nursery. It was looking very festive. The windows were smothered in cut-out snowflakes and Mandy could see paper chains and streamers strung from every corner inside.

Susan greeted them at the door. She looked rather hot and there was a fingerprint of glitter on her cheek, but she beamed at them as they stepped inside. 'Thanks for coming,' she said. 'I'm sorry it's so early, I know Christmas is ages away, but all our parents get so booked up. This was the only convenient date for the party!'

Raj put Taresh down and Susan took his coat and hung it on a spare peg, marked with a duck. 'Come on in,' she said, walking ahead of them down the hall. 'Douglas is about to start singing,' she said, and grinned.

'Though on second thoughts, you might want to stay outside for that.'

The folding doors between the baby and toddler rooms had been pushed back. A long table full of finger food stood along one wall and the whole room was bright with glittery Christmas paintings. Douglas was dressed as a gigantic elf, complete with a red felt hat and green trousers. Mandy couldn't decide whether he looked funny or faintly terrifying, but the children didn't seem to share her doubts. They were standing round him as he played an electric keyboard and belted out 'Jingle Bells' at the top of his voice. Most of them were singing too, though some were giggling as Douglas turned and made faces in between verses.

Harriet Ruck, another of Mandy's old school friends, was unloading chocolate biscuits onto a paper plate at the table. Her triplets were eighteen months old now. They were toddling around, and dancing in the uninhibited way Mandy was starting to love.

Susan bustled up. The glitter was gone from her face but someone had made her a tinsel halo, which was sitting on her head at a jaunty angle. 'Any chance you could give us a hand on the Lucky Dip, Mandy?' She led her over to a huge basket. 'Just remember,' Susan whispered into her ear, 'the basket isn't full of wood shavings. They're definitely snowflakes.'

There were lots of eager little hands waiting to plunge into the basket to find a prize, and for the next few minutes, all of Mandy's attention was taken up with supervising the long line of giggling children. She was pleased when Vicky Beaumont appeared with Connie and helped marshal the queue. The colourful parcels were eagerly opened and Mandy was amused to see that the prizes were pots of bubbles in all different colours. By the time all the children had found their treasure, the air was thick with exhaled detergent and some of the older toddlers were rushing round, trying to catch bubbles on their hands.

'What a great idea,' Vicky commented. 'At least the children will go home clean!'

Mandy laughed. The cheerful festive chaos was the best distraction she could have wished for. When Susan announced it was time to eat, she started wiping hands and faces and helped distribute sausage rolls and carrot sticks. She even found herself consoling two-and-a-half-year-old Simon, who had been distraught as he held his paper plate. He sat on Mandy's knee with tears running down his cheeks, trying to tell her in between sobs what was wrong.

'He says Connie told him that the olives are reindeers' eyes,' Mandy whispered to Vicky, when she finally understood.

Vicky looked abashed. 'That's Ben's fault,' she said. 'He sent us in with a plate of edible reindeer faces made out of tomato macaroni and veg.'

Roo Dhanjal was there with her son Kiran. She had provided the Pass the Parcel, which was wrapped in beautiful layers of sari cloth instead of paper. Douglas was supervising, switching the music on and off and checking that only one layer was unwrapped at a time. The music was playing again when Mandy glanced at her watch. Her heart sank. It was time to get back for her afternoon appointments. She stood up quietly, waved to Raj and Taresh, who were sitting opposite, and began to make her way to the door.

Susan followed Mandy to the entrance. 'Thanks for coming,' she said.

'Thank you,' Mandy said. 'It's been fun.'

'If you can wait a couple of minutes, I'll give you a couple of slices of Christmas cake for your mum and dad. Someone donated one and none of the children seem to want to eat it.' She rushed off and returned with a plastic container stuffed with cake. Mandy took it with a rather strained smile. 'Mum and Dad' felt wrong now, when she thought of Adam and Emily. She sighed inwardly. She couldn't put off seeing them much longer. She was being crushed by the weight of too many secrets.

She was walking down the path towards the green when she heard footsteps behind her. It was James. 'I saw you leaving,' he puffed. 'Is it okay if I walk to Animal Ark with you? Lovely as the party is, my ears could do with a break from the noise!'

Mandy nodded. 'I know what you mean. I'm going to have "Jingle Bells" ringing in my head all day!'

'Is Geraldine back yet?' James asked as soon as they had passed through the nursery gate. 'Have you had a chance to speak to her?'

Mandy couldn't think of an easy way to explain everything that had happened since Taresh knocked over the bookcase. She took a deep breath. 'She's my mother,' she said.

James stopped walking and stared at Mandy. 'What?'

'She's my biological mother.'

'But she can't be,' James protested. 'Your parents died in a car crash when you were a baby.'

Mandy raised her eyebrows. 'Do you think I don't know that? But Adam and Emily lied. My parents were still alive when I was adopted. Geraldine told me I was removed by Social Services because she and my father were drug addicts.'

James's face had gone very red. 'Are you certain it's true? Have you spoken to your parents yet?'

Mandy felt a surge of anger. She had called them Adam and Emily deliberately. James had referred to them as her parents. She shook her head. 'I don't know what to say,' she told him. They walked on in silence for a minute. 'I don't know how to even start the conversation,' she admitted. 'Why didn't they tell me the truth?'

'Maybe they thought it was too difficult,' he said. 'You were only a baby, after all.'

Mandy fought down the heat growing inside her. 'I know I was a baby,' she said. 'Obviously they couldn't tell me straight away. But there was no need for them to keep on lying. They had no right to make me think my mother was dead!'

James rubbed a hand through his hair. 'I can see why you're upset,' he said, 'but your mum and dad probably thought it was easier to let you think that. They would have known Geraldine was a drug addict, and totally unfit as a mother. Had she stayed clean at all when she was pregnant?'

Mandy clenched her fists and walked faster. How could James even begin to defend what the Hopes had done? 'It's not about what my mum did,' she protested tightly. 'She's clean now. And no, she didn't manage to get off the drugs when she was pregnant. But that makes it even worse that Adam and Emily lied. I deserved to know that I was born with foetal drug syndrome. It could have affected my health.'

James turned his head and glared at her without slowing down. His eyes were flashing as if her anger had spread to him. 'Maybe they thought they were able to monitor your health well enough without telling you,' he snapped. 'It hasn't made the slightest difference that I can see.' He matched her step for step as they turned into the lane that led up to the clinic. 'And I don't know how you can suddenly call that woman mum when you still have a mum. The one who raised you. The one who's done everything for you.'

Red rage flared inside Mandy. 'You don't get to tell me who my mum is!' she shouted. 'When Adam and Emily lied to me, they denied me a family. I didn't even get to meet my dad. He's dead. They had no right to decide that for me. They're not my real parents!'

Silence crashed like breaking glass. Mandy found herself wishing that James would go away. Why was he still there, walking beside her? She had hoped talking to him would help, but it had just made everything worse. She was walking faster and faster, trying to get away, but when she reached the last bend, as Animal Ark came into sight, James caught Mandy's elbow and turned her to face him. They stood in the lane, glaring at one another.

'Is that how you see me and Raj with Taresh?' James asked. His voice was quiet. So quiet that Mandy had to lean towards him to hear. The wind was rising, rushing through the hedgerows that lined the lane.

Mandy felt tears rising in her eyes, though whether they were tears from rage or pain, she wasn't sure. 'Of course I don't think that.' *Why would he think that? It's not the same.*

'Really?' James gazed at her as if he was looking into her soul and didn't like what he saw.

Mandy's hands were trembling. She shoved them in her pockets to hide them. 'It's different,' she said hoarsely. 'You'll always be honest with Taresh about his mother, where he came from. And he's related to Raj. It's not the same at all.'

'He is related to Raj,' James pointed out, 'but not to me.' He sounded so pained that Mandy wanted to reach out to him, but it seemed as if he was a million miles away. 'And yet I love him more than I've ever loved anything before, not just because he's mine, but because he needs me for everything.' He paused, shaking his head as if what he was saying was still almost incomprehensible. 'That amount of trust is incredible, Mandy. Nobody knows that better than you. You've always said that the owners of the animals you treat have to have a huge amount of trust in you. It's not so very different: like that, but more. I can't explain it, but it is.'

A stray leaf blew out of the hedge and scattered across the ground, coming to a stop by Mandy's foot. 'It's not the same,' she whispered. 'That trust was there in the beginning, but Adam and Emily betrayed it. Why can't you see that?'

'I can see you're hurting.' James's hands were tight fists by his side. 'And they probably made a mistake, but have you really forgotten how much they've done for you? You had a wonderful childhood. I know because I was there. Then you came back as an adult and they welcomed you into Animal Ark and did everything they could to set up Hope Meadows. I've read about foetal drug syndrome. They were there to nurse you through that. Don't you see?' He took a step closer, the colour rising in his cheeks. 'That's what Geraldine left you with. And they got you through it. You always said they couldn't have loved you more. Nothing has changed.'

Mandy felt sick. How could he say that nothing had changed, when everything had been turned upside down? 'That's just stupid,' she said, feeling suddenly tired. 'Once they had me, they must have decided it was too difficult to tell me the truth. And it's not just me. It's my mum too. Don't you see they've denied her a daughter as well?'

'She denied herself a daughter. She was a drug addict.' He spat the words out slowly. 'She couldn't take care of you.'

Mandy could see Geraldine's face in her head, her expression when she had explained about her addiction and her love for Mandy. 'They never gave her a chance!' she argued. 'They took me away, even though Geraldine wanted me. If I'd been allowed to stay, maybe she'd have got clean years earlier. She's my mother, for God's sake.'

'Is she really?' James sounded as weary as Mandy felt. 'Blood isn't everything.' He looked away, and Mandy knew he was trying to hide the tears in his eyes.

'Not everything,' she conceded, 'but it is *something*. You can't deny that.'

They had reached the driveway. The old wooden Animal Ark sign hung overhead, creaking in the wind.

'I'm sorry that you feel that way,' James said stiffly.

Mandy wanted to reach out to him. She could see the hurt written all over his face, but the pain in her own heart was too much to deal with. 'I'm sorry too,' she replied, all the fight draining out of her. 'I know you want to make this better, but I need to work out what I'm going to do. Nobody can help with that. I'm going to have to deal with this on my own.'

She turned away and walked under the sign, towards the grey stone house where she had grown up, and the clinic where she worked, and the rescue centre she had opened with Adam and Emily's help. Whatever James thought, they had lied to her. How could she ever get past that? Everything in her life was tied up with Adam and Emily and she had no idea how she was going to untangle it.

Chapter Twenty-two

The wind whipped at her hair as she walked up the drive, carrying with it a few droplets of rain. Mandy saw Adam driving towards her with Emily in the passenger seat and she stepped to the side to let them pass. To Mandy's dismay, Adam stopped and lowered the window.

'We're going Christmas shopping,' he announced. He sounded so cheerful that Mandy forced herself to smile back at him.

'Any additions to your Santa list?' Emily leaned across to look up at her. Mandy found herself searching Emily's face. Her eyes were clear and the bruise-like rings around her eyes had almost disappeared.

You knew my mother was alive. Mandy took a step back. She felt as if she might choke if they didn't drive off soon. 'Don't spend too much,' she joked weakly.

'Don't worry, we won't eat into your inheritance,' Adam quipped, and Mandy felt another bolt of pain. How could he not see that there was something wrong?

She held onto her smile, but she was glad when Adam put in the clutch and drove on.

By the time she was ready to see her first patient, there were four already waiting. For at least the third time that day, Helen sent her a questioning look from behind the reception desk. Though Toby was often a minute or two late, Mandy was invariably on time. Avoiding her gaze, Mandy hurried into her consulting room.

Her first patient was a dog with a urinary tract infection. Mandy prescribed a course of tablets, then waved the client off. As she finished writing up the details on the computer, Helen came in. 'Reverend Hadcroft's here with Tallulah,' she said. 'It's just a vaccination, but you know what Tallulah's like. I wondered if you'd like a hand?'

Mandy did know what Tallulah was like. She was a monster black and white cat with claws that could whip round and catch you faster than Mrs Ponsonby nipping into her favourite church pew at a busy midnight mass. 'I would appreciate some help,' she told Helen. Though she wasn't remotely upset with Helen, she could hear her voice sounded stiff and formal.

Helen pulled the door to for a moment, then walked across to stand opposite Mandy. 'Is everything okay? You seem a bit tense.'

For a moment Mandy felt an urge to tell her everything. But after the disastrous conversation with James, and knowing that Reverend Hadcroft was waiting, she didn't know how to start. 'I'm fine, really,' she said. 'Just a bit frazzled.'

'It's not Jimmy, is it?' Helen prompted, and Mandy was glad to be able to give her a firm reply.

'Not Jimmy.'

Helen looked at her sympathetically. 'I guess lots of people feel frazzled at this time of year,' she said. 'Christmas does that to everyone.'

Despite her attempt to stop it, an image of Geraldine rushed into Mandy's head. She'd said this was going to be her best Christmas ever. Now Mandy knew why. She'd found her daughter, and it would be their first Christmas together.

Helen called Reverend Hadcroft through, and Mandy reached into the fridge to pull out the box of vaccines. She grabbed a syringe and needle from the drawer and took the two vials of vaccine from the box. Poor Geraldine, she thought. All those lonely Christmases, wondering where I was, if I was happy, who was putting a stocking at the end of my bed. There was a lump in her throat and her vision blurred with tears.

'Mandy.' Helen nudged her. 'This vaccine's for Tallulah, remember?' She nodded towards the vials Mandy was holding. Turning her head away, so that Reverend Hadcroft couldn't see, Helen mouthed, 'Wrong vaccine.'

Mandy looked down at the tiny bottles and read the name. *Canivet*. She had been about to draw up a dog vaccine. She felt her face go red. Without making a fuss, Helen took the dog vaccines from her, set them back in the fridge and drew out the correct carton.

Concentrate, Mandy told herself.

'That's the lot,' Helen said as Mandy made her way into reception after seeing her sixth client out. 'Everyone must be Christmas shopping,' she added with a cheery smile. 'Shall I make the coffee, or will you?'

'I'll do it,' Mandy said. It was better to keep busy. Once she'd had the coffee, she would find something else to do. As she walked back in with two mugs, Helen's phone rang. Mandy put Helen's coffee down on the desk and sat down.

'Hi Seb.' She frowned and took the phone away from her ear. 'There's been a fire at a farm,' she told Mandy. 'Seb has three animals that urgently need housing. Would we be able to find space for them?'

'Of course.' Mandy took the phone. 'The barn in the orchard is clean and ready,' she said to Seb. 'What do you have, cows, sheep?'

'Actually, it's alpacas.' Seb sounded amused, despite the situation.

Mandy found herself unexpectedly smiling. It wasn't often that Seb managed to surprise her. She knew there was a local farm that had a few alpacas, but they were with a different veterinary practice and she had never had direct contact with them. 'No problem,' she said.

'They'll need to be kept separate,' Seb warned. 'One's a male, the others are two young females. Their owner is planning to start a herd eventually, but this doesn't seem like the best time.'

Mandy blinked. 'Okay. I mean, I'm outside my immediate comfort zone, but we'll manage. No accidental alpacas on my watch!'

Sky, Lucy and Isla followed Mandy and Helen out to the shelter in the orchard. It was big enough for three alpacas, but there was no way to keep them separated. There was a pile of wooden gates propped in the corner that she had planned to use for an outdoor sheep pen. 'Do you think we could use those to divide the barn?' Mandy suggested.

'I'm not sure they're high enough,' Helen said.

Mandy had told Seb he could bring the alpacas, and she was determined to follow through, but their special requirements looked like they might defeat her.

Helen tapped her lip. 'We could ask Jimmy if he could help?' she said tentatively. 'He often has spare timber we could borrow.'

Mandy hesitated. It felt wrong, having to ask Jimmy for a favour. She had no doubt that he would say yes, but she didn't like admitting she needed his help with something so basic. Then she pictured the poor traumatised alpacas, already on their way from the ruins of their familiar stables. She had to do it for their sake, she thought. Taking her phone out of her pocket, she dialled Jimmy's number.

'Hello, Mandy.' Jimmy sounded more cheerful than he had the last time they'd met. 'What can I do for you?'

'How did you know I wanted something?' Mandy retorted, feeling stung.

'Whoa, it was just a way of saying hi,' Jimmy said. Mandy pictured him holding up one hand as if he was trying to calm a frightened horse. 'Is everything okay?'

Mandy cringed. 'Yes, sorry. I'm in a bit of a rush, that's all. Seb's bringing me some alpacas and we need to put a barrier in the barn to keep the male away from the girls. We don't have anything here we can use to build a high enough partition. I thought you might have some spare wood at Running Wild?'

'Yes, plenty,' Jimmy said. 'We've just finished up, so I'll load the Land Rover and come straight over.'

'Thanks,' Mandy said. She felt a pang of guilt as she ended the call. She would have to get used to managing without Jimmy, she reminded herself. She couldn't move back into Wildacre without him, but still expect him to be there when she needed his help.

Helen had shaken fresh straw onto the floor of the barn and was studying her phone. 'I'm Googling alpaca basics,' she explained.

'Good idea,' said Mandy. 'I'm sure Seb will tell us what we need to know but it would be great to make sure we're ready.'

Helen used her fingers to enlarge the page on her screen. 'One, a good shelter.' She looked up at the barn roof. 'Check,' she said. 'Two, provide vet care.' She looked at Mandy, eyebrows quirked. 'I think we can provide that one between us.' Mandy grinned. 'Three . . .' Helen frowned. 'Feed them well. That's not very specific.' She read some more. 'They eat hay,' she said, 'and we've got plenty of that. Apparently alpaca food is readily available. I'll see whether Seb can arrange for some to be brought here, and failing that, we can get onto Harper's first thing.' Harper's was the local animal feed wholesalers.

'Number four,' Helen went on, 'breed them carefully.' She laughed. 'Let's hope we don't carelessly breed them,' she said. 'And if we do, we can always blame Jimmy's faulty barrier.' She took in a deep breath. 'Last but not least, shear them once a year.'

'Given it's the beginning of winter, today will not be shearing day,' Mandy pointed out.

Jimmy pulled up outside the barn a few moments later. He had several pieces of wood and a pile of planks in the back of his Land Rover as well as a large toolkit. Helen extended her Google search to look up ideal measurements for the fencing. Jimmy listened carefully and within a few minutes, he had made a start.

Helen turned to Mandy. 'I'll feed the rescue animals,' she offered, 'and then I'll head over and close up the clinic.'

Mandy found herself alone with Jimmy. It didn't feel awkward, being in the softly lit barn with the scent of clean straw in the air. She helped him without being asked, handing him tools, holding the planks in place and placing screws while he held up the heavier boarding.

Jimmy turned his head and smiled at her. 'We should go into business.'

Mandy managed a rather wry smile in return. If only they could. In spite of everything, she still loved him with all her heart. Several weeks apart had done nothing to dull the feelings. 'How are Abi and Max?' she asked, changing the subject.

'They're fine. Very excited for Christmas.' Mandy thought for a moment that he was going to add that they were missing her. She didn't know whether she was happy or sad when he didn't.

By the time Seb arrived, the shelter was neatly divided by a five-foot-high partition, with enough rails that the male alpaca couldn't climb through. Seb pulled into the car park in a truck with a livestock trailer towed behind. Mandy and Helen lowered the ramp and unloaded the alpacas one by one. They were considerably smaller than llamas, with similar upright necks and short backs, but smaller heads with round noses. They looked very sweet with their long hair and their little red headcollars.

'This is Inca,' Seb indicated the largest of the three animals, 'and those two are Fable and Meera, the females.'

To Mandy's relief, the alpacas seemed very used to being handled. They allowed Mandy and Helen to lead them around the rescue centre and across the orchard to the field shelter. Inca tested the partition with his head a couple of times, then snorted and wandered off to eat his hay. Meera and Fable looked around their new home with big curious eyes before nibbling at the pile of hay.

Seb and Helen headed off and Mandy and Jimmy stood side by side for a while, looking into the glowing barn. Mandy felt more peaceful than she had in days.

Jimmy shifted slightly. 'Is Geraldine expecting you back?' he asked.

'I've moved out,' Mandy forced herself to say. The brief moment of calm had gone.

Jimmy looked surprised. 'Why?'

Mandy braced herself. The news wasn't getting any easier. 'She's my mother.'

Jimmy drew in his breath, then opened his arms. Mandy stumbled towards him and clung on. Through her sobs, she could feel him patting her back. He smelled of aftershave and hay and Mandy found herself wishing this moment would never end and he would hold onto her forever.

But eventually he let go and stepped back. Mandy shivered in the sudden rush of cold air. She straightened up and dug in her pocket for a tissue. 'Sorry,' she said, wiping her eyes.

'You've nothing to be sorry about.' He took her hand. 'Come on,' he said, 'tell me what's happened. I'll help if I can.'

Mandy sent him a watery smile. 'I don't think anyone can help,' she said, 'but I would like to talk.'

They sat down on a hay bale. Jimmy was still holding her hand when she finished talking. He had listened without interruption and let out a long breath. 'You haven't said anything to Adam and Emily yet?'

'I don't know what I can say,' Mandy admitted.

A shadow crossed Jimmy's face. 'No wonder,' he said. 'Your whole life must feel like it's been turned upside down.' He sat for a long moment and Mandy stayed very still beside him, feeling the heat from his palm seep into her fingers. The alpacas had lain down in the thick straw. It had begun to rain and the gentle sound of raindrops on the roof made Mandy feel sleepy.

'What do you think you're going to do?' Jimmy asked eventually. 'Is there anything you do feel sure about?'

'I think I'd like to get to know Geraldine better,' Mandy said. 'I know I need to take things slowly, but I can't turn her away. She's spent so long without me. And she's my mother.' The words still felt strange in her mouth, like fractured glass.

Jimmy squeezed her fingers. 'That sounds like a good place to start. What about this evening? Do you have somewhere to go? I guess you're not staying with your . . .' he checked himself, '. . . with Adam and Emily.'

Mandy shook her head. 'I was at Molly's last night. She's been very kind. I'll go back there.'

'Are you sure?' Jimmy was watching her carefully. 'You can come back to Wildacre, if it would be easier?'

'Not just yet,' she said. She took a wobbly breath, feeling tears just below the surface again. 'I still love you with all my heart, but I know it's over. We'll have to get things sorted out, once I have the headspace. But thanks for letting me talk.'

Chapter Twenty-three

Mandy sat in her car outside Hope Meadows for several minutes after Jimmy had driven away. Though she knew she wanted to speak to Geraldine, it was incredibly difficult to know what to say. Eventually she began to type a message into her phone.

'I know it can't have been easy but thank you for telling me the truth. I'm sorry I left so quickly. I've had some time to think and I hope to see you soon.'

She wondered how to sign off, and in the end put 'Mandy x'. She waited, trying to decide whether she might change her mind, but she knew she wanted to do this. With a steady hand, she clicked send.

She felt exhausted as she drove back to Six Oaks. There was no sign of Molly in the house and Mandy thought longingly about going upstairs and getting into bed, but it was too early. She wandered out to the yard and was unsurprised to see that the light was on in Bill's stable. The big horse's rug was folded on the straw and Molly was running a soft brush down his flank. She smiled when she saw Mandy.

'Just giving him a bit of a pamper,' she said. She

looked sad for a moment. 'Dear old boy,' she murmured. 'I'm going to miss him. It sounds weird, I feel so privileged that he's sharing the end of his life with me. I feel like he has faith in me to do the right thing.' She stopped her brushing and leaned her forehead against Bill's face.

Mandy could feel a lump forming in her throat. However many animals she saw to the end of their lives, she was never numb to the emotions involved. This time would be doubly poignant because she had so much love in her heart for both Bill and Molly.

'Right then,' Molly said, straightening up. 'Time to leave the poor old lad in peace. I'm going to make a stir-fry, if you're interested.' She started putting the brushes back into the grooming box. 'I even bought some halloumi if you want to risk it.'

'That sounds great,' Mandy said. She gave Bill a pat, then followed Molly indoors.

Mandy arrived early at Hope Meadows the following morning. She wanted to check on the alpacas before she brought the dogs outside. The soft-furred creatures were looking over the gate to the barn in a row, three sets of bright eyes gazing at her. The grass outside was white with frost, but the shelter felt warm and cosy.

Mandy brought out Sky and Mustard first. The little collie stood for ages gazing at the alpacas as if she was trying to work out whether they were overgrown sheep.

Mustard seemed scared of them as Mandy led him across the grass. She watched his body language carefully and stopped as soon as his ears began to go back. Once he seemed to feel comfortable again, she fed him treats until he had calmed down enough to move closer. The alpacas peered down their noses at the dogs, looking aloof and judgemental. Mandy found herself smiling. They clearly weren't afraid of these small fluffy visitors.

When all the dogs had been exercised, Mandy concentrated on dishing up breakfast. It was Friday and Geraldine was officially supposed to be coming in, but she hadn't arrived by the time Mandy had to head to Animal Ark. When she arrived in the clinic, yesterday's feeling of unreality still hadn't diminished.

'Look at this!' Emily was opening more Christmas cards. She held one out to Mandy. It was a photo of a cute rabbit reaching up and nibbling the carrot nose off a snowman. 'From Mrs Chan and Lettuce,' Mandy read inside. Mrs Chan was a delightful Chinese lady who had adopted Lettuce from Hope Meadows in the summer.

Emily smiled at Mandy. 'Would you like to have lunch with me today, love?'

Mandy felt her shoulders go tense. She forced herself to breathe and waved towards the daybook which lay open on the desk. 'Not sure where I'll be, to be honest. I'm due at Upper Welford at nine-fifteen so I'll have to rush off now, sorry.' Feeling her cheeks burn, and aware of Emily watching her curiously, Mandy scooped up the equipment she needed and hurried out to her car.

Jimmy was pulling into Running Wild as Mandy drove past. He waved at her and she waved back, but there was a sad, twisting feeling in her stomach. It was doubly hard to see him around when she missed him so much, but there was no going back.

The courtyard at Upper Welford was positively heaving with Christmas cheer. A huge fir tree had been erected in the centre of the cobblestones, decorated with thousands of tiny Christmas lights. Each of the shops had chosen a different theme for their festive windows. Some were snowy, some were filled with greenery, another bursting with rows of tiny elves made from red and green felt. The cheese shop, for some bizarre reason, had opted for a toy goat dressed up as Father Christmas. The scent of hot chestnuts wafted over Mandy and she breathed in deeply. She had missed her breakfast this morning and her stomach was rumbling. She would treat herself to a bag on the way out. Did Geraldine like hot chestnuts, she wondered? There was so much to learn about her.

Mandy suddenly felt a thrill of excitement. She had always assumed she had no chance of meeting any blood relatives. She stood still for a moment, the courtyard whirling around her. Maybe Geraldine was just the start. She could have a whole family waiting for her! She looked around at the sparkling shops. Perhaps she could come back here to buy Christmas presents.

All at once, the festive season seemed full of delight and anticipation instead of mounting dread.

It only took half an hour to trim the cow's foot. Mandy climbed back into her car clutching a warm paper bag of chestnuts and feeling determined. She would call Geraldine directly, she decided. She put the bag on the passenger seat and pulled out her mobile. There was a sense of excitement as she tapped in Geraldine's number. *Pick up, pick up.* The phone rang and rang. There had been no answer from yesterday's text either and Mandy suddenly felt alarmed. Had Geraldine changed her mind about everything?

'Hello? Mandy?' Geraldine sounded breathless when she finally answered.

'Yes, it's me.' Mandy found there were tears in her eyes.

'Oh!' There was so much warmth in the exclamation that the tears spilled down Mandy's cheeks. Her fingers gripped the phone tightly. 'It's so good to hear your voice,' Geraldine went on. 'Sorry I took so long to answer. I was upstairs and my phone was in my bag in the kitchen.'

Mandy hadn't thought about what she was going to say, but the relief at hearing Geraldine's voice was enough to tell her all she needed to know. 'I . . . I wondered if you were coming to Hope Meadows today?'

'Oh!' That happy exclamation again. 'Thank you, I'd love to,' Geraldine replied. 'I'm sorry I didn't contact you. I wanted you to be sure you were ready. I dropped a bombshell, I know that. I should have done things differently, I'm sorry . . .'

'The way you told me doesn't matter,' Mandy assured her, feeling tears drip onto her collar. 'I just wish I had known about you a long time ago.'

'Me too.' There was a pause, then Geraldine spoke again, her voice cracking slightly. 'We can't change the past,' she said, 'but I'm so glad I get the chance to put things right.'

'We can't change the past,' Mandy agreed, 'but we can change the future. Please will you come today? I need to introduce you to our new residents!'

'That would be wonderful,' Geraldine said. 'I can't wait! I'll be there in half an hour.'

Animal Ark's reception looked almost as festive as Upper Welford Hall when Mandy returned. The latest Christmas cards had been hung across the window and the Christmas tree lights were flashing in a complicated red, blue and green sequence. Helen was at the desk, entering something into the computer.

'Where is everybody?' Mandy asked.

'Toby's dealing with Fancy Ponsonby's dew claw.' She quirked an eyebrow and grinned up at Mandy. Regular client Amelia Ponsonby was very taken with the young vet and insisted that he see her indulged Pekinese every time. 'Your mum has gone home and your dad's been called out to a calving at Twyford and it's going to be a Caesar, so he might not be back for a while. There's nothing else in at the moment.'

'In that case, I'll be at the rescue centre,' Mandy said. She couldn't help feeling relieved that Adam and Emily wouldn't be around when Geraldine arrived. She couldn't face the extra complication of seeing them all together.

She walked along the flagged stone path, feeling a growing sense of excitement. 'Mum,' she said out loud as she unlocked the door. It didn't feel right when she had a picture of Geraldine in her mind, but she told herself she'd get used to it.

'My mum's coming to see us,' she announced to Jasper, and he looked up and wagged his long thin tail at her.

She heard the sound of the main door opening. There were butterflies in her stomach and it was suddenly hard to catch her breath. Mandy walked out of the dog room to find Geraldine . . . Mum . . . standing in reception. She looked as nervous as Mandy felt.

'I'm glad you're here,' Mandy said impulsively.

'So am I,' Geraldine replied, and she smiled, though there was strain on her face.

Mandy had wondered about hugging Geraldine when she saw her. Wasn't that how it would have played out in a TV show? Now they were both here, it felt too soon. She found herself staring at Geraldine instead, searching for evidence of their connection. It wasn't often Mandy met other women who were as tall as she was. Should she have guessed something from that? She thought she could see a resemblance around the nose. Fair skin, too, though the dyed scarlet hair meant it was impossible to know what colour Geraldine would have been naturally.

Geraldine nodded, as if she knew what was going through Mandy's mind. 'You were the image of your dad when you were born,' she said. 'But I can see myself in you now. I've got some photos of me when I was younger back in Manchester. We can look at them together sometime if you like.'

'I'd love that,' Mandy said. She wondered if Geraldine had a photograph of her father as well. 'Shall we take the dogs out?' It would be easier to talk if there was something else to distract them. As they led Jasper and Mustard to the paddock with Sky bouncing behind, Mandy felt herself beginning to relax. For now, she just wanted to be with her new mum. She had a million questions, but they could wait.

Mustard was much better today with the alpacas and walked right up to the fence to sniff at them. Mandy gave him a treat to reward his courage.

Geraldine reached over the fence to stroke Inca's blunt nose. 'What are they called?' she asked.

'This is Inca,' Mandy said. 'And these two are Meera and Fable.'

Geraldine moved to the other side of the barn and scratched behind Fable's ear. Fable seemed to be enjoying it. 'I went trekking in Peru a few years ago,' Geraldine told Mandy. 'I had an alpaca as a pack animal.'

'That sounds exciting,' Mandy said. They started to talk about countries they had visited. Geraldine seemed to have been to lots of the places on Mandy's wish list and she listened enviously as she talked about Peru and India and Chile and the Victoria Falls in Zambia. 'You're making me feel as if I should take a year out to see the world!' Mandy remarked.

'Travel is never a waste of time,' Geraldine replied. 'Seriously, you should go whenever you get the chance. Even if you're on your own. It's much safer now than it used to be.'

For once, the reminder that she was alone now didn't sting Mandy quite so much. She suddenly had a vision of herself boarding a plane, one-way ticket in hand, ready for adventures in a far-flung location. 'I'll make time for a holiday,' she promised. 'Yorkshire is gorgeous, but I know there are other horizons to explore.' She looked at Geraldine, who was pouring water into Meera and Fable's trough. 'Thank you for finding me,' she said in a rush. 'It was a shock when you first told me, but now . . . now I can't imagine not knowing who I really am.'

Geraldine beamed at her. Mandy took a step forward, held out her arms and for the first time they were hugging properly; a hug filled with warmth and wonder and almost thirty years of love.

Mandy was suddenly aware of hot breath on the

back of her neck, then a wet tongue slobbering in her hair. She looked sideways to find Meera's lips right beside her ear and she jumped back with a yelp. All three of the alpacas were staring at them, their expressions horrified. Geraldine and Mandy looked at one another and started to laugh.

Mandy felt relieved that the next day was Saturday and she was not on duty. Yesterday afternoon in the clinic had felt very awkward, as if the rooms were echoing with unspoken accusations. Not that Adam and Emily knew what was wrong, but it was obvious they could tell something was up.

Mandy's anger with them rose and fell, though the feeling of betrayal remained. The lack of communication with Emily was particularly hard, when all Mandy wanted to do was tell her about Geraldine's bombshell. Without meaning to, Mandy found herself searching her mother's face for signs of increasing illness. How could she begin such a stressful topic when Emily was already unwell? Angry as she was, she couldn't bear to make things worse.

Mandy was in the cat room when the outer door opened and closed. 'Hello, love!' Mandy found herself smiling as she heard Geraldine's cheerful greeting. She appeared in the doorway carrying a pair of plastic carrier bags. 'I thought we could put up a few decorations,' she said. 'If that's okay?'

'That would be lovely,' Mandy assured her, following her into the reception area.

'I brought some Christmassy music.' Geraldine waved her mobile and a small speaker. She set the speaker on the desk and opened the music app on her phone. 'Carols from King's,' she announced. A moment later, the room was filled with music.

As she taped a foil star to the window, Mandy gazed at the fells. It was a chilly day and sparkling sunshine shone on the early morning frost. Maybe when summer came round, she and Geraldine would walk up the steep tracks and explore the hills together. She breathed in deeply. Geraldine had brought scented candles in glasses and the sweet aroma of cinnamon and vanilla hung in the air.

'Can you give me a hand to arrange these?' Geraldine was holding the manger from a wooden nativity scene.

Picking up the tiny blue-clad figure of Mary, Mandy felt a burst of festive excitement. Whatever else happened, this would be the first Christmas when she knew that her real mother was alive and loved her. She glanced at her watch. She needed to finish her Christmas shopping, and there was time to get to Walton before lunch. 'I have to go out,' she told Geraldine. 'I still have to get a present for Taresh.'

She half expected Geraldine to offer to go with her, but Geraldine just beamed. 'You should have told me,' she said. 'I'm more than happy to hold the fort for a few hours. You work so hard, you deserve a break.'

Mandy headed to her car with an unexpected feeling of lightness. As she passed the cottage, she saw Emily waving through the window. After only a moment's hesitation, Mandy waved back, then tapped her watch and shook her head to indicate she had no time to spare.

The car park in Walton was heaving. Mandy circled a couple of times and stopped when she saw the reversing lights of a Mini come on. She backed into the space quickly. One of the benefits of manoeuvring round farmyards every day was an uncanny ability to fit her RAV4 into any available space.

There was a toy shop near the car park and Mandy decided to head there first. She had been feeling awful about the row with James. She had no idea how she was going to build bridges, but she was determined to get a lovely gift for her new adopted nephew. Mandy wandered round the shop for several minutes, looking for inspiration. In the corner furthest from the door, she spotted a fire engine toy and picked it up to have a look. As well as flashing lights and a siren, there was a hose that sprayed water from a small tank that could be filled up.

Mandy found herself grinning as she took it to the till and watched it being packed up. She would have loved a toy like that. She hoped Taresh would too. It was only as she set off down the high street, weighed down by the enormous parcel, that she began to regret buying Taresh's present right at the beginning of her trip.

She had thought long and hard about presents for Adam and Emily. She had decided that the bathroom set she'd bought in York for Emily was too old-fashioned, and Grandma would appreciate it more. Though Mandy was still in limbo with them, still angry and hurt, she couldn't imagine not getting them anything. She had already decided to get a sweater from the artisan knitwear store at Upper Welford Hall for Adam, but she had no idea what she should get for Emily.

She was passing a brightly decorated boutique when a silk scarf caught her eye. It had a handprinted butterfly pattern in subtle shades, muted pink on powder blue. As soon as Mandy saw it, she felt sure Emily would love it. She walked inside and picked it up. It felt smooth in her fingers, and the butterflies were exquisitely detailed. She took it to the counter and paid for it, feeling relieved.

As she was walking out, she stopped. Just beside the door there was a rack of distinctive gold blouses. Mandy lifted one and held it up against herself. It was more dramatic than anything she would have bought to wear for herself, but with Geraldine's height and presence, and her distinctive red hair, Mandy thought the blouse would look stunning. She checked the price tag and winced. It was expensive: almost painfully so. Way more than Emily's scarf.

She held it up again, gazing at her reflection in the mirror. She could picture Geraldine in it so clearly. Digging in her bag, Mandy pulled out her credit card and strode back to the till. Even if it was dear, even if it was more than Emily's present, so what? She had nearly thirty years of Christmas presents to make up, didn't she?

The shop assistant smiled. 'Beautiful, isn't it?' she said as Mandy handed over the blouse. 'It'll suit your height and figure really well.'

Mandy felt her face reddening, but she could hardly argue. She and Geraldine had the same build. 'Thanks,' she mumbled as the assistant popped the blouse into a bag and handed it over.

'Mandy!' It was Abi's voice. Mandy spun round and spotted Abi and Max in the doorway of a shop with Belle.

'Hi!' Belle smiled at Mandy. 'Christmas shopping is crazy, isn't it? Thank goodness it's only once a year. Otherwise I'd go completely mad!' She looked as well-groomed as ever in a belted red mac and knee-high suede boots.

Mandy nodded. 'I know what you mean,' she agreed, conscious that her bodywarmer was covered in alpaca hair and there was a clump of straw stuck to her shoe.

'Can we go shopping with Mandy, please?' Abi begged her mum.

Belle raised her eyebrows. 'I don't think Mandy wants

259

to drag you around with her,' she began, but Mandy lifted up a hand.

'It'd be fine with me,' she said. 'They can help me with gift ideas!'

Belle beamed. 'Well, if you really don't mind,' she said, 'you'll be doing me a favour. It'll give me a chance to get more done. Are you absolutely sure?'

'Absolutely,' Mandy replied.

She set off along the pavement with a twin on either side of her. Max grabbed her hand while Abi offered to carry the bag with Taresh's fire engine.

'We met Taresh when Daddy took us to York,' she announced.

Mandy looked at Abi in surprise. There was no reason James and Jimmy shouldn't meet, of course. They were good friends now, but it felt strange to think of them hanging out when she had known nothing about it.

'Taresh is so cute,' Abi went on. 'He was trying to say my name and he called me Babby.'

'Would it be okay for us to buy something for Taresh too?' Max asked.

'And Dad?' Abi said. 'Can you help us choose something for him?'

'Of course,' Mandy said, starting to feel flustered. She clearly wasn't going to get any more of her own shopping done. But it was a treat to be with the children again, and their festive glee was infectious.

They went back to the toy shop and Abi picked out a set of three books for Taresh. 'We had these when we were babies,' she explained to Mandy, holding them out to show the titles.

First Words, *First Numbers* and *First Colours*, Mandy read. 'Very useful,' she declared and Abi's face lit up.

'It's really important that Taresh learns to read and write,' she said.

'It certainly is,' Mandy agreed.

'I thought I could get a calendar for Dad,' Max said, tugging on Mandy's hand. 'One for his office.'

They walked to the stationers and began to look through the racks of calendars. 'I like that one,' Max said, pointing to a Yorkshire Dales calendar. It had a stunning photograph of Axwith Tor in winter on the front cover. Mandy lifted it down and they looked through it together. 'Look,' Max said. It was a scene from the top of Malham Cove. 'That was in Harry Potter!' He sounded so amazed that Mandy wanted to laugh.

'You're right,' she said. 'Maybe we can go there some day.' She kicked herself as soon as she'd said it. Despite their accidental meeting today, it was possible she and the twins would not be meeting much at all in the future, and certainly not going for long days out.

They bought the calendar, then it was Abi's turn to find something for her dad. She had seen a carved wooden model of a sparrowhawk in another shop and she led Mandy back there with a determined look on her face. 'Please can we buy it? Please?' Abi said. 'I've almost got enough.' She held out her purse to show

Mandy how much she had. Like the blouse, the sparrow-hawk was quite expensive but Abi seemed so keen that Mandy relented.

'Oh, go on then,' she told Abi. 'I'll give you the difference.'

Abi beamed. 'Daddy will love it, won't he?'

Mandy nodded, feeling a little sad that she wouldn't be there to see him open it. 'Yes,' she said. 'I'm sure he will.'

Chapter Twenty-four

Though she had enjoyed the twins' company, Mandy had a feeling of relief as they headed back to the central arcade where they had agreed to meet Belle. Neither Abi nor Max had mentioned the fact that she wasn't living at Wildacre any more, and Mandy hoped they could wait until after Christmas. She didn't want them to be upset and spoil the festivities.

'Will you be at Wildacre for Christmas?' Max asked, startling her to a standstill.

Mandy looked down at him. His face was anxious, his eyes wide. Mandy forced herself to smile. 'I'm not sure,' she said, choosing her words carefully.

'Don't you and Daddy love each other any more?' Abi said.

Mandy felt on firmer ground with that. 'We still like each other very much,' she said. 'But grown-up lives can be complicated. We have to make sure we want the same things.' Abi looked confused. 'It's a bit like you trying to be friends with someone who wants to spend all their time playing computer games, when you'd rather be outside,' Mandy explained.

Abi nodded, but Max was frowning. 'But you and Daddy both like being outside,' he pointed out.

'We do,' Mandy agreed sadly.

'Hello!' Mandy was rescued by Belle appearing. 'Have you had a nice time?' she asked and Abi and Max started showing her what they had bought in a flurry of carrier bags.

'I'm off now, you two,' Mandy said. She bent down and gave them each a hug. 'Be good for your mum. I'll see you before Christmas, I'm sure.'

'With our presents?' Abi checked, and Mandy wanted to laugh at her hopeful face.

'That's not very polite . . .' Belle began.

But Mandy smiled. 'Of course there'll be presents,' she said.

Mandy had to rush back to the car because her parking ticket had almost run out. She placed her gifts in the back seat and headed towards Welford. Although it was only lunchtime, the sky had clouded over and it was starting to get dark. Brightly coloured lights flashed from garden plants and there were Christmas trees in almost every window.

A car pulled out from under the wooden Animal Ark sign as Mandy turned in. The woman who was driving lifted a hand and Mandy lifted hers in return. Morning surgery must have run over, she guessed.

Geraldine's car had gone. Mandy decided to do a last check of the animals before heading back to Six Oaks. She was walking back from the rescue centre when Adam opened the front door of the cottage and waved to her. 'Come in for some lunch! I'm making cheese and pickle toasties.'

Mandy was desperate to make an excuse, but nothing came to her. With a sickly smile, she kicked off her boots at the door and followed him into the kitchen. Emily was laying the table. 'Hello, sweetheart. Lovely to see you.'

'I'll give you a hand,' Mandy offered, and went over to the cutlery drawer before Emily had time to refuse.

'The toasties are ready,' Adam announced as Mandy laid out plates. Mandy kept her eyes on her food and concentrated on chewing. The toast seemed to stick in her throat and she took frequent sips of water to wash it down. The clock on the kitchen wall ticked away the time in long, slow seconds. Mandy found herself wishing lunch was over and she could escape.

Five minutes in, Adam sat back in his chair and set his toastie on his plate. Mandy saw him glance at Emily. She felt herself stiffening. This was it, she thought. They were going to insist that she told them what was wrong.

'There's something we want to mention,' Adam said. Mandy noticed that her hands were shaking. She put down her toastie and shoved them between her knees. 'It's about a couple that were here just before you arrived,' Adam said. 'Maybe you passed them on the way out?'

Mandy nodded, feeling confused.

'They called into the clinic to register their new cat,' Adam went on.

'That's good, surely?' Mandy said. She looked at him, trying to work out what he was trying to say. 'We've got room on the list for new clients, haven't we?'

'It *would* be good . . .' Emily was speaking now, '. . . except that they don't have their cat yet. They said they're adopting one from Hope Meadows. I know things haven't been great communication-wise recently . . .' She looked as if she wanted to say more but was restraining herself, '. . . but usually you tell us when you're working on an adoption.'

Mandy frowned. 'What were their names? I don't have any new adopters at the moment. I usually don't let animals go this close to Christmas in case they are unwanted presents.'

'That's what I thought,' Adam said. He sighed and fiddled with his knife. 'It seems they visited for the first time today, and Geraldine said they could have one of the cats. They've fallen in love with Sixpence and think they'll be able to pick him up in the next couple of days.'

Mandy stared at Adam. She would never tell anyone they could have an animal before the house visit. 'They must have misunderstood what Geraldine told them,' she said.

'They seemed pretty certain.' Emily's voice was gentle. 'Geraldine had helped them fill in the forms.'

Mandy clasped her hands together under the table. 'Did they say anything about a home visit?'

Adam made a wry face. 'Apparently Geraldine said you'd do that on Sunday, but it would only be a formality as they sounded perfect.'

Mandy shut her eyes for a moment. Geraldine was obviously trying to help, but if this was all true, she had definitely overstepped the mark. At least she hadn't just handed out one of the animals, Mandy told herself.

Adam's voice broke into her thoughts. He was looking very serious, the way he had looked when Mandy had done something wrong as a child. 'I'm sorry, love, I know it's difficult,' he said, 'but Geraldine hasn't been here all that long. It sounds like she's taken on too much responsibility. She needs to understand that it's not just a case of finding willing owners. We have to put the animals' needs first.'

'Geraldine knows that!' Mandy objected.

'Well, she's only worked here for a very short time,' Emily said. 'It's great that she's keen but perhaps you shouldn't leave her in sole charge just yet?'

Mandy swallowed. 'I only went shopping. I trust Geraldine. I can't be here all day every day.'

Adam raised his eyebrows. 'We're not suggesting that, love. Just that you need to be a bit less trusting, perhaps. Nicole was different, we knew she was younger so we didn't give her too much responsibility. But Geraldine's more mature. Perhaps you feel that she can handle things that she's not ready for. I mean, you hardly know her.'

Mandy's hands had formed into fists under the table. She could hear her blood ringing in her ears. 'So now you're blaming me,' she said. She glanced from Emily to Adam. 'You're way out of line, both of you.' She took a breath. 'It does sound like she's overstepped the mark a bit, but nothing that can't be sorted out. I'll ring the people who came today and talk to them. This is not Geraldine's fault.' Her voice rose as she spoke.

Emily stretched her hand towards Mandy. Her eyes were troubled. 'Calm down, sweetheart. We're on your side. I'm sure Geraldine meant well, but you have to make it clear to her that she can't be responsible for rehoming animals. I love that you are so eager to trust people, but you just need to be a bit more careful. We both think so.' She glanced across the table at Adam, who smiled encouragingly.

Mandy could feel the rage flowing through her, right down to her fingertips. How could they talk to her about trust? How dare they? 'If I am too eager to trust people, it's down to you.' Mandy was startled by the coldness in her voice. 'After all, I trusted you and Dad, didn't I? When you told me my parents were killed in a car accident when I was a baby? You knew that wasn't true, didn't you? Both of you.'

She took a deep breath, trying to get her feelings under control. Emily's face had gone very white and Adam's was red. He looked as if he was choking.

'Who . . . who told you that?' Emily stammered. 'You weren't supposed to know . . .'

Adam seemed to have frozen in his seat. He opened his mouth, but no words came out.

Mandy looked from Adam to Emily and back again. Tears were spilling down her face, but when she spoke her voice was steady. 'Geraldine told me,' she said. 'Geraldine is my mother.'

If they had been shocked before, Adam and Emily now looked as if they had been shot. Mandy felt a feeling of dread creep over her. At that moment, if she could have taken back the words, let them believe that they had kept their secret, she might have chosen to do so. But there was no way back now.

'Geraldine knew I'd been adopted by a couple in Yorkshire who were vets. She . . . she also knew your name. She's known where I am for years, and she finally decided to come and find me. She wanted to know if . . . if I was okay.' She couldn't look at the devastated faces on the other side of the table. She rearranged her knife on her plate. 'She visited Hope Meadows and we got on well and when she saw my advert, she volunteered to help out, and . . . well, here we are, I guess.'

'When did she tell you who she was?' Adam sounded as if he had a lump of toast stuck in his throat.

'A few days ago. I found some clippings about Hope Meadows in her room and asked her about them.' Mandy realised the red mist was rising behind Adam's eyes. She knew exactly how that felt, and she braced herself for the explosion.

'That's not the way she should have gone about it!' He banged his hands on the table. 'There are procedures for this. She should have got in touch with Social Services so they could ask you if you were willing to make contact.'

Mandy shook her head. She was calm now, almost unnaturally so. 'What difference does it make? She told me she waited and waited for me to try to get in touch, but I couldn't have done that, could I? Because I didn't know she existed.' She stared into their horrified eyes. 'Geraldine told me everything. How she and my father were drug addicts and the Social Services wouldn't let her keep me. They could have helped her, but they took me away instead.' She stopped. A wave of pain was rising inside her, but she put her hands flat on the table, pressing down hard with her fingertips. 'You know, you were half-right about one thing,' she said, glancing up at them. 'My father did die. From a drug overdose.'

Emily gasped. Adam thrust his chair back and for a moment, Mandy thought he would storm out, but instead he started to clear the plates away, his movements jerky. He threw the knives into the dishwasher, then turned slowly and rested his hands on the table, face thrust forwards.

'Then you'll know why we didn't tell you the truth, won't you?' he growled. 'I won't call them your parents.

Neither of them were fit for that. They were drug addicts! You were so sick when we brought you home, and it was all because of them. You were born addicted to heroin, did you know that? You could have died! Paint it whichever way you like, but she lied to you too. She was beyond help. Staying with your birth mother was never an option.'

Mandy held his gaze, though inside she was shaking. 'But Geraldine wasn't beyond help,' she said. 'She got herself clean, went to university and works as a therapist. How could you have written her off?' she whispered. 'She was barely a child herself! She told me that as soon as she saw me she wanted to get herself clean, to be a proper mother. But instead of helping her, they took me away. She's been searching for me ever since.'

Adam's mouth was a thin line, and now Mandy could see the pain behind his anger. 'And what about you?' he said. 'Did you want to be found? Do you think she has your best interests at heart, or is this still all about her?'

Emily laid her hand on Adam's forearm, as if to calm him down. 'Does she have other children?' she asked.

'I don't think so. I mean, she hasn't mentioned it.' Mandy winced. Surely Geraldine would have told her if she had brothers and sisters? Why hadn't she asked? How could she still know so little?

Emily shook her head, her face hollow with sadness. 'I'm glad Geraldine is well,' she said. 'Really I am.

Of course I knew she . . . I knew her circumstances when we went through the adoption. But it was a closed adoption, Mandy. Geraldine didn't ask to stay in touch with you, and we agreed it was best for you to have a fresh start.'

Mandy swallowed. 'I can see why you might think that, but you didn't have to lie.'

Adam sighed. 'Maybe not,' he said, 'but please believe me when I tell you we did what we thought was right at the time. We didn't want you to grow up wondering why you'd been abandoned, hoping that one day your biological parents would appear and sweep you away.'

Mandy frowned. 'That's not what Geraldine is doing.'

'No,' Emily said. 'She isn't.' There was so much sadness in her voice that Mandy could scarcely bear to hear it.

Adam sat down and put his head in his hands. 'We couldn't have loved you any more than we did,' he said, his voice muffled. 'And we love you just as much as we ever did. You were our daughter from the moment we set eyes on you, the answer to all our prayers, the most perfect little girl we could have imagined.'

Mandy felt her mouth twist angrily. Was he not even able to listen to himself? 'Really?' she said, and she could hear the bitterness in her voice. 'I was addicted, wasn't I? Hardly perfect! That must have been hell for you.'

Emily shook her head. 'Your dad's telling the truth,'

she said. 'It was a challenge, but we knew from the start it was worth it.'

'What would you have done if I had been permanently affected?' Mandy argued. 'How did you know I'd make a full recovery?'

Adam lowered his hands and smiled at her. 'We didn't,' he admitted. 'But it wouldn't have mattered. We already loved you so much, we knew we would love you and care for you, however things turned out.'

'But how could you be so sure?' Mandy whispered. 'You didn't see me the moment I was born. You didn't know who my parents were, my grandparents, where I truly came from. How did you know?'

Emily's eyes were filled with tears. She reached across the table and took Mandy's cold fingers in hers. 'You're right,' she said. 'We didn't know all those things. But we had you and that was all that mattered. You were there in our hearts. It's where you've always been.'

Mandy pulled her hand away. 'I'm sorry,' she said. 'I know you did what you thought was right, and I can see how much you loved me. I had the most wonderful childhood anyone could hope for. But you *lied to me*. And now . . . now I don't know what to think.' She pushed back her chair. 'I need to go,' she said. 'Can I have some leave, please? I'll be here for Hope Meadows, but I don't think I can face doing clinics at the moment. Is that okay?'

She saw a flash of panic cross Emily's face, but Adam said heavily, 'Whatever you want. We can handle Hope

Meadows too, if you want to get away. We'll be waiting here for you if you need anything. Always.'

Mandy could hear the devastation in his voice, but she told herself not to give in. 'I don't need you to look after Hope Meadows,' she said. 'I'm not going away, but I need some time and space. Please don't try to contact me.' She glanced at them both one more time, then turned and walked to the door. With a deep breath, she pushed down the handle and stepped out into the cold air.

Chapter Twenty-five

Mandy's eyes were blurred with tears as she drove towards Six Oaks. Heavy clouds had covered the sky and though it was only mid afternoon, it was almost dark. All she wanted was to curl up in bed with Sky and stay there forever. When her phone began to ring, she almost ignored it, but then with a sigh she pulled over and picked it up.

It was Jimmy and she sat there for a long moment, looking at the screen, feeling torn. Much as she wanted the comfort of his voice, it didn't feel right to pour out her problems to him. Reminding herself that she didn't need to drag him into the tangled mess of her life, she took a deep breath and pressed reply. 'Hello,' she said. In spite of her efforts, her voice was high and wavering.

There was a very brief pause. 'What's happened?' His voice was so gentle that Mandy's good intentions fled.

'I told my folks . . . I mean, Adam and Emily.'

'Shall I come over?' he offered.

Mandy fought with herself for only a second. 'Yes, please,' she said. 'I'll be at Six Oaks.'

It started to rain as she drove into the yard. Paul

was wheeling a barrow of hay nets across the yard as she climbed out of the car, but to Mandy's relief he just nodded at her and carried on towards the stables. She made a dash for the kitchen door and pushed it open. It was a relief to be inside away from the stingingly cold shower. The stove was lit and the kitchen was warm. Mandy peeled off her wet jacket and hung it over a wooden chair. There was a scrawled note on the table: *Hot date with that sexy farrier from Ripon!!!!! Free shoeing forever!!! Ice-skating by the cathedral then dinner and . . . ? Don't wait up!*

Despite the general awfulness of everything, Mandy smiled. *Never change, Molly*, she thought. Putting the message back on the table, she switched on the kettle to make tea. She collected a few dirty mugs and moved them into the dishwasher, then straightened the tea towels on the Aga rail, finding comfort in small tasks.

The kitchen was almost tidy by the time Jimmy pulled up in the yard. He strode into the kitchen and held out his arms. Without thinking about it, Mandy walked into his embrace and leaned her head on his chest. It felt safe and secure and wonderful as he held her close.

'Thanks for coming,' she said, pulling away slightly to look up at him. 'And I'm sorry. I know I shouldn't have asked you to come . . .'

'Hush.' Jimmy lifted a hand and stroked her hair and for a moment, she thought he was going to kiss her, but he smiled instead. 'You can still call me, if you need to. I'd always help a friend.'

A stab of cold pierced the warmth he had wrapped around her. *A friend* . . . Mandy stood very still. You have to get used to this, she told herself. This is how it is now.

There was a tentative knock on the door. Sky began to bark and Mandy went over to open it.

Paul was standing on the doorstep. The rain had stopped but his hair was slicked to his head and there was an anxious look on his face. 'It's Bill,' he said. 'Can you come, please . . . his breathing . . . he doesn't look right.'

Mandy grabbed her wellies and slipped them onto her feet. 'On my way,' she said.

Bill was standing in the middle of his stable. His neck was stretched out, his eyes wide and alarmed, and his breath was coming in gasps so heavy he was almost groaning. Paul undid the stable rug with unsteady fingers. When he slipped the rug off, Mandy was shocked. The weight seemed to have dropped off the big horse. The hollows above his eyes had deepened and the hair over his ribs was standing out as he strained to breathe.

Paul stood beside Bill, stroking his nose. 'It's all right, old lad,' he murmured and Bill's ear twitched.

'He doesn't look good,' Jimmy said. He had shut Sky and Bertie in the kitchen and followed Mandy across the yard.

'No.' Mandy narrowed her eyes, assessing the poor creature. 'But we knew this was coming,' she added sadly. 'I need to get in touch with Molly. She'll want to be here.' She rushed back indoors, grabbed her phone from the table and punched in Molly's number.

Molly was laughing as she answered. She sounded breathless and happy. 'Hello?'

'I'm sorry to disturb you,' Mandy began.

'Mandy!' Molly squealed down the phone. 'Are you coming to join us? We're having a fab time.'

Mandy took a deep breath. 'I'm really sorry. I'm afraid it's Bill.'

There was silence on the other end of the line. Mandy could hear voices in the background but they faded. Then Molly's voice came again, somewhere quieter. 'Is it time?'

'Yes,' Mandy replied. There was a tight feeling across her forehead, but she felt very calm.

'On my way,' Molly said. 'I'll be there in thirty minutes.'

Mandy hurried back to the stable. Bill was still struggling to breathe. His respiration was rapid and shallow. Mandy often sedated animals before she euthanised them, but there was no way she could sedate Bill because it would affect his blood circulation or worsen his breathing. She had to give Molly a chance to get there first.

'Molly will be here in half an hour,' she told Paul and Jimmy. 'I'm going to give Bill some injections to see if we can make him more comfortable.'

'Wouldn't it be better if we could get him to lie down?' Jimmy asked.

Mandy shook her head. 'He won't lie down now. Not while he's distressed like that. He's already struggling to breathe and lying down would put even more pressure on his lungs.'

It was raining again. Wrapping her arms around herself, Mandy went to her car and pulled out several bottles. She would give him steroids, she decided, as well as a non-steroidal anti-inflammatory. She wouldn't use them together for an animal in good health, but for now they might help. She added in a dose of clenbuterol to open up Bill's airways and put a catheter on the growing pile. She could put a line into his vein before Molly arrived.

When she returned to the stable, Paul was still at Bill's head. 'Are you okay to hold him?' she asked. 'I'm going to put a catheter in his vein. It'll stay in so I can inject him safely. Then I'm going to give him something to help his breathing.'

Paul nodded and unhooked a huge leather headcollar from the wall. He slipped it over Bill's nose and buckled it loosely.

To Mandy's relief, the catheter slid into place without difficulty. She taped it in place, then drew up the injections. 'Good boy,' she murmured to Bill. He didn't flinch as she produced the syringes one by one and injected them quietly. Paul kept smoothing the hair on Bill's neck as the horse's gasping breaths gradually quietened.

It was just over the half hour when Molly arrived.

There was a screech of wheels on the yard and a moment later, Molly rushed in. She was wearing high-heeled boots, skinny jeans and a faux-fur gilet over a cashmere polo neck, but she seemed not to care as she plunged into the straw. She wrapped her arms around Bill's neck and laid her cheek on his soft coat. 'Poor old boy,' she murmured. 'It's all right. I'm here. You're safe.' She turned to look at Mandy. 'He seems so calm,' she said.

'I've given him some injections to help his breathing,' Mandy explained, 'but he was in a bad way when I called. He's comfortable now, but I think the time has come.'

'Okay.' Molly's mouth crumpled for a moment, but she pulled herself together. 'What do you need me to do?'

'Stay with him, but get ready to jump out of the way. I can't sedate him, but with the injection I'm using, he should hopefully go down gently.'

There were tears in Molly's eyes, but she nodded. Mandy gave Molly's shoulder a squeeze, then pulled out the first syringe from her pocket.

Molly held Bill's face between her hands and kissed his nose. His ears twitched forwards and he wobbled his top lip at her. 'Good boy, good old boy, good boy, it's all going to be okay,' Molly said, over and over, like the softest lullaby.

Mandy attached the syringe to the catheter and began to inject as smoothly as she could. The big syringe was unwieldy, difficult to press home, but she kept pushing on the plunger until it was empty. Removing the first syringe, she picked up the second.

Molly was still talking, sing-song gentle. 'Good old boy, best boy ever.'

Mandy looked up at Bill's calm face as she pushed home the final dose. 'You're so good,' she murmured, putting a hand on his neck. The horse blinked once and then his eyes widened. Slowly, very slowly, his legs began to buckle and he dropped onto the straw. With one last sighing breath, he lay his head down and was still.

Molly knelt beside him, cradling his head. 'Sleep well, my precious,' she gasped. There were tears on her cheeks and as she watched, Mandy felt tears in her own eyes, but she stayed where she was. Though she had loved Bill too, this was Molly's time with him. She reached into her pocket for her stethoscope. Carefully, so as not to disturb Molly, she moved to Bill's side and put the stethoscope against his barrel-like chest. She listened to the silence with relief. His heart had stopped and he was at peace.

She felt a warm hand on her shoulder. When she turned, Jimmy was standing behind her. Without thinking, she reached up her own hand to hold his. After a moment, she stood up. Her legs felt stiff and she leaned on Jimmy as she stumbled. She sent him a quick smile, thanking him with her eyes, and he nodded.

Paul picked up Bill's stable rug. Tenderly, he pulled

it over the huge body, then gave a twisted smile. 'He always liked to be warm,' he said. He looked at Molly, who had pushed herself to her feet. 'Shall I ring Brandon Gill?' he offered.

Molly nodded and Paul let himself quietly out of the stable. 'Brandon always comes and buries my horses for me,' Molly explained. 'He knows where I want Bill to go. He's got a big enough digger to cope with the cold ground, fortunately.' As ever, she seemed to take comfort in practicality, though Mandy could see the sadness in her eyes.

'Brandon's a good guy,' Jimmy said. His voice was filled with sympathy.

Guessing that Molly needed a last few minutes with Bill, Mandy opened the door and left with Jimmy. She paused to glance back into the stable. In the faint glow of the electric light, Molly was bent over Bill's head, running her hands over his gleaming neck.

With a lump in her throat, Mandy made her way to the kitchen. Jimmy put on the kettle and started to make a pot of tea. Mandy sat down at the table, watching him move round the room. Now that there was nothing else for her to do, she felt utterly drained.

'Tough day for you,' Jimmy remarked softly.

'Not the best,' Mandy agreed. 'It was pretty awful, talking to Adam and Emily. I wish it had gone better, but at least it's out now.'

Jimmy poured the tea into a mug and set it on the table in front of her. He sat down and looked into her eyes, his expression serious. 'I know it's difficult for you,' he began, 'but it must be hard for Adam and Emily, too.'

Mandy felt her body stiffen. 'It's . . .' she began, but he held up his hand.

'Harder for you? Of course it is. But never underestimate how much they love you. They've been there for you for a long time.' He pushed the mug of tea towards her.

Mandy took a sip. It was strong and sweet. Jimmy must have put sugar in it. 'Geraldine loves me too,' she said. 'She's loved me all my life without even knowing me.' She stared at him, willing him to understand.

'She has,' Jimmy agreed. 'That's what happens when you're a parent. At least that was how it was for me. All this love just bursts into life the moment your child is born.' He smiled. 'It's like your heart suddenly belongs to someone else, this tiny creature who is completely, utterly dependent on you. It must have been awful for Geraldine to lose you. I can't imagine how that must have felt.' He drew in a long breath. 'But I can imagine how Adam and Emily felt when they first held you. There's nothing like wanting a baby more than anything else in the world.'

Mandy swallowed. 'However much they loved me, I wish they hadn't lied,' she said, running the tip of her finger along a crack in the table.

'Right now, I bet they do too,' Jimmy pointed out.

'We all make mistakes. Everybody does. But most things can be forgiven, I think.'

Mandy felt the muscles in her jaw working. She stood up and put her empty mug on the side. 'I know it should be possible to forgive them,' she admitted. 'I just don't feel like I can. Not yet.'

Jimmy stood up too. 'I do understand,' he said. 'And I think Adam and Emily will understand too. But this is the middle of the storm, right? And one thing you do when a storm is raging is stay exactly where you are. No rash moves, no dramatic decisions. Just hold on until the wind dies down. Okay?'

Mandy nodded. His words made sense. For now, she needed to stop and wait.

'The right time will come,' he promised.

She managed to smile, though her voice trembled as she spoke. 'No rash moves,' she echoed. 'I think I can manage that.'

Chapter Twenty-six

Mandy wanted to believe that having everything in the open might ease the situation a little, but she was still apprehensive as she drove towards Animal Ark the next day. The car park was empty when she arrived and she was glad when nobody appeared from the cottage as she drew up.

She had texted Geraldine yesterday evening, telling her that she had spoken to Adam and Emily. It was better that Geraldine stayed away until the situation was resolved, Mandy decided, but she had promised that she would go to Barn End Cottage after the morning routine.

As she went into the reception area, she saw a white envelope on the desk. Frowning, she walked over and picked it up. Her name was written on the envelope in Emily's beautiful handwriting. She tore it open and unfolded the single sheet of paper.

'My dear Mandy,' it said. 'I am so sorry we lied to you about your biological parents. I know it was a mistake. But please know that your father and I love you more than anything else in the world, and would never have done *anything to hurt you. We could not be more proud of the young woman you have become, and we will always be here for you. We will wait for you to come to us, though, as you asked. All our love, Mum and Dad xxx'.*

Mandy sat down at the desk, holding the paper tightly in her fingers. She lifted the note, read it again, then put it down and sat back in the chair with a sigh. A moment later, she felt a cold nose being pushed into her empty hand. Sky was sitting right on Mandy's foot. The little collie put her head in Mandy's lap and gazed up with her soulful eyes. As Mandy reached out a hand to stroke her ears, her furry tail began wagging softly on the stone floor. 'I'm glad you're here,' Mandy murmured, and Sky's tail flicked back and forth a little faster.

She glanced at the letter one last time, then folded it up and slipped it back into its envelope. The letter had come from Emily's heart, that much she could tell. But however much Adam and Emily loved her, she couldn't pretend that nothing had changed. The knowledge of what had happened in the past had altered everything. They couldn't just go back.

She caught sight of someone walking past the window, and for a moment, she felt a stab of panic. Hadn't Geraldine got her message to stay away? But the door opened and Helen walked in, smiling gently, her eyes filled with compassion. 'Molly called me and told me about Bill,' she said. 'I thought you might like some company.' She walked over to Mandy and they hugged. Helen had been fond of Bill too, Mandy knew. 'Seb's outside,' Helen went on. 'He's looking at the alpacas and he said he'd be happy to exercise the dogs if you like.'

Mandy was grateful for their quiet thoughtfulness. 'That would be great,' she said.

'Is everything okay?' Helen asked as they stood side by side in the small furries' room, cleaning out the guinea pigs' cage. 'Other than Bill and Jimmy, I mean? You've been awfully quiet lately.'

Mandy shook her head. 'I'm not really okay, no, but it's something private I need to deal with.'

Helen reached out and squeezed Mandy's shoulder. 'I'm here if you want to talk,' she said. 'Any time.'

Mandy knew she meant it. 'Thanks,' she said.

The drive to Barn End Cottage took Mandy through the centre of Welford. It wasn't just the pub looking festive now. A tall Christmas tree had been erected on the green, laden with white lights and oversized blue baubles. A crowd of people were gathered around it singing, all muffled up in coats and scarves. Reverend Hadcroft was among them, his greying hair shining under the lights, and he waved at Mandy. As she drove past, she caught the cheery strains of 'The Holly and the Ivy' and she drove onwards feeling a little brighter.

By the time she arrived at Barn End, threatening clouds hung over the fells and the wind was rising. As she drew up, Geraldine appeared in the doorway and Mandy's heart lifted. Geraldine opened her arms as Mandy walked towards her and a huge smile lit up her face. Without hesitation, Mandy hugged her and this time it felt warm and easy and wholly right.

Geraldine released her arms first. There was warmth in her eyes as she looked at Mandy. 'Thanks for letting me know what happened,' she said. 'I know this must be difficult for you.' She paused, tilting her head. 'I'm so glad I found you, but I'm sorry it's brought so many problems.'

'Don't be sorry,' Mandy said. 'It isn't your fault that someone else lied. I'm still thrilled that you found me.'

They walked inside together and sat down. 'So what now?' Geraldine asked. 'I'm glad you told me about Adam and Emily,' she added, 'and thank you for coming, but are you sure you want to do this now? If you need space, you should take it. I've waited all these years to get to know you and I can wait a bit longer if you need.'

No rash moves. Jimmy's words came back to her. But what did that mean right now? Stay or go? Each one required a decision.

As if sensing her discomfort, Geraldine pushed back her chair and stood up. She grabbed her coat from behind the door. 'I fancy a quick walk while the rain's still holding off,' she said. 'How about you?'

Even Jimmy couldn't object to some fresh air and exercise, Mandy thought. 'Great idea,' she replied.

They strode up the hillside on a narrow track. Sky raced in circles around them; a streak of black and white, excited by the gusty wind. Though the track was steep, Geraldine matched Mandy's long stride step for step. They were both breathing hard by the time they reached the top of the ridge. They stopped and looked down over the valley. A long line of houses marked the main road into Walton, but Welford was still the same huddle of stone houses and grey slate roofs that Mandy remembered as a child.

Geraldine turned to Mandy. 'I'm starting to realise what people mean when they describe Yorkshire as God's Own Country,' she said. 'Even in winter it's beautiful.'

Mandy grinned. 'It sounds as if you've brought your rose-tinted spectacles,' she said. 'Like anywhere, it can be pretty grim when the weather's bad.'

Geraldine glanced at the sky as a gust of wind lifted her hair. 'Speaking of weather, if those clouds get any lower, we're going to get very wet.'

The clouds were indeed piling up over the Beacon, but the wind was coming from the west. 'It won't rain yet,' Mandy said. 'Not here, anyway. Not unless the wind drops.'

Geraldine looked at Mandy with her head on one side. 'You think not?'

'Pretty sure,' Mandy said.

There was fascination in Geraldine's eyes. 'It must be amazing to know so much about the place you live,' she said. 'Natural things like the wildlife and the weather, I mean.'

Mandy smiled. 'I didn't set out to learn it,' she admitted. 'Just picked it up over the years.' There was a stab of memory: Adam standing on a rock near the top of a fell, pointing at the sky, describing the clouds. She pushed the thought aside. 'James and I were out in all kinds of weather. We used to go all over the place, just him and me and his labrador Blackie,' she told Geraldine.

'It sounds like the pair of you roamed wild,' Geraldine said. 'Were you really allowed to go wherever you wanted?'

Again, Mandy felt a prickle of unrest. She couldn't tell whether there was a veiled criticism of Adam and Emily in what Geraldine had just said. She had never felt in danger when she was rambling the countryside as a child. 'It might seem risky now,' she said, 'but Adam and Emily taught us how to keep ourselves safe and we always let them know where we were going.'

Geraldine seemed to read the wariness in her tone. 'I didn't mean to criticise them,' she assured Mandy. A wistful look came into her bright blue eyes. 'It must have been wonderful growing up with the whole of the Dales as your playground.'

Mandy nodded. 'It was a fabulous place to grow up,' she agreed.

They walked along the edge of the ridge, stopping

now and then to navigate the stepping stones and narrow gaps that were built into the drystone walls. The wind picked up until it was snatching their words and they had to shout to make themselves heard. Mandy was glad when the track sloped down into a sheltered patch of woodland.

'I've been wanting to ask,' she began hesitantly. 'Do you . . . I mean, we . . . have any more family?'

Geraldine nodded. She seemed pleased Mandy had asked. 'I have a brother,' she said, 'your uncle. He's called Leo.'

'Does he know about me?' Mandy made herself ask. They were walking single file down a narrow path through the trees and she strained her ears to hear the reply.

'Of course he does.' Geraldine looked over her shoulder with a smile. 'You've never been a secret. He's already told me he'd love to meet you. He's a dentist and he lives in Macclesfield, near Manchester.'

Mandy felt a rush of joy. Adam and Emily were only children. Mandy had always felt it would have been lovely to have had an aunt or uncle.

'You have three cousins too,' Geraldine went on. 'Leo and his wife have three boys: Charlie, Thomas and Patrick. They're . . .' She paused for a moment, frowning. '. . . twenty-three, twenty and eighteen, I think. Lovely boys, though Thomas made his mother's hair turn white when he was a teenager.'

Mandy was finding it hard to take everything in. She

wanted to shout out loud, sing carols to the trees, dance like Harriet's toddlers at the Christmas party. She didn't just have a mother. She had a whole family, proper blood relatives. She wondered what her new family would think of her, what they were like. 'I'd love to meet them all,' she said.

'That would be fabulous. I'll fix something up when I get back. They'll all be around for Christmas, I'm sure,' Geraldine said. 'There's no rush to decide,' she went on, 'but would . . . would you consider spending Christmas with me in Manchester?'

The question took Mandy by surprise. Though she had enjoyed seeing Welford's decorations and had loved shopping with the twins, she had been trying not to think about Christmas Day. It hadn't crossed her mind that she might spend it with Geraldine. She couldn't imagine spending it at Animal Ark now and Jimmy was out of bounds, so she had no easy excuse, but the idea of being paraded in front of a whole new family over the festive season was overwhelming.

She took a deep breath. 'Ummm . . . I'll think about it,' she said.

Geraldine nodded. 'Well, the offer's there,' she said. 'They'd all love to have you, I know that.'

There was a volley of barking and Mandy looked around. Sky had disappeared but a moment later she burst out of a rocky gully. She stopped in front of Mandy and barked again. 'What's up, girl? What have you found?' Mandy walked over to the gully and started to scramble down into the narrow trench with Geraldine close behind her.

'Ugh!' Geraldine exclaimed as a soggy white bundle emerged from the bracken at the bottom. 'Is that a dead sheep?'

Mandy nodded. 'It is, poor thing. I'll ring Bert Burnley when we get back,' she said. 'Pretty sure she'll be one of his on this fellside.'

They headed back up through the wood and down the hill. As they walked, Geraldine linked her arm with Mandy's. 'Thanks for coming out with me,' she said. She stopped and turned to look at Mandy as if drinking her in. 'I can't believe I'm walking with my daughter,' she said faintly. She had tears in her eyes. 'I've never been happier in my life!'

Mandy smiled back, but the memory of Adam and Emily had slipped back into her conscience. She stared across the valley, trying to spot the roof of Animal Ark on the far side of the village. Had she ruined everything for two of the people who loved her most? What about their happiness?

When they reached Barn End Cottage, Geraldine unlocked the door and turned to Mandy. 'You will come in, won't you? It'd be lovely to have a coffee together. I've bought a Christmas cake too, if you'd like a piece.

Mandy nodded, but waved her mobile. 'I'm just going to ring Mr Burnley about the sheep,' she said. 'Better reception out here.'

'See you in a minute,' Geraldine warbled and headed inside.

Bert, like most Yorkshire farmers, was stoical in his response. 'Thanks for letting me know, lass. I'll be collecting the rest in anyway in a day or two. Supposed to be snow by the end of the week.'

He rang off and Mandy put the phone back into her pocket. She opened the door, kicked off her boots and walked into the kitchen. There was a plate in the middle of the table piled with fruit cake and the kettle was coming to the boil. Geraldine was sitting at the table with a pen and paper. She looked up when Mandy came in, her face flushed with excitement.

'Do you have a favourite alternative to turkey?' she asked. 'I could do a nut roast, perhaps? Leo and the boys are very traditional but Leo's wife Janet – you'll love her, she's a sweetheart – is practically vegetarian.'

Mandy stood very still as a chill crept over her.

'Any strong feelings about Christmas pudding?' Geraldine went on, looking down at her paper. 'I know some people can't stand it but I have to have it as an option. Oh, and don't worry about buying presents for everyone. They won't expect it, and I'll warn them not to go overboard for you, though I know Leo will ignore me!' She stood up, seeming to mistake the shock on Mandy's face for excitement. 'I can't wait!' she said. 'Our first family Christmas.' She paused. 'I mean, I know you might not be free on Christmas Day, but you will come to Manchester to see everyone, won't you? I'll save my Christmas dinner for then. And you'll have to indulge me and let me do you a stocking.'

Mandy felt the tiniest glimmer of relief. She wasn't going to be paraded like a prize heifer on Christmas Day, then. But Geraldine's enthusiasm was still over-whelming. Mandy's Christmases invariably revolved around being at Animal Ark with Adam and Emily. The idea of trying to recreate that with a family she didn't know was more daunting than exciting.

Geraldine was looking at her, her face bright with happiness, and Mandy felt a nasty sense of unease. If she didn't go, would it spoil everything for Geraldine? It wasn't as if she had any plans of her own, beyond feeding the animals in Hope Meadows. For the past two years, she and Jimmy had spent Christmas Day together. The first year, Adam and Emily had been away, but last year they had all eaten together. Gran and Grandad had joined them in the evening. If Mandy wasn't there, would Adam and Emily have Christmas dinner on their own?

Her phone vibrated in her hand before she could say anything. It was a text from Jimmy: 'Are you free right now? Trapped bird at RW! Need help!'

With a guilty flash of relief, Mandy began to type: 'On my way.' She gave Geraldine what she hoped was a conciliatory smile. 'Sorry,' she said. 'Animal emergency.'

'Oh, that is a shame,' Geraldine said. 'I was hoping we could spend the evening together. I've got a box set of Ealing comedies I thought you might like.' She straightened a tea towel on the rail. 'But I understand. The animals have to come first.'

Mandy was relieved Geraldine hadn't suggested coming with her. 'Let's do that another time,' she said.

'Okay.' Geraldine smiled. 'Call me when you're finished. It'd be lovely to make more festive plans.'

Mandy drove as fast as she dared to Running Wild and pulled into the car park.

'Hi Mandy.' Kimberley, one of Jimmy's assistants, jogged over to her. 'Jimmy said you were coming,' she said breathlessly. 'He's on the far side of the wood. I'll take you. Is there anything you need to bring?'

Mandy gave Sky a handful of food. 'Stay here,' she told the collie. Closing the door, she walked round to the boot and grabbed the rucksack that she kept there for wildlife emergencies. Then she followed Kimberley into the dim green light of the woods.

Though she could hear shouting from people on the ropes course, Mandy didn't see anyone until she caught sight of Jimmy. He was crouched down, facing away from them, near the bottom of a large suspended stretch of netting. It looked like part of the course but it was deserted. He glanced over his shoulder as they approached. 'Come over,' he urged, beckoning. 'Nice and slow.'

'I'll leave you to it,' Kimberley said. She patted Mandy on the shoulder and slipped back into the trees.

Mandy pushed her way through the undergrowth. As she neared the net, she caught a glimpse of something moving. Close to where Jimmy was crouching, a magnificent bird was caught in the ropes. 'Is that an *eagle*?' Mandy breathed.

Jimmy grinned. 'Yep,' he whispered. 'A golden eagle, young 'un by the look of it.'

Mandy couldn't take her eyes off the bird. 'Where has it come from?' There were no local nests that she knew of, and she was sure she would have known if there had been any unexpected sightings.

'Judging by the hood and tresses, a falconry centre,' Jimmy said, 'but other than that, I've no idea.'

Mandy shifted closer. Sure enough, the eagle was wearing a leather hood and there was a thin strip of leather hanging from its leg.

'I've never seen display birds around here before so I reckon he got lost,' Jimmy whispered. 'Maybe he got blown off course. He's a bit battered. I think one of the local kites might have had a go at him. He hasn't got those injuries from being tangled here.'

There was a smear of blood on the ropes and Mandy could see the eagle's leg was injured. Suddenly the huge bird began to flap its wings, struggling to free itself. It let out a shrill call that bounced off the trees.

'Careful!' Mandy exclaimed as she saw the eagle's talons thrashing close to Jimmy's head. She thought fast, recalling everything she knew about handling large birds. 'If we can wrap its head in a cloth and pin its wings to its body, we should be able to slide it backwards out of the net. We could do with some sort of cage to transport it.'

'Will you take it to Animal Ark?' Jimmy asked.

'Not unless it's badly injured. It's best if we can take it back to where it came from. They'll have the facilities to treat minor scrapes. I'm not sure we've even got a cage that would hold it at the rescue centre.'

The mighty wings began to flap again and feathers started to drift into the air, rubbed by the ropes. There was no time to look for a suitable cage. Mandy took a step back, found a clear space and emptied her canvas bag out onto the woodland floor. 'If we can get his wings secured,' she told him, 'I think this bag might be just about big enough to carry him. We just need some fabric to hold him still.'

Without a word, Jimmy took off his coat, then his shirt, then his T-shirt. Though she was trying not to watch, Mandy caught a glimpse of his wonderfully familiar body. The urge to run her hands across his muscular back was almost overwhelming. Jimmy seemed to be all too aware of her eyes on him. He pulled his shirt and coat back on at double speed.

Mandy took a long strip of bandage from her kit. She stood as close to the eagle's head as she dared. Jimmy glanced at Mandy and grinned. 'Does this remind you of anything?'

Mandy frowned. 'What?'

'This is how we first met, rescuing an animal from

a climbing net,' Jimmy prompted. 'Remember the deer?'

Mandy looked at him with a mixture of pleasure and sadness. As if she could ever forget. It was winter now, but back then it had been summer. The woods had been dappled with evening sunlight and a frightened doe had been caught in a spool of net waiting to be put up. How angry she had been with Jimmy when he'd told her about the Outward Bound centre. She had been sure he would destroy the countryside and upset all the local wildlife with his ropes course. She had been so very wrong.

The eagle began to thrash again, and Mandy pushed her bittersweet memories aside. 'Ready?' she whispered to Jimmy and he nodded. 'One, two, three, now!' she breathed.

She quickly wrapped a loop of the bandage around the eagle's beak. She had done it many times before with snapping dogs, but the size and shape of the hooked beak made the task far more difficult. Once she got the loop into place, she tightened it, then wound it round again. In a flash, Jimmy wrapped his T-shirt tightly around the eagle's body, pinning its wings to its side.

The bird had become very still. With infinite care, Jimmy began to pull the sleek body out of the net. He looked surprised as he finally lifted it clear. 'I thought he'd be heavier,' he said.

'Birds have hollow bones,' Mandy reminded him.

She grabbed her bag and held it open while Jimmy slowly slid the eagle inside. As soon as he let go, the eagle began to thrash. Mandy pulled the zip closed, then sat back on her heels, panting. Though it was a thick canvas bag, she was afraid that the eagle might tear it with his talons, but to her relief, the material held and after a few seconds the writhing stopped.

Jimmy puffed out his cheeks. 'This is a new experience. Shall I carry it?'

'Please,' Mandy said. She began to pick up the contents of her bag, pushing them into the plastic carrier that she carried as part of her kit. Then she followed Jimmy back through the undergrowth, watching the eagle swing silently in his unusual transport.

Kimberley was waiting for them in the portacabin. 'I think I've found where he comes from,' she said. 'The falconry centre over at Bells Malton. He's called Sebastopol, apparently.'

'Big name for a big bird,' Mandy commented.

'Certainly is,' Kimberley agreed. 'Anyway, the good news is that someone is on the way to collect him.'

Jimmy seemed a little awkward now that they were no longer alone. He set the bag down in his office and locked and closed the door. 'I'll drop your bag back at Animal Ark,' he said to Mandy. 'I really appreciate you coming over.'

'No problem,' Mandy replied. It felt odd to return to this cold politeness. Only a few minutes ago, they had worked together as if nothing had ever changed. She waited to see if he would say anything else, but he stood beside her looking awkward so Mandy sketched a wave and headed for her car. She sighed as she climbed into the driver's seat. One day, she told herself, I'll be able to meet him and we'll be friends and it will all be normal. But though she tried hard, she couldn't even begin to imagine how that would feel.

She turned the key in the ignition and listened to the engine fire. Look on the bright side, she told herself. Sebastopol's rescue was something exciting to put on the website.

The thought of Hope Meadows brightened her until she remembered tomorrow's home check for the clients that Geraldine had rashly promised could have Sixpence. Mandy let out a low groan. She still needed to talk to Geraldine about the importance of letting Mandy make all rehoming decisions. With a sigh, Mandy put the car in gear and pulled out onto the narrow lane. All she could do was cross her fingers and hope that Geraldine's instincts had been right about these people, the same way she had been with the Andersons and Olive. Though Mandy would still have to talk to her, it would be much easier to do if she didn't have to break bad news to her first.

Chapter Twenty-seven

Mandy picked up the clipboard from the seat beside her to double-check the address Geraldine had written down. It was definitely the right place. She looked up again at the townhouse. It was an attractive Georgian building which had been divided into several flats, if the multiplicity of the doorbells was to be believed. She could see a Christmas tree through the window of one of the ground-floor rooms and there were white lights threaded round one of the smaller windows on the top floor. Not so appealing was the fact that the front door led out onto a busy road. Mandy had been lucky to get a parking space outside.

She climbed out of the car and walked up the steps that led to the door. There were six buzzers outside and she checked her list again. Fiona and Jono Barnes. Theirs was the top buzzer. She pressed on it until the speaker crackled into life. 'Hello?'

'Hi,' Mandy said. 'It's Mandy Hope here from Hope Meadows.'

'Come on up.' The voice that replied sounded cheerful and friendly. 'We're on the top floor, right-hand side.'

Mandy pushed open the door and walked inside. Though the stairwell was bright and clean, she couldn't help feeling concerned as she walked up the three flights of stairs. It wasn't an absolute no-no to have a cat in an apartment where it was difficult or impossible to go outside, but that and the busy road were already ringing alarm bells.

The door swung open as Mandy arrived on the top floor. A short, broad-shouldered woman in her mid-twenties stood in the doorway. She beamed at Mandy. 'Hi, I'm Fiona. Come in.'

Mandy followed her into the narrow hall. 'Jono's through here,' Fiona said over her shoulder. She led Mandy into the kitchen. Though it was small, it was bright and clean.

A tall young man with carefully gelled hair walked over and offered his hand. 'Hi, I'm Jono,' he said. 'It's good to meet you.' He smiled, showing a straight set of very white teeth. 'It was great looking round Hope Meadows the other day. Both of us fell in love with little Sixpence.' His face softened and he glanced round and met Fiona's eye. They shared a smile, then Jono looked back at Mandy. 'I'm making some coffee, would you like some?'

He had warm brown eyes, and Mandy found herself smiling back. No wonder Geraldine had liked them, she thought. She glanced round, thinking for a moment. Normally she would have run through her adoption questionnaire at the rescue centre before carrying out the home check, but now she was here, it might be good to get the inspection done first. Though the lack of outside access was less than ideal, it might still be possible for them to adopt.

'Maybe you could show me round,' she said to Fiona, 'and then we can sit down and have a coffee while we go through some questions.'

'Fine,' Fiona replied. 'Okay with you, Jono?'

Jono nodded and smiled. 'Sounds good to me.'

Fiona showed Mandy around the flat, which didn't take very long. Like the kitchen, the other rooms were small but very clean and well-organised. In the sitting room, Mandy realised that the tasteful Christmas lights she had seen outside belonged to Fiona and Jono. There was a small, rather old-fashioned iron fireplace with a wreath hung over it and in the corner nearest the door there was a Christmas tree on a table.

'I thought we could get a bed for Sixpence in that corner.' Fiona pointed to a cosy space beside the fireplace. 'And I thought we'd get a couple of litter trays for in here and the bathroom. I don't want one in the bedroom or kitchen.' She led Mandy through to the back of the apartment. 'This is the bedroom,' she said, pushing open another door.

The bedroom was even smaller than the sitting room. A wardrobe and a small bedside cabinet on either side of the double bed pretty much filled the room. 'We've already got him a bed in here,' Fiona announced. Her face reddened as she spoke. 'I know Geraldine said we had to wait for the inspection to be absolutely certain, but she seemed to think it would all be fine.'

Mandy spotted a covered cat bed tucked beside the wardrobe. 'It's like the one Sixpence was using already,' Fiona explained. 'We thought he'd feel at home if it was the same.'

'That sounds like a good idea,' Mandy replied. She was starting to relax. So far, the inspection had gone perfectly. Fiona seemed both kind and sensible. Sixpence was a nervous cat, so perhaps an active indoor life would suit him. As long as there was nothing unexpected in the answers to the questionnaire, it looked as if Geraldine's rather rash promise might not backfire.

They sat down at the tiny kitchen table. With all three of them, it was a little tight, but Mandy managed to pull her clipboard and a pen from her bag.

'We're just going to run through some questions,' she told them. 'I'll write down the answers, if that's okay?' Jono and Fiona nodded.

Mandy looked at the list, though she knew the questions off by heart. 'Have you had a cat before?'

Jono and Fiona glanced at one another, then smiled. 'My parents always had cats when we were growing up,' Fiona said.

'No cats,' Jono said, 'but there were always animals around. I had a pet rabbit when I was seven and I had to look after him myself, then after that we had a dog.' He leaned forwards and pushed down the plunger on the cafetière.

'Well, that answers my next question, which was about other animals,' Mandy said, writing furiously. She finished, then sat up, tapping her pen on her knee. 'So why do you want to have a cat?'

Jono looked at Fiona as if it was her turn to respond. 'I was at med school until last year,' Fiona said. 'I knew we couldn't have a pet while I was studying, but I finished in the summer and then we got married. I'm a junior doctor at Ripon Hospital now. We were thinking about a dog, but there are times we both work irregular hours, so we decided a cat might be more suitable.'

Mandy frowned. She would ask more about the irregular hours in a moment, but she wanted to find out a bit more about the couple first. 'And what do you do?' she asked Jono.

'I'm a nurse,' he replied. 'We met when Fiona was on one of her rotations.' He reached out and took Fiona's hand. 'We feel that having a cat will complete our family for now,' he said.

Mandy shifted in her seat and straightened the clipboard in front of her. She looked up and the two friendly smiles met her gaze. 'Can you tell me a bit more about your working patterns?' she said. 'Will someone be here every day? How about overnights?'

For the first time, Fiona began to look uneasy. 'It's not really easy to predict,' she admitted. 'For the next few years, I'm not sure where I'll end up. We can request certain areas, but the NHS can literally send you anywhere. Jono's a bit more settled, but he does night shifts as well. As I said before, we did think about getting a dog, but we knew our lifestyle wouldn't suit a dog just yet. In a few years, things will settle down. But we really hoped that we could get a cat for now. Both of us love animals. It's something we've always wanted.'

Mandy felt her apprehension rising. She wished she could move onto the next question, but she needed to get a straight answer. Lovely as Fiona and Jono were, Sixpence needed a home where there was a consistent routine, and where he wouldn't be left on his own for long periods. 'So . . .' She paused, trying to think how to word her next question. 'So on any given day, would there be someone around for at least part of the time? Or would Sixpence be here sometimes for more than a day on his own?'

She knew Fiona could see where this was going. Her face had turned rather red. Jono was still smiling, but there was tension in his face. Fiona looked at Mandy. 'I'm afraid there might be times when both of us are out all day,' she admitted. 'We both work twelve-hour shifts sometimes. We're not supposed to, of course, but it does happen. Jono's home more than I am because he works in Walton, but I have to drive over to Ripon. Sometimes it's so tiring that it's easier to stay over.' Disappointment shadowed her eyes. 'You're going to say we're not suitable, aren't you?' she said.

Mandy sighed. She liked the couple very much, but there was no way she could bend the rules to fit their situation. 'I'm awfully sorry,' she said, 'but I'm going to have to say that it's not a suitable home. Not for Sixpence, not just now. If one or other of you would be home more often, I'd love to let you have him, but otherwise it really wouldn't be good for him.'

'Is it just Sixpence?' Jono asked. 'Or do you think it wouldn't suit any cat?'

Mandy glanced down at her clipboard for a moment, giving herself time. She looked up and found a sympathetic smile. 'Sixpence is a bit of a special case,' she said. 'He came from a squat, so he had a chaotic life and he needs absolute stability and a regular routine. But to be honest, I think, for now, it wouldn't be the best for you to have a pet. I understand how difficult it is. Really I do. But until one or both of you has a job that has more regular hours, I think it would be better to wait.' She sat back in her chair. She had been worried that Fiona and Jono would take her refusal badly. They both looked sad, but neither seemed angry.

Fiona picked up her coffee, cradling it in her hands. 'I know you're right,' she said, 'but I miss animals so much. I always wanted to be a doctor, but nobody tells you how crazy the first few years are. It'd be so relaxing to have a cat to stroke or a dog to walk. And we thought that any home would be better than being in a rescue centre.'

Mandy swallowed the last of her coffee. 'I understand,' she said. 'It's absolutely nothing personal. In different circumstances, you'd be marvellous cat owners, I'm sure. But for now, it has to be a no.'

There were tears in Fiona's eyes, but she blinked them away.

Mandy gazed at her kind face. 'I don't know if it would help at all,' she said, 'but you would be very welcome to come over to Hope Meadows whenever you're free. I'd love some help walking the dogs and it's vital that plenty of people come in and see the cats. Some of them have never been played with or stroked. If you'd like to come now and then . . .' She stopped, feeling a little embarrassed, hoping that Fiona wouldn't feel it was an imposition to ask for help when she had just turned them down for adoption.

But Fiona's face had brightened. 'Would that really be possible?' she said. 'That would be amazing! I know it's not the same as having a pet of our own, but it would be a lovely thing to do.' She looked at Jono. 'What do you think?'

'Count me in,' Jono replied. 'That way we can help loads of animals rather than just one.'

Mandy wanted to hug him. 'You absolutely would,' she said. 'You don't have to come at any regular time. Just let me know when you have a spare few hours and we'll fit you in.'

Fiona followed Mandy to the door.

'Thanks for showing me round,' Mandy said. 'It's a lovely flat.'

'Thank you,' Fiona said. She pulled open the door. 'Can you pass on my best wishes to the lady who showed us round last week?' She frowned, looking at

Mandy. 'She looked quite like you,' she said. 'Is she your mum?'

Mandy felt a lump rise in her throat. A picture of Emily had risen in her mind so fast that she hadn't been able to stop it. She could hardly say 'kind of', which was the reply that had leaped into her head, and she couldn't bear to start to explain. She decided to ignore the question. 'I'll pass on your thanks,' she said. 'Give me a call next week and we'll fix up a time for you to come in.'

She sketched a wave and turned away before Fiona had time to say anything else. She held onto the rail as she trailed downstairs, then walked over to the car and climbed in. The sense of delight she had felt when Fiona and Jono had agreed to help at Home Meadows had vanished.

How had everything ended up like this? She no longer knew who her parents were. She had fallen out with James; Jimmy and she were trying to form some kind of odd friendship from the ashes of their relationship and she'd hurt Adam and Emily beyond words. To top it off, Geraldine was busy planning the greatest Christmas with a family Mandy had never met. Her world was upside down and she had never felt less Christmassy in her life.

Jimmy had told her not to rush into anything. Not until she was ready. But she couldn't carry on like this, in a weird state of limbo. Putting in the clutch, she put her foot on the accelerator and drove off.

Chapter Twenty-eight

It was still dark when Mandy pulled up at Animal Ark on Monday morning. The weather had changed overnight; suddenly it was properly cold and the air tasted of snow. The lights were on in the kitchen. Though the curtains were closed, Mandy pictured Adam and Emily sitting together at the old scrubbed oak table, eating toast and drinking coffee. For a moment, she felt a yearning to be sitting there with them. So many years of memories, but the past was gone.

She had asked to be free of veterinary work for a week, and Adam had been as good as his word, despite the fact that Christmas was just around the corner. But she had made the decision that one way or another, she had to face them as soon as possible.

With a last glance at the softly glowing window, she crossed the car park to Hope Meadows. Even though Mandy had asked Geraldine to stay away until she'd had a chance to speak to Adam and Emily, she had decided she needed to talk to Geraldine about the disappointing visit to Fiona and Jono as soon as possible. Though it had ended okay on this occasion, it was a situation that should never be repeated. Mandy had asked Geraldine to come in early and meet her in the orchard – she didn't want to risk Geraldine encountering Adam and Emily in the clinic when there was so much that still needed to be discussed.

Mandy had thought very carefully about how to tell Geraldine that she couldn't make decisions about rehoming the animals. Mandy had always taken Adam and Emily's good leadership for granted, she realised. They had been kind and generous to their staff, but when errors were made, they always followed it up. Now she was going to have to do the same. The fact that it was Geraldine who had stepped out of line made it more complicated, but it still needed to be done. Beyond that, she wasn't sure. More than anything, Mandy knew she needed to slow things down. She felt as if her life was rushing out of control, and she had no chance to figure out how she felt about each dramatic change. She had decided that come what may, she wouldn't spend Christmas in Manchester. She didn't know how Geraldine would take it, but Mandy couldn't let her carry on making festive plans that weren't going to come true.

Geraldine was standing under the yellow light outside the field shelter, speaking to the alpacas. Her breath rose in clouds, and she was swathed in knitted hat and scarf. She turned as Mandy approached. 'How did the home check go?' she called.

'Not too bad,' Mandy hedged. 'If you come inside, we can chat about it.'

Geraldine followed her in and unwound the scarf from her neck. She dropped her hat and scarf on the desk and perched on the edge of it.

Mandy cleared her throat. 'You asked about the home check, but first we need to have a chat about protocols,' she began. 'First things first: can you tell me what happened when Fiona and Jono visited the other day?'

Geraldine's face had fallen a little as if she suspected what was coming. 'Well, they came in,' she said, 'and asked about rehoming a cat. I'd seen you asking questions before and I did my best to remember what they were.' Her eyes flicked upwards, as if she was trying to recall the precise conversation. 'I asked about previous pets and some things about their house . . .' She looked back at Mandy. 'Once I'd asked about them and why they wanted a cat, I took them through to see the cats. They looked at Luna, and they seemed to like her, but then they went over to see Sixpence. It was like they fell in love. All three of them. I've never seen Sixpence go to anyone as quickly.'

She stopped talking and rubbed at a spot on her trousers. 'That was it, really,' she said. 'I took down their details and I told them you would come out and do a house visit. Then they said that if they were going to get a cat, they should register it with Animal Ark in case it needed any medical care. I was pleased,' she added. 'I thought that was a very responsible thing to do.'

Mandy was watching closely. She was telling the truth, so far as Mandy could tell. She thought for a moment, choosing her words carefully. 'Adam spoke to me after they had been into the clinic,' she said. 'According to him, they seemed to be under the impression that they would definitely be able to have Sixpence.' Her eyes searched Geraldine's face. 'Did you do anything that might have given them that impression?'

For the first time, Geraldine looked doubtful. 'I'm afraid I might have done,' she admitted. 'They were a lovely couple. And I loved the way Sixpence was with them. I thought they'd be great owners.'

Mandy sighed. 'You were mostly right,' she agreed. 'They seemed a good fit to me too, only when I asked them about their work, I found out that they both work long hours and shifts. They couldn't guarantee that they would be there every single day.'

Pink spots appeared high on Geraldine's cheeks. 'Oh,' she said.

'I had to tell them that they weren't suitable to adopt if they were out so much,' Mandy explained. 'Fortunately they were really nice about it. Both of them said they might come into the centre to play with the cats and walk the dogs. They said how lovely you'd been. But there are protocols in place for a reason. I love the fact that you're enthusiastic, but for now I need you to take down details of anyone who comes in and let me take it from there.' She glanced out of the window. Pale grey light was seeping through the clouds. Mandy turned back to Geraldine. 'I want you to take on as much responsibility as you can,' she told her. 'I'm happy for you to be here now and then when I'm not. If people arrive and you feel they're trustworthy, I'm happy for you to show them round and introduce them to some of the animals. But you have to make it absolutely clear that the decisions about rehoming are down to me at the moment.'

Geraldine's face had gone very red, and she looked at Mandy with troubled eyes. 'I'm sorry,' she said. 'I put you in a difficult position, didn't I?'

Mandy nodded, but she managed to smile. 'You did, but luckily there was no harm done,' she said. 'No need to mention it again, okay?' Managing staff was hard, she thought. Yikes.

They went into the food prep room and started to assemble the breakfasts. Geraldine measured out Sixpence's food, then stopped and turned to Mandy. 'I just wanted to say sorry again for putting you on the spot,' she said. 'I've always been a bit too impulsive. Heart over head, that's me. I want to do things right, but I get carried away.'

Mandy grinned at her. 'That'll be where I get it from, then,' she said. 'It's not altogether a bad thing, even if it has led me into a few scrapes.'

Geraldine ran her hand over her hair, and Mandy noticed there were worry lines on her forehead. 'I've been impulsive with you too, haven't I?' Geraldine said quietly. 'Talking about my family, arranging Christmas dinner . . . Just turning up here at all.'

Mandy nodded, not taking her eyes off the spoon

dangling from her fingers. She felt Geraldine's cool hand on her wrist.

'Please look at me,' Geraldine said, her voice earnest.

Mandy lifted her gaze.

Geraldine was smiling, her eyes gentle. 'I'm sorry,' she said. 'I really am.' She paused, searching Mandy's face. 'Do you need some space?' she asked. 'Please be honest. I've been ready for this for years, but you haven't had any notice at all.'

For a moment, Mandy couldn't speak. She took a deep breath. 'Heart over head,' she echoed. 'I think I do need a bit of space, if that's okay.' She stopped, gathering herself. 'Don't get me wrong; I'm thrilled you found me, it's amazing. But it's a lot to take in. And right now, it seems to be hurting other people. I don't want that. I need some time to sort everything out before I can begin to process this, if you see what I mean.'

Geraldine nodded. 'I do,' she said. 'You're a lovely girl, Mandy. The best daughter anyone could want. Adam and Emily did a wonderful job of raising you.' Her eyes glittered with unshed tears. 'I truly don't think I could have done better myself.'

Mandy looked at Geraldine, then reached out to her. 'Please don't cry,' she whispered, wrapping her arms around Geraldine's slim body. 'No more tears, please! It's going to be brilliant. We have lots of time now. I'm not going anywhere.'

'And nor am I,' Geraldine replied. They stood still, clinging tightly to one another. Then Geraldine straightened up and pulled a hankie from her pocket. 'I'll go back to Manchester this week, I think, and stay there for Christmas,' she said.

Mandy felt a weight lift from her shoulders, quickly followed by guilt. Had she just ruined Christmas? Geraldine sent her a rather watery smile. 'Don't worry,' she said. 'I'm not going to sit in a darkened room being lonely. I'll see my brother and his boys, and my friends. I'd like to call you though, if that's okay?'

'Please do,' Mandy said. 'And will you tell my uncle and my cousins that I'll come and see them very soon.' She thought for a second. 'In fact, how about New Year's Eve? Maybe we could ring in the new year together.'

Geraldine looked stunned. 'Really?' she said. 'That would be incredible! Thank you!'

Mandy felt a surge of genuine pleasure. 'It'll be something for me to look forward to as well,' she said. 'A new start for both of us.'

Geraldine grabbed her hands and squeezed them hard. Mandy thought she was going to dance around the room, but she just stood there, glowing as if she couldn't have been happier, and then she sighed and reached out a hand to touch Mandy's face. 'You are a lovely, lovely girl, Amanda Hope,' she said, 'and don't you ever let anyone tell you otherwise.'

Mandy suddenly felt filled with energy and clarity. 'Can you finish up here, please?' she said. 'I want to go over to the cottage. I need to sort some things out.'

Geraldine nodded. 'Of course. Take your time.' She grinned. 'If any visitors turn up, I'll tell 'em you're the boss. I promise not to do anything rash. Oh, and I hope it goes well.' She winked at Mandy, who felt startled by Geraldine's ability to read her mind. *But then, we are related.* Geraldine picked up two of the breakfast bowls and flapped them at Mandy, shooing her out. 'Go on, then,' she said.

As Mandy walked out, she heard Geraldine begin to hum 'Oh Come, All Ye Faithful' as she distributed the food. It sounded like a march of triumph.

Though it was freezing cold outside, Mandy barely felt the chill as she strode back across the car park. She had no idea what she was going to say, but Geraldine's words rang in her head. Adam and Emily had been the best parents she could have asked for. Whatever they had done, she needed to tell them this.

She pushed open the back door and walked into the kitchen. Though she could smell coffee and toast, the old scrubbed pine table stood empty. Mandy frowned as she glanced up at the clock. She had assumed Adam and Emily would still be eating breakfast. Tango jumped down from his usual spot on the windowsill, stretched and padded over to greet Mandy, purring like a train.

'Where've they got to?' she asked him, and he looked up at her with his huge yellow eyes and blinked. They couldn't be far away, she thought. The back door had been unlocked.

She went into the hallway. A folding wheelchair stood beside the front door. Mandy stopped, her eyes fixed on the chair. What was that doing there? Where were Mum and Dad? She strained her ears, listening for signs of life and to her relief, she heard voices from the sitting room.

In two strides, she was at the door. She thrust it open and burst into the room. To her relief, Emily was sitting on the sofa. Though her face was very pale, she was sitting with a tray on her knee. Adam was beside her, spreading a piece of toast. Both of them looked up at Mandy, their eyes wide.

'Is something wrong?' Adam scrambled to his feet, toast in one hand, knife in the other.

'No, nothing – at least, not with me . . .' Mandy waved a hand towards the open door. 'The wheelchair? What's happened?'

Adam sat down again and handed the piece of toast to Emily. 'Your mum had a fall on Saturday,' he said. 'Her leg again.'

'The hospital advised me to use the chair when I'm out and about,' Emily said. 'Until they see whether my muscle strength improves.'

Mandy swallowed. A fall? Hospital? 'Why didn't you call me?' she demanded. There was a tight feeling across her forehead.

Adam looked at her, his eyes pained. 'We weren't

sure if it was the right thing to do,' he said. 'Your mum was never in any danger.'

There was a sick feeling in Mandy's stomach. 'No danger . . .' she echoed.

Emily reached a hand towards her and Mandy rushed over and knelt down on the floor. She gripped the thin fingers and pressed them to her cheek. 'I'm so sorry,' she whispered. She looked up. Despite the exhaustion around her eyes, Emily's sweet, familiar smile was shining down at her. 'I should have been with you!' she said.

Emily lifted her left hand and placed it on Mandy's hair. 'I'm fine, my love,' she said. 'Nothing to worry about.'

Mandy could feel tears prickling behind her eyes. This close, she could see new lines of pain on her mother's face. There were shadows where her cheeks had become hollowed out and the hand Mandy was holding was cold, despite the brightly burning fire.

Still clinging onto Emily's hand, Mandy slid onto the sofa. Adam sat down on his usual wing-backed chair beside the fire. Mandy looked from Emily to Adam and back again. 'If it's okay with you both, I'm going to move in,' she said. She squeezed Emily's fingers. 'I can help you bathe and dress, and do all the cooking,' she said.

Emily stretched her eyes wide. 'I'm not sure you should do the cooking!' she teased and Mandy laughed.

Adam smiled, but there was a trace of doubt in his

eyes. 'Don't think we don't appreciate this, Mandy,' he said. 'But are you sure this is the right time? I mean, we know you have a lot going on at the moment.' There was no threat, no anger in his words, but Mandy could tell he wasn't just talking about Jimmy or work.

Mandy breathed in and out, meeting his gaze squarely. 'Nothing is more important than being here with you two,' she said. She deliberately kept her voice firm but she could feel a wobble inside. There was a tiny movement beside her and she felt Emily's fingers tighten on hers. 'Mum needs us both, Dad,' she said.

'She does indeed,' Adam acknowledged. He sighed and smoothed his hands along the arms of his chair. 'I want to say that I'm sorry,' he said. 'I didn't react the way I should have when you told us about Geraldine.' His voice was earnest, and he stared straight at her, as if willing her to believe him. 'I wasn't fair to you,' he went on. 'It must have been incredibly difficult, but nothing that has happened was your fault. I know I've said it before, and I hope you can believe me now when I say I am always, *always* on your side.'

Mandy blinked away the threatening tears. 'I know you are,' she whispered.

Adam stood up and opened his arms. Mandy felt the tiniest pressure from her mum's fingers again. She returned it, then stood up and crossed the room to her father. He held onto her for a long time. Tears welled up in Mandy's eyes and overflowed onto her cheeks, but she didn't care. She closed her eyes, breathing in his familiar scent, then opened them and drew back very slightly to look up at him. She had more than one tall parent, she reflected. 'I'm sorry, too,' she said.

'Thank you for saying so,' he said, 'though you really have nothing to be sorry about.' He kissed her forehead, then released her. They sat down on the sofa, one on either side of Emily.

Emily took Mandy's hand again. 'Your dad and I have had a long talk,' she said. 'We're both incredibly sorry we lied to you, we really are.' She paused and glanced at Adam. 'We were scared of losing you. But now that Geraldine has found you, we'd like to get to know her – if it's okay with you? We don't want to push you into anything you aren't comfortable with.'

Mandy gazed at her mum's kind face. 'It's very okay,' she said. 'I know it'll be hard, but I think you'll like her.'

Adam's eyes were twinkling. 'If she's anything like you,' he said, 'even just a little bit, I'm sure we'll love her.'

Chapter Twenty-nine

Emily patted her knees. 'I fancy a spin in the fresh air,' she declared. 'Mandy, are you up to giving me a push around the village?'

It was as if she had registered Mandy's shock at the idea of the wheelchair and wanted to confront her with the reality straight away. Mandy almost laughed. Nothing like facing something head on, she thought. 'Of course I will,' she replied.

'No speeding,' Adam warned.

'I promise not to break the speed limit, so long as Mum doesn't use the whip,' she said, grinning.

It was painful to watch her mum get up from the sofa. Mandy wasn't sure whether to offer to help, but she held out her hand and Emily took it. Though each step was slow, she could see the determination in her mum's face. Emily lowered herself into the chair and smiled up at Mandy. 'Thanks, love. I have no plans to be in this chair permanently, I promise. Not for a long while anyway, but it's useful for now. And I'm definitely not going to hide away.'

Mandy nodded. Her mum's courage made her want

to weep. She pulled herself straighter and forced herself to smile. 'You shouldn't ever have to hide away,' she said. 'And wherever you go, I'll be there, if you want me.'

Adam had disappeared into the kitchen. He re-appeared, clutching a hot water bottle. He placed it on Emily's lap then tucked a woollen blanket over her knees. 'Okay?' he said, handing her a hat and gloves.

'All set,' Emily pronounced.

They set off down the lane, then turned left towards the village green. It was still dark and bitterly cold, but there were brightly coloured lights in the windows of the houses. Mandy felt very odd to be pushing her mum in the chair. It was difficult to steer and hard work going uphill. When they reached the centre of the village, Mandy suddenly became aware of how many curbs there were. She had never considered it before. As they walked along the edge of the green, Mandy caught sight of a small boy staring at them, but Emily smiled and waved and the little boy waved back.

'This reminds me of taking you out in your pushchair when you were a baby,' Emily said, twisting around to look up at Mandy, 'though it was springtime then and there was blossom on the trees.'

Mandy was instantly curious. 'Did you look after me right from when I was born?' she asked. 'Was I in withdrawal when I first came?'

Emily's eyes filled with love, mixed with sorrow. 'You were,' she said. 'Poor little darling. I couldn't bear watching you suffer so much, but I knew you had to go through it. Your screams were something else, though.'

Mandy hesitated. Since Geraldine's revelations, she had read about caring for addicted babies online. She had been horrified by the details. 'How did you manage?' she asked. 'Wasn't it hard?'

'It was,' Emily admitted, 'but we knew it was worth it. You were our daughter. We felt it from the moment we saw you. We knew right from the beginning that we would do anything for you.'

'Can you tell me more about it?' Mandy asked. She had never really asked about her past, she realised. She had known she was adopted and that had seemed enough. But now she wanted to hear about everything, however difficult.

'Shall we stop somewhere?' Emily suggested. 'Then we can talk face to face. Under the oak tree on the green, perhaps?'

Mandy pushed the wheelchair onto the path that led across the green. There was a bench under the oak tree and a hedge behind, so they would be sheltered from the wind. She parked Emily's chair beside the bench, and wrapping her own coat tightly round her, perched on the chilly seat.

Emily adjusted the hot water bottle on her lap and took a deep breath. 'Your father and I always knew we wanted a family. We found out quite quickly that it wasn't going to happen naturally for us, and adoption seemed the obvious answer. We both had so much love to give, and even though it was a hard process to get through, hearing that we had been approved was the best day of our lives.' She corrected herself, smiling. 'No, the second best. The best was when we met you.'

Mandy tried to imagine how that must have felt, wanting a child so desperately that you were prepared to take on a complete stranger's baby. 'Was I . . . where was I?'

Emily reached out a gloved hand and took Mandy's. 'In an incubator in Manchester General Hospital. You were in intensive care for the first two weeks of your life,' she began. Her eyes were shadowed, as if even now, the memory haunted her. 'That's where we first saw you. You were so tiny when you were born, only five pounds. They let us cuddle you, but you had to stay there until they felt you were stable enough to cope without immediate medical care. I'll never forget the day we brought you home. You were so beautiful, I could hardly believe you were ours.' She stopped and gazed across the green to where the Christmas tree was shaking in the wind, then looked back at Mandy. 'You were the most beautiful baby I'd ever seen,' Mandy said.

Mandy stroked her mum's glove with her free hand. 'Was I off the heroin by the time you brought me home?' she asked. She couldn't believe what she was saying. She had been born addicted to heroin – it was the stuff of a gritty Channel 4 documentary. The idea that she had started her life as a baby in withdrawal, that she had been through something so awful, seemed both surreal and terrible.

Emily shook her head. 'Not properly,' she said. 'We had to give you medicine every four hours.' Her mouth twisted in a wry smile. 'For the first time ever, we had to get locums in to Animal Ark. You didn't sleep, so we didn't either. We just sat up with you, counting down the minutes until we could give you another dose of methadone and stop the screaming.' She drew in a breath. 'I used to swaddle you in a little blanket your gran had made. You gripped it so tight with your tiny hand. I'd hold you up under my chin and cuddle you as tightly as I could. It seemed to calm you down.'

She lifted her mittened hand to Mandy's face, as if searching for the baby in her now adult daughter. 'You didn't open your eyes for the first two days here,' she said. 'And then on the third day, in the afternoon, you opened them and started to look around. I had tears in my eyes every time I looked at you. It was as if we could see you . . . the real you, for the very first time.' She wiped a tear that glistened on her cheek.

'Everyone must have thought I was an awful mother the first few times I brought you out,' she went on. 'Methadone babies have a very particular cry, high-pitched and agonising, as if you were being tortured. We didn't feel we could tell anyone what you were going through. I can remember making a run for it when Dora Janeki appeared in her Land Rover once as I was pushing you up the lane. Your little face was so red and you looked so angry.'

Dora Janeki had been one of Animal Ark's regular farming clients. Mandy had always been rather intimidated by her. Dora had been kind underneath, but she never smiled at the best of times. No wonder Emily hadn't wanted to talk to her about what was wrong with her baby.

'It was such a relief when you finally started to sleep a bit more,' Emily said. 'Though at first if you went more than an hour, I'd panic and I'd have to poke you awake to make sure you were okay. And then you began to recover properly. We hadn't known what to expect . . . whether you would ever be properly well. When your real personality started to shine through, it was the most wonderful thing. I used to bring you here and we'd sit under this tree and I would sing to you. Your dad was back at work by then, so it was just the two of us.'

Mandy looked around the frosted-white green. James had married Paul here, two and a half years ago. Thirty years ago, Emily had brought her here in her pushchair. So many things would have been just the same. The grey stone war memorial and the ancient church with its square tower. Had the oak tree been smaller then, Mandy wondered? Or were its branches so ancient that it had stopped growing long ago?

She noticed Emily watching her. There was so much love in her eyes that Mandy wanted to laugh and cry at the same time. Despite the frost, she dropped to the cold ground and rested her head in Emily's lap, feeling her mother's hand stroking her hair over and over. 'I'm so sorry for doubting you and Dad,' Mandy whispered.

Emily helped Mandy back onto the bench. 'It's completely understandable,' she said. 'Looking back now, it seems obvious we should have told you. But it was so hard at the beginning. It just seemed easier to tell you that your parents had died, and after a while it felt as if it was so close to the truth that it wouldn't do any harm to let you believe that.' She looked down at her lap and adjusted the blanket with a trembling hand. 'There's no parenting manual, even for babies who are healthy. You just have to try your hardest and hope you don't mess it up too much.'

Mandy touched her mum's arm. 'You didn't mess it up,' she said. She sighed. 'I'm sorry things have been so hard lately. Hard for both of us. But it's made me realise how lucky I am. Geraldine is my birth mother, yes, but you . . . you're my *life* mother. You gave me the life I have had so far, the life I have now, and all the life I have to come.'

A tear ran down Emily's thin cheek. 'Thank you,' she whispered. 'My sweet, wonderful daughter.'

Mandy smiled as her own eyes filled. 'I love you so much, Mum.'

Chapter Thirty

It had been a crazy day at Animal Ark. Mandy couldn't
believe that tomorrow was Christmas Eve, even
though the walls were covered with Christmas cards
and Helen had put a CD of Christmas music in the
stereo.

Rachel had popped in to offer to take the guinea pig
family home for Christmas. 'I'd love to have them for a
few days,' she'd said. 'Then after it's over, maybe you can
put a notice up in the nursery. A guinea pig is for life,
not just for Christmas?' Mandy had accepted her offer
gladly. There would be a rush of unwanted Christmas
pets at Hope Meadows a few weeks after Christmas: there
always was. But sooner or later, kind new owners would
come along, even for long-term residents like Jasper.

Adam was humming in his consulting room. He had
been astonishingly cheerful all day. And when Mandy
had popped into the cottage in between clients, Emily
had been at the kitchen table, knitting what looked like
a miniature sweater. After only a few days on her new
medicine regime, she already seemed much better.

Toby popped his head around his consulting room

door. 'Is that the last?' he asked Helen. 'Only I was hoping to get off a few minutes early.'

'Were you really? I'd never have guessed!' Helen teased. Toby was spending Christmas in Klosters, skiing with a mysterious lady friend. He had been so comically tight-lipped about her that Mandy and Helen couldn't help thinking it must be serious.

Helen and Seb were spending Christmas with Helen's dad. He had recently proposed to a cheerful, motherly woman he had met online. Helen rolled her eyes when she told Mandy. 'She's a lovely lady,' she said, 'but I'm not convinced she'll be able to put up with the steam engines.'

Mandy laughed. 'Perhaps she's always secretly wanted to be a train driver,' she pointed out.

Helen squinted at her, looking thoughtful. 'You could be right,' she said. 'Their first date was on the Pullman. Dad said she spent ages chatting to the driver. He was jealous, I think. I was never sure if he was worried the driver might run off with her, or whether he'd offer her a ride on the plate instead of Dad!'

The connecting door to the cottage opened and Emily walked in. She still used the chair now and then outside, but she was mostly walking with the aid of a stick. She dotted her way across to the desk, holding a brightly wrapped parcel.

'I need to post this to James,' she said. 'Not that it'll get there for Christmas, but he'll get it soon afterwards.'

'What is it?' Helen asked.

Emily leaned against the desk. 'It's a jumper I've knitted for Taresh,' she said. 'He'll probably feel the chill more than most this winter. I wanted to finish it sooner but, well, things got in the way.'

Mandy looked at the parcel with a touch of sadness. She and James hadn't spoken since their row. She had taken Taresh's fire engine to James's café on a trip to York, hoping to bump into him, but James hadn't been there. She had left it with Sherrie, who had promised to pass it on, but as yet, James hadn't called or texted to say he'd received it.

'I'll give you a run to the post office in a minute,' Adam told Emily. 'I'm making a shopping list. We can go there on the way.' He turned to Mandy. 'I've found a recipe for vegan goulash which looks very tasty,' he told her. 'Does that sound good to you for Christmas Day?'

'Sounds great,' Mandy said, then lifted an eyebrow. 'Will there be dumplings?'

Adam drew in his chin, looking offended. 'With goulash? There will of course be dumplings,' he said. 'What kind of a father do you think I am?'

Mandy sent him a wide-eyed look. 'Well, I can't answer that in polite company,' she said, 'and dumplings do sound wonderful . . . but I hope you know that I still want roast potatoes and stuffing.'

Adam let out a loud guffaw as he put an arm round her shoulders and squeezed her. 'That's my girl!' he said.

Mandy's phone buzzed and she pulled it out of her pocket. To her surprise, it was a text from Jimmy. She hadn't contacted him since they had rescued Sebastopol. She had been trying to get used to not seeing him, while wondering if he was looking for somewhere else to live. But even with everything that was going on, she still missed him every day.

'Can you come to Wildacre?' she read. 'I have something for you.'

She felt a stab of frustration. Had he bought her a Christmas present? She had thought for a long time about whether she should get him something. Temptation had been high, especially after her shopping trip with the twins. She had finally convinced herself that it was the right thing not to. They needed some distance from each other . . . or at least she did.

She toyed with the idea of refusing, but that would be illogical. Wildacre was her house, after all. Maybe he was going to tell her he was moving out. With mixed feelings, she typed in a reply. 'There in ten minutes.'

Emily had headed back to the cottage to get her coat on, but rather than getting ready to go out, Adam was engaged in a heated debate with Helen on the merits of brandy butter versus thick cream with Christmas pudding.

'You can't beat cream,' Helen insisted. 'Brandy butter's too sweet.'

'Too sweet?' Adam sounded scandalised. 'Not possible at Christmas.'

Mandy cleared her throat and both Helen and Adam looked at her, eyebrows raised. 'I think I can solve this for you,' she told them. 'The correct answer is to have both cream and brandy butter, and if you still need something else, a small scoop of vanilla ice cream is perfect.'

Helen made a face. 'Ugh! What kind of savage would have ice cream on their Christmas pudding?'

But Adam was looking at Mandy with admiration in his eyes. 'Good call!' he said. With an ostentatious flourish, he added ice cream to his shopping list.

'I'm going out,' Mandy told him. 'To see Jimmy.'

Adam nodded. There was a look of approval on his face. 'That's good,' he said.

Mandy felt a little sad. Though she knew her dad was rooting for her whatever she decided, she hadn't explained fully how she was feeling about Jimmy. She sensed that on some level, he was still hoping they would get back together. And until Jimmy moved out of her home, it was impossible for Mandy to tell her dad that was never going to happen.

It seemed natural to steer her car into its usual spot at Wildacre, but a stab of sadness hit Mandy as she gazed through the windscreen. The house looked as welcoming as it had every day since she'd bought it. It had always felt like coming home, and she missed being here more than she could say. But Jimmy and the twins needed the space, and she couldn't bring herself to hurry him out.

Sky's reaction to coming home was less complicated. She bounded across the lawn and pushed her way through the front door. Jimmy must have left it ajar, Mandy thought. There was a flurry of barking, then the ecstatic scrabbling of four dogs rushing in circles. Mandy stepped into the hall and crossed to the kitchen door, which was open.

Jimmy was standing in the centre of a sea of dogs. To Mandy's amusement, he was holding a tray of burned biscuits above their heads. Her eyes started to water and she waved a hand in front of her face. The kitchen was filled with smoke.

'You didn't have to bake for me,' she said, laughing. Taking pity on him, she opened the back door to let out the smoke and shooed the dogs into the garden. 'Quite a welcome,' she remarked, looking around. There was flour on the counter and no less than three bowls smeared with biscuit mixture. A tea cloth had slipped from its hook and was lying on the floor. 'How many cookies did you bake?'

'Twenty-four,' Jimmy said mournfully. He surveyed the crispy shards on the baking tray. 'I think I cremated every single one.'

'I hope this isn't what you wanted to show me,' Mandy teased. In spite of everything, it still felt way too easy to be back here with Jimmy.

'You're at least going to try one, aren't you?' Jimmy

said, his eyes wide and innocent. 'I'll be highly offended if not.'

'Be as offended as you like,' Mandy said. 'Mineral licks are all very well for animals but charcoal really isn't to my taste.'

They were still grinning at one another when Mandy heard a car pull up outside. She looked at Jimmy, whose grin developed a guilty edge.

'Who can this be . . .' he began, but he was interrupted by a volley of frenzied barking in the garden and Mandy looked out of the window. Two new dogs had joined the melee. She would have recognised them anywhere. 'Seamus and Lily!' she exclaimed.

A knock sounded on the front door. She followed Jimmy into the hall. As the door swung open, Mandy could see James and Raj on the doorstep. Taresh was in Raj's arms and he was clutching a huge black-and-white toy dog.

'Come in,' Jimmy said, pulling the door wide, and before Mandy had a chance to say a word, he swept Raj and Taresh straight through into the kitchen, closing the door behind them.

James walked into the sitting room and after a moment, Mandy followed. For an age, they stood there looking at each other. Mandy could feel her face glowing with embarrassment and from the uncomfortable expression on James's face, he was struggling too.

'I'm so sorry,' Mandy began, but James held up his hand.

'Please let me speak first,' he said. 'I'm really, really sorry. I was totally insensitive. I was so busy being Taresh's dad that I forgot to think about you.' He looked pleadingly at Mandy. 'I'm supposed to be your best friend,' he said. 'I let you down when you needed me. Can you forgive me?'

Mandy almost wanted to cry at his worried expression. 'Of course,' she said at once. 'You didn't say anything wrong,' she added. 'I don't think there really is a wrong or right. It's all been so weird and hard to get straight in my head. I mean, who suddenly finds they have a new mum at the age of thirty?'

James sagged with relief. 'I can't even begin to imagine what it's been like. Just know,' he said, 'that you can talk to me any time, okay? No judgement ever. I promise.'

'Thanks,' Mandy said. 'To be honest,' she admitted, 'I feel all talked out, but it's good to know you're there.' She put her head on one side. 'Believe it or not, it's okay now, it really is. Geraldine's in Manchester for Christmas, and I'm going there for New Year. Family to meet!' James's eyebrows disappeared under his hair, but he didn't say a word. 'And as soon as Christmas is over,' Mandy continued, 'Mum and Dad and I are going to sit down and tell Grandad and Gran about Geraldine. I mean, they know I'm adopted, of course, but they deserve to know what's happened.'

James patted her on the shoulder. 'You sound just like yourself again,' he said. 'I'm so glad everything is sorted out.'

Mandy smiled, though a touch of sadness washed through her as she glanced towards the kitchen door. Not everything had been sorted out. There was still the problem of Jimmy and Wildacre hanging over her.

They were about to go into the kitchen when Jimmy appeared. 'I just want a quick word with Mandy,' he said, then once James had joined Raj in the kitchen, he closed the door.

Mandy pulled a face at him. 'You set me up!'

For a second, Jimmy looked guilty, but then he grinned. 'James told me what had happened,' he said, 'and as soon as I heard, I knew you'd be too stubborn to approach him first. I ran the risk that you'd be cross with me, but I wanted to help.'

'Thank you. You were right, as it turns out.' She met his eyes and they smiled at each other. Jimmy looked as if he was about to say something when there was a noise behind them and a piercing voice from the doorway.

'Woof, woof!'

Mandy turned to see Taresh looking at her, brandishing his toy. 'Woof, woof, Bandy!' he shouted.

Moving away from Jimmy, Mandy crouched down and spoke to him. 'What did you say?'

Taresh waved the toy dog again, almost hitting Mandy on the head. 'Woof, woof, Bandy!' he announced. There was pride in the big brown eyes and he grinned, showing his new front teeth.

'Aha!' Raj came over, looking rather embarrassed.

'Yup,' he said to Mandy, 'he's named the little doggy after you! I hope you're not offended.'

'Not remotely,' Mandy said, standing up. 'In fact, I'm honoured.' She smiled down at Taresh and he held out his arms to her. With a feeling of delight, she scooped him up. 'Now,' she said, 'would you like to see the chickens outside?'

'Chick chick!' Taresh began to bounce in her arms. 'Chick, chick!' he yelled again.

Mandy held onto him tightly. It felt so good. 'Good boy,' she said, and with a glance at Jimmy, she headed for the back door.

Chapter Thirty-one

The garden was looking rather bedraggled with soggy winter growth, but the chicken run was clean and thoroughly fixed. Mandy put Taresh down beside the cage and he gazed at the chickens, putting his little fingers through the mesh. He seemed transfixed with joy as Butter and Peckerill ran towards him, clucking loudly. Mandy lifted the lid of the grain container that stood outside the run. Jimmy had kept it well filled. She took out a handful of grain and poured a little into Taresh's small hand.

'Now throw it to them,' she prompted. She took some grain for herself and showed him how to throw it through the wire.

Taresh squealed with delight as all six chickens appeared and rushed towards the food. 'Chick chick!' he shouted as the chickens pecked at the grain.

If Taresh was enchanted with the chickens, Mandy was just as charmed by Taresh. She crouched down and put her arm around his tummy and her head against his, breathing in the sweet scent of his baby shampoo. From the corner of her eye, she caught sight of Raj videoing them with his phone. Close beside him, James was beaming with pride. They loved their son so very, very much, Mandy thought.

Taresh caught sight of James and Raj watching him. 'Daddy! Papa!' he called. He pointed at the chickens, then he turned to Mandy, indicating that he wanted her to open her fingers. She held out the grain, and to her delight, Taresh filled both his chubby hands. But instead of throwing it into the hen run, he toddled over to James and Raj and sprinkled it onto their shoes. James burst out laughing and scooped Taresh up.

'That's for the chickens, silly billy!' he said.

'Nilly willy!' Taresh echoed at the top of his voice.

Jimmy walked over to stand beside Mandy. 'The joy of chickens,' he commented with a grin, but Mandy couldn't find her smile.

'Could I have a word with you?' she asked. 'Once James and Raj have gone?'

Jimmy looked at her with a frown, but he nodded. 'Of course,' he said.

It seemed to take an age for James and Raj to leave. Not that Mandy wanted them to go, but she knew she had to talk to Jimmy in private. They stood side by side, waving the little family off and Mandy felt another stab of pain. It felt so poignant, standing there as if they were still together. As if once James had gone, they would head inside, throw some logs on the fire and cuddle up with the dogs all evening. Mandy could feel the prickling behind her eyes, but she blinked back her tears. Maybe this would be the last time she and Jimmy would stand here together, but it had to be done. There was no way she could carry on like this.

They closed the door and made their way back into the sitting room. For the first time, Mandy registered the twins' contribution to Christmas: the riot of paper chains hanging from the ceiling, paper snowflakes sellotaped to the windows. She wanted to cry. *I should have been here when they decorated my house.* She lowered herself into an armchair, feeling very tired.

Jimmy sat down on the sofa and leaned forwards with his elbows on his thighs. 'What did you want to talk about?'

Now the moment had come, Mandy couldn't speak. She looked at Jimmy miserably, willing him to tell her he had changed his mind, that he wanted her forever, to have and to hold, but he just frowned. 'What did you want to tell me? Is it something about your parents? Geraldine?'

Mandy shook her head. The tension in her jaw was giving her a headache. 'It's not about them,' she admitted. 'It's about us.' Something on the ceiling caught her eye. A foil star was hanging from the light fitting, twisting in the draught from the fire. The glowing logs in the grate collapsed and settled, sending a shower of sparks up the chimney. She looked at Jimmy, who was sitting very still. 'I know you meant well today, bringing me and James together,' she said. 'And I appreciate it. Don't think I don't. But every time I see you, every time we get together, it only reminds me of everything I've lost.'

Jimmy was watching her, but she couldn't read the look in his eyes.

Say something. Anything. Please . . .

She took a deep breath. 'I need a break,' she said. 'A complete break. And I'm going to need you to move out of Wildacre. There's no rush, not yet. I can stay with Mum and Dad as long as I need to, but I'd like you to start looking for somewhere else, please.'

Jimmy reached out and tried to take her hand, but she leaned away from him and shook her head. 'I can't,' she said. 'Not any more. Maybe sometime in the future we can be friends, but not yet. Not for a long time.' She swallowed. A tear began to run down her face, but she brushed it away. 'I love you,' she told him. 'I always have and I always will, but I can't live half a life, and that's all I'll have if I come back to you.'

She could see tears in Jimmy's eyes now. He twitched as if he was going to reach for her again, but his hands stayed on his knees. 'Of course I'll move out,' he said hoarsely. 'Thank you for letting me stay here.' He stopped and swiped at his eyes with his thumb. The fire was low. The room was getting chilly, Mandy registered dimly, though her face felt burning hot. There was an acrid scent in the air, bittersweet tones from the incinerated biscuits.

'Will you do one last thing for me?' Jimmy asked, sounding choked.

'Of course.'

Jimmy took a deep breath. 'I'd like to go out one last time,' he told her. 'Tomorrow evening. One last Christmas Eve together, for old time's sake. And after that, I promise you I'll do whatever you want me to.'

Mandy gazed at him. He was trying to smile but he couldn't quite manage it. 'One last time?' he said. 'Please.'

Despite her intentions that this would be the last time she saw him for a while, Mandy didn't see a reason to refuse. She nodded.

'I'll pick you up at eight o'clock,' Jimmy told her.

Chapter Thirty-two

Mandy woke up in her bedroom at Animal Ark. It was Christmas Eve. How many times had she woken here, feeling the excitement of Christmas looming over her? Though her conversation with Jimmy yesterday had been difficult, along with the sadness, she felt a strange feeling of peace. She would have a quiet Christmas here with Mum and Dad, and then at New Year, she would spend time with Geraldine and meet her new family. There would be plenty of time to come to terms with being single again.

She sat up in bed and Sky stood up, stretched and sniffed the air. 'You can smell it too?' Mandy said, and Sky bounded onto the bed, wagging her tail. 'Dad's pancakes,' Mandy told her. Since she had moved back in, Adam had been feeding her up. 'I suppose we'd better go down and give him a hand.'

It was bitterly cold outside. Mandy put on two coats just to feed the alpacas. She gave them a thick bed of extra straw, though she was laughing at herself as she did it. Wild alpacas lived high up in the mountains of

Peru. The Yorkshire frost would barely penetrate their thick winter coats.

The clinic was quiet. After the hectic days of the past week, it was a relief to have some time between the consultations. Mandy found herself hoping the quiet spell would continue through Christmas Day. Not that the odd calving didn't help to work up an appetite for Christmas dinner. Adam had offered to do the on-call tonight and Mandy would be on tomorrow, then they would share Boxing Day.

There were no appointments booked for the afternoon. They waved Helen off at three o'clock and Mandy and Adam did the rounds at Hope Meadows, then retreated to the cottage. Emily was curled on the sofa making a patchwork quilt. The radio was playing Christmas carols, and the Christmas tree they had put up at the weekend twinkled with lights and tinsel.

'Mind if I join you?' Mandy asked her mum. 'If you can spare the space, that is.'

Emily smiled. 'Can you help me in return? How are your sewing skills coming on?'

Mandy rolled her eyes. 'Marginally better than my cooking, but you know perfectly well that the only things I can stitch neatly are animals.'

Emily laughed. She pulled the quilt towards her, making room for Mandy on the sofa.

'I've been thinking.' Adam threw himself into his chair, his eyes twinkling as he looked at them. 'Why don't we turn one of the consulting rooms into a craft room? You can quilt, Emily, and Mandy can make wooden toys.' He grinned. 'I hear you made a great job of mending your chicken coop and were instrumental in making the lovely alpaca dividers.'

Mandy frowned. 'Have you been speaking to Jimmy?' she said and Adam's eyes widened, then he nodded.

'He popped in a couple of days ago,' he admitted. 'He was looking for worming tablets.'

Mandy couldn't help feeling puzzled. Why hadn't Jimmy asked her for the tablets? She was sure there were plenty in the kitchen drawer at Wildacre anyway.

Adam let out a contented sigh as he sat back in his chair and stretched his feet out towards the fire. 'We should have something easy for dinner,' he said. 'Save my energies for tomorrow. How does tomato soup and crusty cheese rolls sound?'

'Perfect,' said Mandy. 'As long as you let me choose my own portion size. If you keep feeding me up, I'll be rolling around like a barrel!'

By the time half past seven came round it was so cosy by the fire that Mandy found herself quite reluctant to go back outside. Sky had fallen asleep at Emily's feet and Emily had stopped sewing and was listening to a carol service on the radio. Mandy glanced at her mum, then stretched her arms. 'I wish I could stay here all evening,' she said with a yawn.

'Perhaps Jimmy is taking you somewhere warm, like the pub,' Adam said, looking up from his book.

Mandy shook her head. 'Not by the sound of it,' she

said. Jimmy hadn't told her where they were going, only that they would be outside and to wear good boots. 'It's forecast to be minus eight tonight,' she added, wincing.

'Make sure you wrap up warm,' Adam told her. 'There's no snow forecast, you'll be fine.'

'It's too cold to snow,' Mandy said. She walked over to the window, pulling back the heavy curtain to look outside. A plump crescent moon was shining brightly on the thick frosted grass. Adam had strung white lights through the bushes and the hawthorn hedge. The tiny bulbs were cold blue white, like starlight, and they lent a magical air to the garden.

Emily looked up from stroking Tango on her lap. 'Everyone says it can be too cold to snow,' she said, 'but there's snow at the South Pole, isn't there?'

Mandy laughed. 'That's probably where Jimmy's going to take me,' she replied. With a feeling of resignation, she headed into the hallway and began to put on her fleece, jacket, hat and gloves.

Jimmy pulled up outside at eight on the dot. He was wearing a fur-lined hat with flaps for his ears and a warm scarf. 'Hi,' he said. They walked to the car and he opened the passenger door for her to climb in.

'Where are you taking me?' Mandy asked as he climbed in beside her and started the engine.

He shook his head, a small smile playing round his lips. 'Wait and see,' he told her as he set off towards the village.

As they turned up the road that led to Upper Welford Hall, Mandy wondered if they were going to Running Wild. She wouldn't put it past Jimmy to hand her a head torch and take her on the ropes course in the pitch-dark just for fun, but she was relieved when they turned sharp right onto the road to Six Oaks. 'We're not going riding, are we?' she said, turning to face him. 'I'll freeze!'

'Nope.' He steered his Jeep onto the side of the road just short of the yard and pulled on the brake. 'Shanks's pony for us,' he announced. 'It'll keep you warmer.'

They climbed out and he walked round to the back of the car. Pulling out a rucksack, he slung it over his shoulder. They crossed the road and Jimmy opened the wooden gate to the path that led up through Silver Dale. 'This way,' he said.

It was a truly beautiful night. As the lights of Six Oaks faded behind them, Mandy found herself looking up at the sky in wonder. The moon was sailing high over the valley, surrounded by millions of frost-hazy stars. Though the track was steep, it was smooth and easy to navigate, despite the darkness. Their feet crunched on the frozen ground and when Mandy turned, she could see the faint trail of their footprints stretching out behind them.

'Where are we going?' she asked Jimmy, but he shook his head and his eyes crinkled.

'Just for a walk,' he said.

The path along the shoulder of the dale steepened and narrowed. They climbed in silence for a while, their breath merging in silvery clouds. Though the air was cold, it was perfectly still. Far behind them at the entrance to the valley, one of Molly's horses whinnied. Mandy found herself thinking of Bill's sweet face. Where was he now, she wondered? She looked up at the stars wheeling in the dark winter sky and felt a deep sense of calm wash over her. Wherever Bill was, he was happy and free from pain, and eternally grateful to Molly for the last years of his life.

They reached the rushing waters of Silver Force and stopped to catch their breath. The fellside beyond the waterfall was dappled with shadows where trees clung to the lower slopes. Far below, in the depths of the dale, a few lights twinkled in the darkness. The air was chilly against Mandy's warm cheeks.

'Look,' Jimmy said, pointing, and Mandy turned to look at Silver Force itself. Huge icicles had formed on the rocks either side of the waterfall. Ice and water sparkled in the moonlight and the sound of the tumbling beck filled their ears.

'It really is Silver Dale tonight,' Mandy murmured, and Jimmy smiled with his eyes, though his mouth was hidden in the folds of his scarf.

They walked on and the sound of the rushing water receded. The top of Silver Tor lay straight ahead. Jimmy glanced at Mandy, then tramped onwards and a moment later, they reached the summit. Jimmy shrugged his arms out of his rucksack and put it down on a rock. Mandy breathed in the clean, frosty air and turned to look back down the valley, following the winding track with her eyes. Far in the distance, she could see the glow of lights from a tiny village. To her delight, the sound of church bells came to her on the still air.

'It's Midnight Mass!'

'Isn't it a bit early?' Jimmy queried.

'I think most churches hold it before midnight now, so people can get some sleep,' she told him. There was a rustling sound behind her. What was Jimmy up to, she wondered? Their last night together, yet he wasn't even enjoying the view.

'What are you doing?' she said, and turned round.

Jimmy was behind her, kneeling on the icy ground. He had pulled the scarf away from his face and his eyes were bright in the moonlight. His hand was stretched out towards her and he was holding a tiny velvet box.

'Mandy Hope.'

She could see his breath in the icy air. How serious he looked.

'Will you marry me?' he asked.

Mandy felt as if the edge of the world was tilting sideways. Below and above, dazzling stars spinning through infinity. 'What?'

Jimmy raised one eyebrow. 'It's usually yes or no,' he pointed out. 'Not what.'

Mandy felt laughter bubbling up inside her. Everything still seemed unreal as Jimmy reached out his free hand and took hers in its white knitted mitten.

'I know what I said before,' he told her, 'and all I can say is that I was wrong. There is nothing that would give me greater pleasure than having a child with you. You are the most amazing woman I've ever met. And you'll be a wonderful mother. Abi and Max are the proof of that, the way you are with them.' He paused and looked anxiously at her, as if he wasn't sure she would believe him. 'I want to share the rest of my life with you,' he said. 'You and our children.'

Though she could see her hand in his, Mandy felt as if she was floating free in the night sky.

'I'm sorry for what I've put you through these past months,' Jimmy went on quietly. 'I knew I needed to move out of Wildacre. It's your home. But every time I started to look for somewhere else, I couldn't do it. And I realised after a while . . . well, I realised it wasn't the house I couldn't bear to leave.'

Mandy felt faint. It was the mirror image of what she had been going through. 'And I knew I ought to ask you to move out,' she said, 'but I couldn't bring myself to do it. It just felt completely wrong.' She could see the moonlight reflected in his sparkling eyes. In the distance, the bell was still tolling.

'Do you really mean it?' she whispered. 'Get married?'

Jimmy nodded. 'Really,' he said. He sent her a rueful look, half grin, half apology. 'I hate to break the romance,' he added, 'but my knee is about to freeze to this grass. Do you have an answer?'

Mandy laughed out loud. She slipped off her mitten

and took a firmer hold of his warm hand. 'Yes!' she said. 'A thousand times, yes!'

She tugged on his hand and he stood up, though his eyes never wavered from her face. She leaned in towards him, breathless and giddy, and he kissed her gently. She inhaled his scent and felt the urgency rise as their bodies pressed together. She closed her eyes. The world was spinning. This was everything: this man; here and now. She wrapped her arms more tightly around his neck and they clung to one another as the stars whirled overhead.

Jimmy loosened his arms and took a step back. 'Moment of truth,' he said and he opened the box.

Mandy gasped. Inside was the most perfect engagement ring: a simple gold band with a single pear-shaped diamond. 'It's beautiful!' She held out her hand and watched as Jimmy slid it onto her finger. It felt cold and smooth and absolutely right, as if it had always been there.

'It's perfect,' Mandy breathed. 'Thank you.' She sighed, staring at the stone. It was flawless under the moonlight. A thought came to her and she looked up at Jimmy with her head on one side. 'Did Dad know about this?'

Jimmy shot her a mischievous smile. 'Of course,' he said. 'You don't think I'd do this without asking his permission first, do you?'

Mandy stared at him. 'You didn't!' In this day and age? So much for feminism. He really was incorrigible.

Jimmy nodded. 'Yup,' he said. 'Father's privilege. One day I'll do the same for our daughters. And anyway . . .' He rubbed his hand down his cheek. '. . . I wanted to check that you'd say yes.'

Mandy pretended to glare at him. 'And you thought my father could answer for me?'

Jimmy shook his head, grinning. 'Not really,' he said. 'But he didn't dismiss the idea so I figured I was in with a chance. Though after everything you said yesterday, I was terrified you'd tell me it was too late and I'd lost my chance.'

Mandy raised her eyebrows. 'If you're going to spend the rest of our lives speaking to Dad instead of me, perhaps I should have done,' she said.

Jimmy put his arms around her again, looking into her eyes. 'I'm so glad you didn't,' he said softly.

Mandy smiled up at him. 'So am I,' she said.

They turned again to look at the view, Jimmy standing behind her, his arms around her waist. 'So how many children are we having?' he murmured. 'Just a ballpark figure, you understand . . .'

'Would it be okay if they outnumbered our dogs?'

'Sounds perfect.'

Mandy couldn't ignore a tiny, niggling worry, lingering from Jimmy's trip to Canada. Perhaps this wasn't the right time to bring it up, but if not now, when? She took a deep breath. 'You . . . you seemed really happy when you were away with Aira,' she began.

She felt Jimmy smile against her hair. 'It was an

incredible experience,' he agreed. 'I can't believe how lucky I was to see those bears up close.'

Just the bears? Mandy wanted to probe, but forced herself to tread gently. 'I would never stop you from going away with Aira,' she said. 'Adventuring is in your blood, it's who you are and something I love about you. But . . .'

'But will I leave you with the kids and gallivant off to the ends of the earth?' Jimmy finished for her.

'Well, yes. Will you?'

Jimmy laughed softly. 'Of course I won't! Okay, I get why you might be worried, but this trip . . . it was a last hurrah, a big tick on my bucket list to see polar bears in their natural habitat. I don't have the same wanderlust as Aira, that's for sure. Home is where I want to be now, and home is wherever you are.' He kissed the top of her head and added impishly, 'You're not jealous of the postgrads, are you? Silly girl. Liz spent the whole time pining for her boyfriend back in Seattle, and I just heard that Megan got engaged to her girlfriend the week after she got back.'

Mandy felt herself sag with relief. That was exactly what she needed to hear, she realised. Not that the students had been otherwise distracted – deep down, she'd always known she could trust Jimmy – but that he wasn't hankering after endless far-flung travels. They would travel together, she was sure of that, but not alone.

The tolling of the bell came to an end, the last chime hanging in the frosty air. Mandy could hear the rushing

355

water of Silver Force on the edge of the silence. Jimmy's
arms were wrapped tightly around her. She could feel
the beating of his heart, the warmth from his body and
the smoothness of the new ring on her finger. She
breathed in deeply, smelling snow on the wind. Perhaps
there would be a white Christmas, she thought. But
she knew that even if it rained, it would still be perfect.

'So,' Jimmy said, 'what happens now? Shall we head
back?'

A shiver went down Mandy's spine as she felt his
breath against the side of her neck. Home was here,
she thought, in Jimmy's arms. There was nowhere else
she'd rather be. But down in the valley, her parents
were waiting. Hope Meadows. Animal Ark. Wildacre.
All the things that made up her life. She turned to him
and smiled, feeling the depths of his love in his steady
green gaze.

'Yes, please,' she said. 'It's time to go home.'

Summer at Hope Meadows

Lucy Daniels

Newly qualified vet Mandy Hope is leaving Leeds – and her boyfriend Simon – to return to the Yorkshire village she grew up in, where she'll help out with animals of all shapes and sizes in her parents' surgery.

But it's not all plain sailing: Mandy clashes with gruff local Jimmy Marsh, and some of the villagers won't accept a new vet. Meanwhile, Simon is determined that Mandy will rejoin him back in the city.

When tragedy strikes for her best friend James Hunter, and some neglected animals are discovered on a nearby farm, Mandy must prove herself. When it comes to being there for her friends – and protecting animals in need – she's prepared to do whatever it takes . . .

HODDER

Christmas at Mistletoe Cottage

Lucy Daniels

Christmas has arrived in the little village of Welford. The scent of hot roasted chestnuts is in the air, and a layer of frost sparkles on the ground.

This year, vet Mandy Hope is looking forward to the holidays. Her animal rescue centre, Hope Meadows, is up and running – and she's finally going on a date with Jimmy Marsh, owner of the local outward bound centre.

The advent of winter sees all sorts of animals cross Mandy's path, from goats named Rudolph to baby donkeys – and even a pair of reindeer! But when a mysterious local starts causing trouble, Mandy's plans for the centre come under threat. She must call on Jimmy and her fellow villagers to put a stop to the stranger's antics and ensure that Hope Meadows' first Christmas is one to remember.

HODDER

Springtime at Wildacre

Lucy Daniels

In the little village of Welford flowers are blooming, the lambing season is underway . . . and love is in the air.

Mandy Hope is on cloud nine. Hope Meadows, the animal rescue and rehabilitation centre she founded, is going really well. And she's growing ever closer to handsome villager Jimmy Marsh. What's more, James Hunter, her best friend, is slowly learning to re-embrace life after facing tragedy.

But when an unexpected crisis causes Mandy to lose confidence in her veterinary skills, it's a huge blow. If she can't learn to forgive herself, then her relationship with Jimmy, and the future of Hope Meadows, may be in danger. It'll take friendship, love, community spirit – and one elephant with very bad teeth – to remind Mandy and her fellow villagers that springtime in Yorkshire really is the most glorious time of the year.

HODDER

Snowflakes over Moon Cottage

Lucy Daniels

As far as Susan Collins is concerned, this Christmas is all about quality time with her family, especially her son Jack. After a string of terrible dates she's given up on love, and Susan's certainly got plenty to keep her busy.

That is, until she meets handsome children's author Douglas Macleod. Dishevelled in appearance with bright red hair he is the opposite of Susan's usual type, but an undeniable spark soon lights up between them. But then Michael Chalk, Jack's father, turns up on the scene wanting to be a family again – and Susan finds herself torn.

With snow settling on the ground and the big day fast approaching, who will Susan and Jack be choosing to spend Christmas at Moon Cottage with this year?

HODDER

Summer Days at Sunrise Farm

Lucy Daniels

Veterinary nurse Helen Steer adores her job at Animal Ark, and with the summer ahead things couldn't be better.

That is until her best friend goes travelling, leaving Helen unexpectedly jealous and questioning her own stable life with her boyfriend Seb. Charming new vet Toby Gordon, with his flirtatious wit and mysterious family background, suddenly seems a much more exciting prospect.

But just as Helen and Toby's friendship starts to become something more, Sunrise Farm, the beautiful fruit farm where Helen lives, is hit by crisis leaving its future in the balance. Along with her friends Mandy and James, who put aside their own problems to help, Helen throws everything she has into saving her home.

Though with so much at stake, is there time to think about a new relationship? Or will Helen be forced to let her second chance at love slip away?

HODDER

Bookends

When one book ends, another begins...

Bookends is a vibrant new reading community to help you ensure you're never without a good book.

You'll find exclusive previews of the brilliant new books from your favourite authors as well as exciting debuts and past classics. Read our blog, check out our recommendations for your reading group, enter great competitions and much more!

Visit our website to see which great books we're recommending this month.

Join the Bookends community:
www.welcometobookends.co.uk

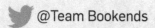 @Team Bookends   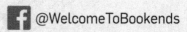 @WelcomeToBookends